T0245677

PENGUIN BOOKS

THE FRAUGHT LIVES OF NATHAN KWAN AND LAPSANG SOUCHONG

Tutu Dutta is a writer of Children's and YA literature. She was born in India but grew up in Malaysia. As she started life as a STEM student, she has a B.Sc and an M.Phil in Environmental Science.

Her publishing journey started with *Timeless Tales of Malaysia* (2009) by Marshall Cavendish (republished as *The Magic Urn and Other Timeless Tales of Malaysia* in 2017). This was followed by *The Jugra Chronicles*, set in 17th Century Borneo, published by MPH Group Publishing. A picture book, *Phoenix Song*, illustrated by Martina Peluso, was published by Lantana Publishing (UK) in 2015.

Her fascination with dark folklore resulted in *Nights of the Dark Moon*, published by Marshall Cavendish Asia in 2017. The culmination of her foray into dark folklore was *The Blood Prince of Langkasuka*, published in 2021 by Penguin Random House SEA.

In 2019, an anthology she co-edited with Sharifah Aishah Osman, *The Principal Girl: Feminist Tales from Asia*, was published by Gerakbudaya Enterprise. This book was a hit with YA readers and a second edition of the book, *The Principal Girl Redux* was published in 2023.

Dutta has been a speaker at the Asian Festival of Children's Content in Singapore and at Folklore related conferences organized by the University of Malaya, National University of Malaysia and University Tunku Abdul Rahman. She was also one of the Plenary Speakers at the IBBY2022 International Congress in Putrajaya, Malaysia.

Tutu Dutta also had another life as the spouse of a diplomat, and lived in far-flung cities where she researched some of her stories: Singapore, Lagos, New York, Havana and Zagreb. At present, she lives in Malaysia's Klang Valley with her husband, daughter, and three dogs.

Also by Tutu Dutta

The Blood Prince of Langkasuka (2021)

ADVANCE PRAISE FOR *THE FRAUGHT LIVES OF NATHAN KWAN AND LAPSANG SOUCHONG*

'The prose seems to feel especially rich and sensitive when conveying elements of personal relationships, domestic dynamics; and the opening section about the dead bird seems especially resonant and symbolic.'

—Don Bosco
Singaporean Children's Author and Entrepreneur

The Fraught Lives of Nathan Kwan and Lapsang Souchong

Tutu Dutta

PENGUIN BOOKS

An imprint of Penguin Random House

PENGUIN BOOKS

Penguin Books is an imprint of the Penguin Random House group of
companies whose addresses can be found at
global.penguinrandomhouse.com

Published by Penguin Random House SEA Pte Ltd
40 Penjuru Lane, #03-12, Block 2
Singapore 609216

First published in Penguin Books by Penguin Random House SEA 2024

Copyright © Tutu Dutta 2024

All rights reserved

10 9 8 7 6 5 4 3 2 1

This is a work of fiction. Names, characters, places and incidents
are either the product of the author's imagination or are used fictitiously,
and any resemblance to any actual person, living or dead, events or
locales is entirely coincidental.

ISBN 9789815202007

Typeset in Garamond by MAP Systems, Bengaluru, India

This book is sold subject to the condition that it shall not, by way of trade
or otherwise, be lent, resold, hired out, or otherwise circulated without the
publisher's prior consent in any form of binding or cover other than that in
which it is published and without a similar condition including this condition
being imposed on the subsequent purchaser.

www.penguin.sg

Dedicated to all cat lovers, especially to my old friends in Havana, Cuba whose dedication to their pets was an inspiration to me; and finally to all defenders and lovers of animals.

Contents

1

The House at the Corner of Aranda Lane

'Nathan! *Mari sini! Lekas mari sini!*' The summon to appear came from a husky voice, raised in consternation, from a sturdy, middle-aged woman. She was dressed in a cotton *batik* blouse, patterned in earthy brown, ochre and black—recognizably Javanese—paired with comfortable loose black trousers. Her long hair was tied in a neat bun behind her head. Whenever she raised her voice like this, it usually meant trouble for Nathan.

Nathan dashed out of his bedroom in alarm. He raced down the stairs and stopped short in front of the woman who was standing near the front door. He caught sight of her agitated face and replied breathlessly, '*Kenapa*, Kak Yam?'

Kak Yam pointed to the front door, which was ajar. She replied emphatically, '*Tengok ini*, Nathan! *Kuching awak buat pasal lagi!*'

Nathan looked towards the doorway, the reason for Kak Yam's hysterics becoming clear. His beloved pet Siamese was standing just outside the threshold. Jewelled green feathers glinted from between its jaw. He drew in his breath and called out sharply, 'No Souchong! Let the bird go! Let it go, now!'

Lapsang Souchong looked at Nathan calmly with piercing ice-blue eyes. Nathan felt his heart pounding inexplicably—a strange mixture of fear, alarm, and anger gripped him. He glared at the cat. Angry brown eyes confronted inscrutable blue ones. The cat finally lowered his gaze and nonchalantly walked indoors.

Souchong crossed the spotless marble floor, making his way towards Nathan, and dropped the little bird at the boy's feet. Then he sat on his hind paws and looked up. Nathan understood the gesture—Souchong was offering him a gift. It was a sign of true affection, as cats seldom let go of their prey willingly. Nathan felt strangely panic-stricken. He recognized that this was a stress response and forced himself to calm down. *Breathe,* he told himself.

The maid cried out, her voice even more agitated than before, '*Aiyah! Macam mana boleh? Saya baru saja mop lantai ini!*'

Nathan ignored her—Kak Yam's agitation over the dirt stains on the usually spotlessly clean floor, was stressful, and he needed to focus. He gently picked up the bird in his hands. It fluttered weakly against his palms. The bird appeared to be intact from the outside, although it was barely breathing. He murmured to himself, 'Poor little bird! Maybe we can save you . . .'

He carried the bird in his cupped hands and walked upstairs, with the cat following behind. '*Eh, tak boleh bawa burong itu ke dalam bilik* . . .' Kak Yam's voice, raised in protest, reminded him of her presence. She didn't want him bringing a bird into his bedroom.

'*Saya akan lepaskan dia, sebentar lagi*, Kak Yam,' Nathan replied, trying to appease her.

She sighed in exasperation and complained loudly, '*Sekarang saya mesti mop lantai sekali lagi*!'

Nathan didn't allow Souchong into his room—he was afraid the temptation to seize the bird might overcome the cat. He stopped the cat with one foot, quickly stepped into the room and closed the door behind him with his elbow. Souchong looked a bit put out but settled down to wait just outside the door. Once inside, Nathan rummaged in the drawer of his study table, discovering a tin box he'd used for storing trading cards. It was brightly painted and had a blue dragon and the name Yu-Gi-Oh on it; he had forgotten that he even had this. He emptied the box, spilling all the cards into the drawer, and gently placed the bird in the box. He left the box on his study table and rushed to the bathroom with an empty plastic cup. He turned on the tap and allowed a little water to collect in the cup and hurried back to the dormant bird. Nathan dipped his finger in the cup and allowed drops of water to fall on its beak but the bird seemed unable to swallow anything. He tried again, murmuring encouraging words to the bird, 'Come on . . . just drink the water . . . please!'

It was futile. The bird did not swallow even a single drop. He sat on the bed and sighed in frustration. Then an idea occurred to him. He picked up his hand-phone and called his cousin, 'Junie, can you come over now?'

The voice on the other end said, 'Why? What's the matter, Nathan?'

Nathan ran his fingers through his dark, wavy hair and sighed. He answered with a catch in his voice, 'It's Souchong. He caught a bird . . . I think it's dying . . .'

There was a momentary silence at the other end then Junie replied, 'Hold on! I'm coming right over!' Nathan breathed a sigh of relief; he was glad that Junie did not waste time asking questions; she always knew when something was urgent.

Nathan paced his room while waiting for Junie, anxiously checking on the bird, every now and then. The fifteen minutes it took her to arrive seemed endless.

Junie lived in the same row of terrace houses as Nathan, in a township called Kota Kemuning, located in the Klang Valley. This particular section of Kota Kemuning was known as Aranda—all the sections were named after orchids. It was a quirky and charming neighbourhood with quirky and charming little terrace houses. The charm came from the fact that every row or semi-circle of houses enclosed or bordered a small park or community garden. This gave the place a laid-back, rural feel; in fact, the whole of Aranda was built on a small hillock, with terrace houses constructed in horseshoe patterns or meandering rows along the contour of the land, rather than the geometric grid patterns found at other housing estates.

Junie was Nathan's cousin and best friend, but more importantly at the moment, she was the best student in Biology class. Junie loved animals and always knew what to do when her friends' pets sustained minor cuts and scratches. He rushed to the door when he heard footsteps rapidly climbing up the stairs.

Nathan opened the door and Junie walked in, slightly out of breath. She was of medium build with perfectly cut straight hair—she had maintained the same Page Boy hairstyle for the past three years. On her pert nose was a pair of rimless glasses; she could have been considered pretty if not for her intensely serious air. Her no-nonsense attitude was reflected in her clothing—a crisp white cotton blouse paired with a denim skirt. They were the same age—fifteen going on sixteen—and almost the same height but had quite different looks. Nathan had warm brown skin, large, slightly dreamy eyes and features which reflected his Indian-Chinese heritage. Junie had pale skin and dark, alert almond-shaped eyes which rarely missed anything. But they both shared certain characteristics—strong, well-shaped eyebrows and eyes that slanted ever so slightly at the corners which gave them a cat-like look.

Junie asked straightaway, 'Where is it?'

He took her to the box on his desk. Junie drew in her breath at the sight of the bird—its crown, shoulders and tail shone with an iridescent metallic green in the sunlight streaming in from the window. 'Wow! A blinged-out bird!'

Nathan asked her, 'Do you think it's a hummingbird? It looks like one.'

Junie replied absentmindedly, 'Umm . . . no. Hummingbirds are native to the Caribbean, only found in the Americas . . .' She frowned and bent over the box.

Meanwhile, Lapsang Souchong took the opportunity to slip into the room. He headed towards Nathan and rubbed himself against his legs. The cat had the round head and sturdy body of the old-style Siamese cats. Nathan had not forgotten his annoyance with the cat and pushed him away with his leg. He muttered under his breath, 'Why did you have to do something like this . . . it's not like you don't get enough to eat . . . fatboy!'

Junie replied without taking her eyes away from the bird, 'You can't blame Souchong for this . . . he was just following his instincts. Cats are born hunters.'

She picked up the bird in her hand and tried to gently dip its beak in the cup but she had as little success as Nathan. The bird was completely still by now. Junie put it down gently back into the box and turned towards Nathan. She said with a sigh, 'I'm afraid it's too late. I think it's dead.'

Nathan protested, his voice raised in distress, 'Are you sure, Junie? I mean there is no blood or bite mark on its body!'

Junie replied, 'It doesn't seem to be breathing. Even though there's no blood, it might be injured inside. Maybe a broken neck . . . wait let me check on something online.'

She walked to his laptop and googled Malaysian birds online. She scrolled from page to page; her fingers moving with extraordinary rapidity—she seemed to know exactly which keys to press, without even looking. Finally, she seemed satisfied she had found what she was looking for. She remarked, 'It's a sunbird . . . a ruby-cheeked sunbird, to be exact; *Chalcoparia singalensis*. Totally protected, it's illegal to capture or kill this bird.'

'We might get fined by the Wildlife people for this . . . why would anyone call a green bird, ruby-cheeked?' He sounded high-strung at first, but a deflated sigh followed his question.

Seeing his downcast face, she said, 'Maybe we should give Ruby Cheeks a proper burial in the garden?'

Nathan steeled himself and picked up the box. They walked solemnly down the steps and out of the front door into the garden. The house was the corner lot of a row of terrace houses and had its own garden—Junie's house was also a corner lot at the opposite end of the terrace, but Nathan's house had a much larger garden. Lapsang Souchong followed closely behind, glancing curiously at the box in Nathan's hands. It was a well-maintained garden with a large bougainvillaea tree, covered with masses of bright violet flowers as a centrepiece. The tree was surrounded by a semicircular bed of tuberose. The creamy flowers were in bloom and filled the garden with a heady scent—a strange combination reminiscent of fresh sweet gardenias with rich decadent musk.

However, Nathan chose a quiet shady spot at the edge of the garden under a frangipani tree. It was also in bloom, bearing white trumpet-shaped flowers with a yellow centre. A high wire mesh fence, bordered by bushes of *strelitzia* bearing bright orange-yellow flowers, surrounded the entire garden. Splashes of bright red *heliconias* interrupted the *strelitzia* row at regular intervals.

He handed the box to Junie, walked to the tuberose patch, and picked up a small hoe which was always left there with its tip buried in the soil. He walked back to the frangipani tree and started digging a hole. When the hole was large enough, he gestured to her to place the box in the hole. Junie placed the box carefully in the ground and turned to him, 'Do you want to say anything?'

He shook his head and started covering the box with earth, Nathan could not help saying, 'I'm so sorry . . .' Then he stopped abruptly and said, 'No, I can't do this. I'm going to keep the bird!'

Junie replied, 'What? You can't keep the bird—it's really, actually dead!'

He said stubbornly, 'I can preserve it, just like the Egyptians!'

Junie sighed, Nathan was going through his Egyptian phase now—he was reading up on all things Egyptian and was determined to put some of his knowledge into practice. She said resignedly, 'Okay . . . so what do you propose to do now? Mummify the bird?'

'Err . . . yes. I mean if they can mummify cats, why not birds?' he replied determinedly.

'Hmmm . . . that's complicated. Until we find out what to do, maybe we should just err . . . deep freeze it first?' she suggested tentatively.

Nathan nodded vigorously in agreement. The truth was he had no idea what to do. He just didn't want to bury the bird, at least not just yet. He brushed away the earth covering the box, picked it up and handed it to Junie, while he covered up the tiny hole he had dug up. He took back the box with the bird from Junie when he had completed his task, sweat dripping from his brow.

'But how are we going to stop Kak Yam from poking around the freezer? She'll have a fit when she sees the dead bird! You know how obsessed she is about keeping the house clean . . .' Junie continued.

Nathan looked thoughtful, then he said with a gleam in his brown eyes, 'You just leave it to me! Come on, let's go back to the house!'

They walked back slowly towards the house, carefully making sure that Kak Yam was out of the way before Nathan dashed upstairs into his room. Once inside, Nathan carefully took the bird out of the box and wrapped it in several layers of toilet paper from the bathroom. Sometime later, Junie came into the room and handed him a zip-lock bag and a plastic container she had picked up from the kitchen. She sometimes packed food and she knew where Kak Yam stored her plastic food containers. Nathan placed the bundle into the zip-lock bag and sealed it shut. He placed the bag into the small rectangular plastic container and shut the lid tightly. Finally, he placed masking tape all around the container and wrote 'SCIENCE EXPERIMENT' all around it with a red marker pen. He said with satisfaction, 'This will keep Mum from trying to open the box and even Kak Yam recognizes the word "science experiment" by now!'

Junie couldn't help smiling. She said, 'Wow! You've outdone me. Why am I not surprised?'

They poked their head outside to make sure Kak Yam was out of the way and silently sneaked downstairs. They could hear Kak Yam in the kitchen; it was almost afternoon and time to prepare lunch. Nathan signalled to Junie, who slipped out into the garden and called out, 'Kak Yam! Kak Yam! *Mari sini*!'

Kak Yam dashed outside through the kitchen door and said, '*Apa pasal*, Junie?' She sounded alarmed, almost as if she expected another alarming 'gift' from Souchong.

Junie pointed at the freshly covered 'grave' and replied, '*Kita kebumikan burong itu di sini! Jangan bagi* Souchong *kacau tempat ini ya*, Kak Yam!'

Kak Yam looked amused and replied, '*Kebumikan? Kita tanam haiwan! Tapi saya tak kisah; kebun bukan kerja saya!*' Gardening was not part of her duties, and she calmly walked towards the kitchen. Before she entered indoors, Kak Yam turned her head and added, '*Jangan lupa makan ya;* Kak Yam *buat nasi lemak untuk* Junie *juga!*'

Junie gave her a big smile, she loved *nasi lemak*.

While she was outside, Nathan tiptoed to the refrigerator. It was a large one, with a separate freezer compartment. Nathan placed the sealed plastic container in the spot normally reserved for his 'science experiments' and washed his hands at the sink.

Junie stayed over for lunch that afternoon—Kak Yam's *nasi lemak* was impossible to resist. Nathan cheered up considerably when she decided to stay; he loved having her around to chat. It also meant that he didn't have to eat alone with only Lapsang Souchong to keep him company. Although it was a weekend, his mother was at the office, tying up an important case. He had been spending a lot of time alone lately.

The two of them, each took a plate from the kitchen and helped themselves to *nasi lemak*—aromatic steamed rice cooked in coconut milk and flavoured with *daun pandan* or screw pine leaves. The accompaniments were roasted peanuts, fresh sliced cucumbers, and *sambal ikan bilis*—dried anchovies cooked in onion, garlic and pounded chilli. Junie was an ovo-lacto vegetarian and Kak Yam had made her an extra boiled egg to go with her *nasi lemak*, although she did allow herself some sambal. Nathan had chicken *rendang* to go with his meal. They sat in the dining room and munched away quietly, too preoccupied with savouring the food to say anything for a while. They felt quite comfortable sitting together in companiable silence, as really good friends often do.

Lapsang Souchong gave up waiting for Nathan and Junie to offer him some tidbits and sauntered into the kitchen where he knew a small bowl of plain rice and dried anchovies had been set aside for him. He ate his food with slow relish . . . Kak Yam may pretend to dislike him, but she was a kind soul, she knew how to take care of him.

Finally, after they had finished their meal, Junie sighed in satisfaction, looked up and said, 'I have an idea about what to do. But we need to use the school lab . . .' and she explained her idea to him.

2

The Girl from Kazakhstan

Next Monday morning, at 7 a.m. sharp, Nathan waited for Junie's mother to pick him up for school. She arrived in a spacious SUV. As usual, Junie's older brother, Jin, was sitting in the front passenger seat beside his mother. Nathan joined Junie in the back seat—they smiled and nodded to each other, greeting each other without speaking a word. Nathan greeted Junie's mother politely, 'Good morning, Auntie Fei!' She smiled and returned his greeting, 'Good morning, Nathan! All ready for school?'

The car moved smoothly out of the housing estate onto the highway, even this early in the morning traffic was already building up. But the cars were fortunately still able to move, another half an hour and it would have slowed to a crawl. Their school was a private school in a secluded part of Subang Jaya. It was a convenient arrangement because Junie's mother worked in Subang Jaya, and she could drop them off at school in the morning on her way to work and pick them up after work. Her boss, who was a family friend, allowed her to work shorter hours to accommodate her children's schedule. He did not consider this a sacrifice as good secretaries who were proficient in both Malay and English were hard to come by.

Auntie Fei drove into the spacious grounds of Noble Hall International School and came to a halt at the drop-off point in front of the main building. Students didn't get admitted to

Noble Hall just because their parents had money, they had to be gifted in some way or other—be it academically, athletically, or artistically. Of course, there were a few students from enormously rich families who got in through donations, which in turn helped to finance the few especially gifted students on scholarships who came from poorer families.

The main school building used to be an old colonial mansion, flanked on both sides by family and servants' quarters, now extended with the addition of another floor. The architect had been careful to maintain the original features and design, so that the entire complex retained an old-world feel to it. The main building faced south—the most auspicious direction—while the east wing faced the rising sun, and the west wing contended with the long rays of the setting sun. The main building had a centrally located concert hall—which also served as an assembly hall—that was surrounded by administrative offices and the teacher's rooms.

The concert hall curved outwards in a semi-circle coalescing into the garden which surrounded it. Facing north was an entirely new modern block, housing the science laboratories on the ground floor, a computer lab and a library on the first floor, music rooms and a small auditorium on the second floor and a massive gym on the top floor. The grounds to the north were surrounded by trees and also had a tiny lake—which used to be a disused mining pool—that had evolved into a lotus pond at one end. There was also a sports ground—with a swimming pool included—to the east.

Nathan, Jin, and Junie had arrived early and there were only a few cars behind in the queue. The three of them disembarked once they reached the gate and waved goodbye to Auntie Fei as she drove away. Two tall, athletic, and very attractive girls, who were standing around expectantly, flitted towards Jin. Nathan and Junie exchanged glances and grinned; Junie whispered, 'The Jin Jeanies!'

Jin was not just good-looking, he was also one of the stars of the school swim team. The Noble Hall team was the top swim team among all the private schools in Malaysia. Accompanied by the girls, Jin headed for his class, which was located on the second floor of the west wing, where the Sixth Form classes were located. Jin and the girls were in Upper Six, the graduating class. Nathan and Junie, who were in Form Five, headed for their class on the first floor. The east wing was reserved for the First, Second and Third Form students. The students from the lower forms had a separate canteen and toilets and thus rarely ever mixed with students from the upper forms.

Nathan's best friend, Sachin Sundara, was the first to greet them when they entered the classroom, 'Yo, my man Nathan and Junie! What's up, dudes?'

Nathan replied, 'Yo, Sachin! What's up, dude?' and they bumped fists, wriggled their fingers, and gave each other a high five. It was their usual form of greeting. Junie sighed and rolled her eyes in mock despair and mumbled 'Grow up, *lah*!' She went to take her seat, which was right in front of the classroom. Both Nathan and Sachin preferred to sit at the very back. Junie's childhood friend, Zahara Mustafa, walked into the classroom and placed her satchel on her desk. She greeted her with a bright smile, 'Hi Junie! How was your weekend?'

Junie's face lit up when Zahara, or Zara as she preferred to be called, greeted her. She was one of the popular girls; extremely pretty with long super-straight 'rebonded' hair and large eyes fringed with dark lashes. She wore make-up, even though it was against school rules, but none of the teachers bothered to reprimand her. The school had strict rules but the teachers tended to be open-minded about allowing students to express their individuality; self-expression was considered to be important. Everything about Zara said 'high maintenance'. Even though everyone had to wear uniforms—the girls were required to wear a white cotton blouse paired with a dark blue pleated skirt—she managed to stand out with her bespoke uniform and polished put-together looks, accented by discreet but outrageously expensive branded jewellery. She was also the only student in the class with an iPhone.

Junie got up and walked towards her. She was about to reply when she noticed with astonishment that Zara's brown eyes were bright blue now! She gasped, 'Zara! You're wearing blue contact lenses!'

Nathan and Sachin, who were standing behind Zara, discussing the latest computer game, turned around to look but could only see the back of her head.

Zara nodded, 'Yes! I got them during the weekend! What do you think?'

Junie found them a little disconcerting and could not stop herself from staring at Zara. But she forced herself to smile and said, 'Umm . . . cool! Your eyes really stand out . . . and . . . and I love blue eyes!'

Zara finally turned around to look at Nathan and Sachin for a few seconds, with a bright smile on her face; the boys didn't know how to respond. They quickly walked towards their desks and awkwardly took their seats.

The first period was English class. *Three more hours to go before Biology class*, Nathan thought to himself. Biology was not his favourite subject although he did quite well in all his tests. But Junie had insisted that they consult Mr Yeoh, the Biology teacher, for permission to use the laboratory.

The subject that Nathan really liked was History, but he would never admit this to anyone—history was nerdy even among the nerds. It was acceptable to be a gamer or a tech geek, but history was too esoteric; it was considered to be boring and the domain of 'old people'.

At that moment, someone walked into the classroom; Nathan and Sachin immediately fixed their gaze on her—in fact, the entire class fell silent and stared at her. She was extremely pretty, with features that were a beguiling mix of Asian and Caucasian; with clear green-brown eyes complimented by thick, dark brown shoulder-length hair. They had never seen her before. Sachin nudged Nathan, 'She's new!'

Nathan nodded, he liked the fact that despite her good looks she seemed less 'high maintenance' than Zara. He said thoughtfully, 'That's odd . . . it's already the middle of the term . . . Maybe she came from a different school system?'

'She's obviously a foreigner . . . probably Central Asian,' whispered Sachin. Nathan nodded in agreement, he had seen enough episodes of National Geographic to tell the difference between East Asians and Central Asians.

The girl moved hesitantly towards one of the empty places at the back of the class. Nathan and Sachin got up to lend her a hand but Alex Low beat them to it. Sachin raised his eyebrows in surprise and exchanged glances with Nathan; Alex was an intense bespectacled boy who seldom spoke to anyone much less showed gallantry to girls. His face was slightly flushed as he said, 'Sorry, someone's already sitting there,' and directed her towards another unoccupied desk; 'You can sit here, this desk is not taken.'

The girl looked him in the eye, flashed him a warm smile and said, 'Thank you! I'm Aida.' She placed her books on top of the desk, smoothed her skirt and sat down on the chair, looking a bit self-conscious. 'And you are?'

Alex blushed a little more. He spent most of his time gaming with faceless opponents and was not used to real-life interactions, and he felt especially awkward talking to this pretty girl. Nathan and Sachin exchanged glances again and grinned, but they were careful not to snicker—they hated being laughed at and it was unacceptable to do that to someone else.

Alex took in a deep breath, and stammered, 'Hi, I'm err . . . Alex. Umm . . . if you need any help with your maths . . .' but before he could complete the sentence, Ms Karen Jones—the

English Language teacher—walked in to start the lesson for the day. Ms Jones was slim and bespectacled, with short dark brown hair and an amazingly straight carriage, which made her look taller than her 160-centimetre height. She smiled cheerfully and started by introducing the new girl to the class, 'Good morning, class! I hope you had a good rest during the weekend. We have a new student joining us today. Class, say hello to Aida Anargul!'

Aida stood up and everyone in the class turned to look at her. She looked self-conscious and a little shy but forced herself to smile and say, 'Hello, everyone!'

'Aida is from Kazakhstan, a country from Central Asia and an important part of the ancient Silk Road, which we have been studying in history class. Isn't that exciting?' Ms Jones also taught them history. The entire class looked mystified at the word 'Kazakhstan' apart from Nathan and Junie; Junie turned around to look at Nathan and they smiled and nodded at each other.

Ms Jones continued, 'But I'm going to ask Aida to introduce herself and tell us a little more about herself and her country, Kazakhstan.'

The class listened in rapt attention as Aida said a few things about herself. Her mother was a diplomat and she had been to school all over the world, including New York, the Hague and Bangkok before coming to Kuala Lumpur. She spoke with a slight American accent, but Nathan thought her English was near perfect. The class was fascinated by her extraordinary lifestyle, especially the fact that she had attended UNIS—the United Nations International School—in Manhattan, New York.

Ms Jones asked, 'Would anyone volunteer to be Aida's buddy to show her around the school?'

Junie was about to volunteer but to her surprise, Zara immediately put up her hand. Zara rarely went out of her way to be friendly to new students. Ms Jones gave her a big smile and said, 'Wonderful, Zara! You can show Aida around the school during the break and introduce her to your friends!'

The day went by in a blur and soon it was lunch time. Zara escorted Aida to the canteen. Nathan, Junie, and Sachin walked close behind them. They each took a tray and picked what they wanted to eat. Zara, who was always on a diet, chose *kueh teow* soup with fish cake and green *sawi* leaves while Aida picked up a pack of tuna sandwiches and a slice of apple pie. Nathan and Sachin each asked for three *roti chanai* accompanied by *dhal,* a thick curried lentil; Junie had the same, but she asked for only two *rotis.* However, on the way to their usual table, Zara saw Jin and two of his swim teammates sitting at another table. The two Jeanies were also with him. They waved at Zara, and she smiled back at them.

Zara turned to Aida, 'Sorry, Aida. I have to join my friends over there! I'm sure you can err . . . join our classmates at the back.'

Zara walked towards Jin's table and Aida looked taken aback at being abandoned by her 'buddy' so quickly. The three friends who had been watching Zara and Aida with a touch of envy, were equally surprised. Aida stood in the canteen alone, looking slightly lost. Junie came to her rescue. She walked towards her and said brightly, 'Hi, Aida! Why don't you join us for lunch? I'm Junie, we're in the same class.'

Aida looked relieved to see a friendly face. The four of them took their seats, and sat quietly for a while to tuck into their food. Nathan, who had been waiting for Junie to introduce them to Aida, finally decided to introduce himself, 'Hi, I'm Nathan, by the way, and this is Sachin, and you've met Junie. Sorry, you were abandoned by Zara.'

Aida smiled and said cheerfully, 'Oh, I don't mind! I'm happy to meet three more classmates!'

Sachin said with a trace of sarcasm, 'Zara is one of the popular girls, you know, you can't expect her to eat lunch with uncool nerds like us!' He added quickly to Aida, 'I don't mean you of course, you are clearly not a nerd!'

Junie gave him an annoyed look. She said, 'I know that I've been pigeonholed into the "nerd" category just because I wear glasses, love to read and worst of all, am the top student in science! But I am not a nerd . . . and I like Zara, and I'm glad to have her as one of my friends.'

No one said anything, so Junie continued, 'Zara is not one of them, she's just a bit impulsive sometimes . . . I mean she's not fake like the Jeanies, she's a real friend.'

Sachin said with mock enthusiasm, 'Dare to dream, Junie! Dare to dream!'

Junie shrugged off his comment. The thought that Zara chose to be friends with her just because Jin was her brother did occur to her, but she decided that although it may have started that way, it was not the case now. Nathan tried to smooth things over by adding, 'Anyway, we're more fun to be with, we know lots of cool stuff like sunbirds and sacred cats and we actually enjoy eating our food!'

Sachin nodded his head vigorously, 'It's miserable eating with people who are afraid to eat!'

Aida looked relieved. She agreed enthusiastically, 'I love food too! I'm going to try all the local food once I know more about them.' Then she changed the subject, 'Have you all been friends for a long time?'

Nathan replied, 'Forever. But Junie and I are cousins, so we've known each other since . . . well, since we can remember.'

Aida looked surprised and said, 'Really? You look quite different!'

Sachin grinned and said, 'That's because he's a hybrid—a Chindian—and Junie is just plain Chinese!'

'What's Chindian?' Aida asked.

'Chinese-Indian. Junie's dad and my dad are brothers, in fact, they're identical twins. So, we're more closely related than most first cousins, in fact we're like step-siblings,' Nathan replied nonchalantly while tearing up a piece of *roti chanai*, dipping it into a bowl of *dhal* before popping the piece in his mouth.

Aida looked slightly mystified. Sachin explained, 'Don't worry about it, everyone gets confused at first even if they're not from another country. Anyway, allow me to introduce myself, properly. I'm Sachin Sundara and I'm just a plain Indian Malaysian, although my dad was born in India.'

Aida smiled and said, 'I guessed that . . . I mean that you're Indian. But Sachin sounds familiar . . .'

Sachin said, 'Yup. My dad is cricket-mad and decided to name me after Sachin Tendulkar, considered to be the greatest batsman in the history of cricket. Actually, the original family name is Sundararamamurthi but he had it shortened to Sundara before I was born and for that, I'm incredibly grateful to him!'

Aida's hazel eyes widened, and her eyebrows shot up. Nathan and Junie grinned. Then Aida broke into a smile as well. Junie was relieved to see that Aida had finished all of her sandwiches and was about to eat her apple pie—she always felt a little guilty when she finished all her food and Zara didn't. The group fell silent again as they finished the last bit of their meal.

Sachin, who completed his meal first, wanted to know more about Aida's life before she came to Malaysia. But both Nathan and Junie looked slightly shocked when Sachin said, 'Isn't Alimati the capital of Kazakhstan?'

But Aida replied good-humouredly, 'It's Almaty, not Alimati! Almaty is the largest city in Kazakhstan and used to be the capital until 1997. The new capital is Astana. Astana is a modern city with tall buildings, offices, and malls. '

Junie nodded and said, 'It's the same here—Kuala Lumpur used to be the capital until the government decided to move to Putrajaya. They built it in the middle of nowhere, I think the land used to be an oil palm estate.'

Nathan added, 'There were rumours that the land was haunted because a war had been fought there centuries ago and the trees harboured spirits.'

Aida opened her eyes wide, 'I've never heard of that but I followed my mother to Putrajaya last week and it's really amazing. The architecture seems to represent buildings from all over the world.'

'By the way, I remember reading that Kazakhstan used to be a part of Russia before,' Nathan said.

'The Soviet Union, not Russia. We used to be part of the Soviet Union, until 1991. That's when the USSR broke up, and Kazakhstan became independent,' Aida explained.

Nathan decided to press on, 'But Kazakhstan is in Eurasia, isn't it? Where Europe merges into Asia? And it used to be part of the ancient Silk Road, connecting China to Europe.'

Aida nodded, looking surprised and pleased with what Nathan had said. She said, 'Not many people know that!'

'That's because we're doing a project on the Silk Road for extra credit for our history class, and it would be cool if we could ask you some questions,' Nathan added.

'Happy to answer all your questions, it's not often people actually show an interest in my country,' she said, looking even more pleased.

'So, Marco Polo must have passed through Kazakhstan on his way to China,' Junie speculated.

Aida nodded. 'Yes, he may even have passed through Almaty. It's one of the most ancient settlements on the Silk Road and used to be a centre for trade. The name, Almaty, comes from the Kazakh word for "apple" and the area around Almaty is thought to be the ancestral home of the apple.'

Nathan, Junie, and Sachin visibly perked up at this bit of information. This was something new. Nathan said, 'I've always thought that the apple originated from . . . err Europe . . . you know, Medieval pictures have apples painted on them.'

'Apples have been growing wild around the Almaty region for ages and ages. Travellers on the Silk Road probably brought apples with them to Europe and planted the seeds there,' Aida asserted firmly.

'Interesting,' said Nathan. 'But how do people really know that Almaty is where the apple originated from?'

'Well, the local people believe that apples have been growing in Almaty for thousands of years . . . and the wild *Malus sieversii* is thought to be the ancestor of the modern apple,' Aida explained.

Junie nodded. She said, 'Bananas originate from Southeast Asia and we have, or used to have, all kinds of wild bananas being sold in the villages.'

By now the three friends were genuinely impressed by Aida, they felt that she could be one of them, despite her 'glamourous' look she was a cool nerd.

A peal of laughter came from the table across and all four of them looked up. It was Zara and the Jin Jeanies. Nathan said under his breath, 'Jin must have said something funny.'

Sachin said, 'I don't think he's smart enough to make a joke . . .'

Aida seemed to have noticed them for the first time. She remarked, 'The guy at the table with Zara is kind of cute . . .'

There was an awkward silence before Junie said, 'That's my older brother, Jin.'

Aida replied, 'Oh really . . . but he's . . .' but she stopped short.

' . . . too cute to be my brother?' Junie completed the sentence for her.

Aida looked abashed and said, 'I didn't actually mean that.'

Junie said good-naturedly, 'Don't worry, I'm used to that by now. My superpower is being Jin's invisible sister,' and the three friends burst out laughing.

Sachin added, 'Do you have any brothers or sisters?'

'No, I'm an only child although I've always wanted a younger sister,' Aida replied.

Sachin added, 'I have a younger sister, but luckily she's still into amassing as many Barbies as she can, so we don't have much of a sibling rivalry!'

Aida looked amused but Junie gave him an annoyed look, she hated being reminded of her rivalry with her elder brother.

'I'm in the same boat as you, Aida,' Nathan chimed in. He wondered if he actually wanted to have a sibling. Oddly enough, Souchong suddenly appeared in his mind. Perhaps he did have a sibling, after all, a cat sibling.

The bell rang at that moment, and everyone got up, put their trays away and walked back to their respective classrooms. On the way, Junie reminded everyone, 'We have bio lab now.'

Mr Yeoh, the Biology teacher was of medium build and medium height. He was not excitingly handsome but could be considered as pleasant looking, affable, and bespectacled. He was popular with most of the students and Junie's favourite teacher, she always thought he looked too young to be a teacher.

Mr Yeoh had already placed microscopes, clean test tubes and glass slides on the rows of lab tables. He announced, 'Your assignment today is to identify freshwater micro-organisms. Please take a test tube and a dropper with you—we are taking a walk to the lotus pond today. Each one is to fill the test tube with pond water, seal it and bring it back to the lab.'

Everyone looked pleased at the prospect of spending some time outdoors. Each student picked up their test tubes obediently, and led by Mr Yeoh, walked out of the laboratory and across the lawn to a footpath. They walked through the secluded tree-lined path which led to the pond. The lotus pond was a remnant of the old tin mining pool, which had been filled up many years ago. It was bordered by a footpath and surrounded by tall flowering trees which hid it from view. The pond was fairly large and circular in shape and was almost completely covered with green lotus pads, some of them were crowned by resplendent pink lotus flowers in full bloom. A few bore fruits in the form of large green pods and in some cases, the pods had shrivelled and turned black. Nathan, Junie, and Sachin loved the lotus pond and they sometimes walked there during lunch or their free periods.

While waiting for the rest of the class to catch up with them, Aida asked Junie, 'Who are the "Jeanies" you mentioned during lunch?'

Junie whispered, 'The "Jeanies" are Minji Lee and Maiandra de Souza. They are Six Formers and all the boys think they are the prettiest girls in the school and the girls think they are the coolest. You know, they wear the trendiest stuff, and they hang out with the swim team. But they can be . . .' Junie did not finish her sentence because Mr Yeoh had started speaking.

Mr Yeoh said, 'Okay class, listen up! The pond is an ecosystem by itself, but not a closed one—water evaporates from it and it receives water and nutrients from the surrounding environment, especially when it rains. The dominant species is of course the lotus plant. Can anyone tell me the scientific name of the lotus?'

Both Junie and Alex raised their hands. Mr Yeoh said, 'Yes, Jun Mei?'

Junie said, 'It's *Nelumba nucifera*, also known as the sacred lotus.'

Not to be outdone, Alex added, 'And also commonly known as *teratai* in Malay.'

Mr Yeoh beamed at them and said, 'Excellent, Jun Mei and Alex! *Nelumba nucifera* . . . and *teratai* in Malay. Remember that class!' He added, 'An interesting fact about the lotus is that its seeds, when dried, can survive for a long time. In fact, seeds estimated to be over 1,000 years old, recovered from a dried-up river bed in northeast China, were recently germinated *in vitro* by scientists.'

Junie raised her hand and asked, 'Mr Yeoh, how did they know for sure, that the seeds were that old?'

'Good question, Jun Mei. A group of scientists, led by J Shen-Miller, succeeded in germinating lotus seed pods recovered from a lakebed in 1995. Located in Xipaozi Village, the dry lakebed used to be a large shallow lake used for lotus cultivation at least 1,300 years ago.'

Junie immediately put up her hand and Mr Yeoh added quickly, 'They did carbon dating, of course, to determine the age of the seedpods.' Junie put down her hand and looked slightly disappointed.

Noticing that all the students were paying attention to him, apparently intrigued by a biological fact, Mr Yeoh decided to continue with his story about the lotus seeds of Xipaozi village.

'In fact, there is an interesting story connected to the Xipaozi lotus seeds. A Japanese botanist called Ichiro Ohga was the first person to report the presence of old viable seed pods in the lakebed, during the 1920s. He was the Government Botanist of South Manchuria during the Japanese Occupation of Manchuria in the 1920s.'

Sachin nudged Nathan and whispered, 'Oh-ga sounds like an expression from—' a sharp nudge from Junie cut him off.

Mr Yeoh continued, 'Ohga was helped in his fieldwork by a local farmer. Farmer Liu collected most of the lotus fruit specimens Ohga used in his studies from the soil of his ancestral village. Unfortunately, Farmer Liu was executed after the war for being a Japanese collaborator. Perhaps this goes to show that no good deed goes unpunished.'

The students looked slightly shocked at the fate of Farmer Liu. Mr Yeoh quickly changed the subject and added, 'But we are studying micro-organisms today. They play an important role in every ecosystem and your task is to identify as many as you can.'

The students positioned themselves at different locations along the banks of the pond and used the dropper to fill their test tubes with pond water and sealed it. Once everyone had completed their task at a leisurely pace, Mr Yeoh led them back into the classroom.

Mr Yeoh said, 'Your next step is to prepare some slides. Place a drop of pond water on a slide and examine it under a microscope.

When you spot something interesting, add a very small drop of dye into the specimen and cover it with a glass piece. Then examine the specimen under the microscope and make a sketch of the specimen in your lab book. The next step is to identify the micro-organism you have sketched, correctly!'

Everyone set to work with enthusiasm, Junie, of course, being ahead of everyone. She successfully identified a strand of algae, a green *hydra* and even an actively swimming *paramecium*, which moved by rotating its body. Once she had finished with her slides, she decided to help Aida who was struggling with her sketches. Most of the students managed to identify the algae and *amoebas*, some spotted *hydras* and a few even managed to identify the elusive *euglena*, shaped like elegant ladies' slippers.

When the class was over, the students packed their things and left the laboratory for the next class. Nathan and Junie, however, lingered behind to have a word with Mr Yeoh. He looked at them enquiringly. Junie asked him hesitantly, 'Umm . . . Mr Yeoh, Nathan and I were thinking of doing a new science project for extra credit!'

Mr Yeoh seemed pleasantly surprised, 'You don't really need extra credit, Jun Mei, you're already the top science student this year . . . but we always encourage student initiative. What project do you have in mind?'

Junie took in a deep breath and said, 'Err . . . we are thinking of preserving a dead bird.'

'We want to use the same methods as the ancient Egyptians!' added Nathan.

Mr Yeoh's eyebrows shot up, 'Hmm . . . it sounds interesting; but why ancient Egyptian methods? There are more effective scientific methods for preserving biological specimens.'

'Well, we think the ancient methods might be more interesting. Besides, it will involve history as well as chemistry and biology,' said Junie. She did not mention the fact that Nathan thought the ancient Egyptian preservation method helped to ensure the soul of the bird would be happier in the afterlife.

'And research into Egyptology, which is also a branch of science,' added Nathan.

Mr Yeoh raised his eyebrows and said, 'Hmmm . . . you're not going to kill a bird for this project, are you?'

Junie replied quickly, 'No way, Mr Yeoh! We would never even think of killing a bird,' and she glanced at Nathan.

Nathan replied, 'Mr Yeoh, my cat . . . err . . . accidentally caught a sunbird in the garden. Junie identified it as *Chalcoparia singalensis* and we wanted to preserve it . . . for posterity!'

Mr Yeoh said, 'Ah, a sunbird! *Chalcoparia singalensis* is quite a rare specimen and totally protected . . . an unfortunate loss. Did you know that outdoor domestic cats are the number one threat to birds and are thought to kill 2.4 billion birds in the US alone? And we have no idea what the figures are like for Malaysia. Even the IUCN lists cats as the world's worst non-native invasive species. Even well-fed cats will kill birds . . . and I hope you realize all outdoor cats should be belled and neutered!'

Nathan was genuinely horrified and alarmed to hear what Mr Yeoh had to say. How could the beloved pet cats of so many people kill so many birds? 2.4 billion birds to be exact . . . How many cats did it take to kill so many birds in the US? He couldn't imagine it but he felt compelled to speak out for his cat and said defensively, 'Mr Yeoh, Souchong is actually an indoor cat, he accidentally escaped that one time . . . and we intend to get him a really loud bell . . . like today!'

Mr Yeoh looked sceptical. Before he could say anything, Junie cleared her throat. She already had an inkling about the predatory behaviour of cats, but the information provided by Mr Yeoh shocked her as well. She chimed in nevertheless, 'Err . . . Mr Yeoh, cats had a positive role in society; in the past, they helped to control pests. In fact, some people think exterminating cats during mass witch-hunts in Europe may have led to the Great Plague.' Junie had actually learnt this from Nathan some time ago, and Nathan looked at her gratefully for remembering what he had told her.

Mr Yeoh paused and then he seemed to make up his mind. 'I don't find anything objectionable about this project, although you might want to consider modern methods of preservation. But make sure you document the process with photographs and write a report once the project is complete. Hmm . . . you should also display the mummified bird for the science class, so that we can use this as a reminder to students to neuter and bell all their cats. I suppose you will be using the lab for this?'

Both Junie and Nathan heaved a sigh of relief and said, 'Yes, Mr Yeoh!' They thanked him and rushed out of the lab for their next class, smiles on their faces. Junie burst out, 'Preserve for posterity? Couldn't you think of something better?' and she started laughing.

Nathan said with a grin, 'Well, it worked, didn't it?' Then he grew more thoughtful and said, 'Was everything he said true? About outdoor domestic cats being the number one predator of birds?'

Junie replied, 'It's all true, even well-fed cats will kill birds and other small animals. It's an inborn instinct.'

3

Visit to the Mothership

On Sunday, Junie called Nathan in the morning. He was still asleep when his cell phone rang and he picked it up reluctantly, 'Junie, it's only 9 a.m.! I'm allowed to sleep late during weekends!'

Junie replied cheerfully, 'You get more done if you wake up early! And 9 a.m. is not exactly early. I'm coming to your house for dinner tonight. Actually, I'm coming earlier to help you with your homework . . . your mum asked me to.'

Junie arrived at Nathan's place promptly at four in the afternoon; she was carrying her school satchel with her. They went through their homework and even had time to do some revisions. Nathan always did much better with Junie's help because she was quite a ruthless taskmaster. Even Souchong's persistent attempts for attention were ignored. He headbutted Junie's legs and rubbed himself against Nathan's legs and finally jumped onto his lap, but Junie told him sternly to sit on the floor. He finally walked away in a huff and jumped onto a basket that was in the corner.

Nathan gave a sigh of relief when Kak Yam called them down for dinner at eight.

They ate their dinner slowly, savouring the food in silent camaraderie. Nathan didn't even mind that his parents were still not home.

'It's a public holiday in Selangor tomorrow and I'm planning to go to Kino to get the very last issue of *Fruits Basket*. Want to come along? I'm thinking of inviting Sachin and Aida as well. We can have lunch at KLCC,' Junie announced to Nathan.

Nathan hesitated. He liked visiting Kinokuniya, but it was located in the Kuala Lumpur City Centre and quite a distance from Kota Kemuning. He asked her, 'Why do you always visit Kino? There's an MPH in Subang Parade and Popular is in Sunway Pyramid.'

Junie sighed and rolled her eyes, 'If you must ask me that question, you're obviously not a hardcore bookworm . . . don't you know Kino is the favourite hangout of every bibliophile in the Klang Valley? They call it the "Mothership" That's where the cool people who read or pretend to read like to be seen!'

Nathan was about to reply that he wasn't interested in being cool. Instead, he said, 'Why do you bother about such things? As far as I know, you're the most well-read person in the school; I mean, you have nothing to prove. And if we can get the same stuff somewhere nearer . . .'

'Not reaaally. You get stuff there you can't find in other bookstores. Besides, Kino has the best manga collection,' she added with a grin.

Junie took out her handphone and called Sachin and Aida in turn. Then she put away her phone in her skirt pocket and said, 'It's confirmed then. I'm meeting Sachin and Aida at 10.30 tomorrow morning at the station at Subang Jaya. We're going to take the train to the KLCC. Are you in?'

Nathan perked up when he heard that Aida and Sachin would be coming. He never got a chance to talk to Aida outside of school, since she lived quite a distance away. In fact, he was quite curious to know what she looked like in street clothes. The school uniform tended to make everyone look . . . uniform. He replied, 'I'm in, all right. Let's visit the mothership!'

It was nine when Junie decided to leave and Nathan got ready to walk her home. Even though they lived on the same street, he always made it a point to accompany her when she stayed after dark.

He picked Souchong up, put him in a knapsack and carried the cat on his back.

When they were walking on the road leading to her house at the other end of the block, a black cat appeared and crossed their path. Nathan came to an abrupt stop. 'Did you see that? A massive black cat just crossed our path! It appeared out of nowhere!'

'I didn't see it coming either. I wonder who it belongs to? I would've noticed a cat like that in the neighbourhood,' Junie said thoughtfully.

Nathan said in a low voice, 'They say it's bad luck when a black cat crosses your path.'

'According to Zara, the Scottish believe that black cats are actually lucky,' replied Junie.

'Who are you going to believe, the whole world or the Scottish?' Nathan asked her.

'Hmm . . . so what should we do? Utter a counter spell?' Junie asked.

'If we change direction, then it means that the cat did not actually cross our path,' Nathan replied.

'Oh okay. Let's take the long route around the area. Anyway, I could do with a walk after that huge dinner.' Junie groaned, 'I wish Kak Yam didn't cook such delicious food, it always makes me feel so heavy.'

They turned around and walked into a side road, with a small sign Chempaka Lane, which would take them on a wide semi-circle around their neighbourhood. They would have to circle the small park which divided the blocks of houses. The dimly lit road looked unusually dark that night. Nathan wondered why he never noticed how tall the trees had grown in the neighbourhood. He thought they looked twice as tall and twice as dense compared to the last time he walked here. He said, 'It's weird. This place looks different in the dark . . .'

They passed under a tall tree with dense leaves and were assailed by the sweet fragrance of night-blooming flowers, wafting towards them. Junie said, 'That's odd. I don't remember there being a chempaka tree in the neighbourhood.'

'Chempaka tree? How do you know that it's a chempaka tree? I mean it could be umm . . . frangipani or jasmine or something,' suggested Nathan.

'Jasmine is just a bush, and everyone recognizes a frangipani tree,' she replied.

'Well, I'm glad it's not a frangipani, they call it "the graveyard tree",' Nathan said in a low voice.

'Yes, I know. They also call it "the temple tree". In fact, there's one in your garden, remember? Chempaka is actually way scarier than frangipani,' she replied.

Nathan was genuinely curious, 'Why is chempaka scarier?'

Junie spoke in a low voice, 'Some people think that the chempaka tree, especially the one bearing white flowers, is actually the *sundal harum malam*.'

Nathan said, 'What's that? *Sundal harum malam*?' and immediately regretted asking her that question. The name sounded both enticing and menacing at the same time—a perfumed night harlot.

Junie lowered her voice further and somehow managed to sound quite creepy, 'The *sundal harum malam* is a tall tree with strongly scented white flowers which only bloom at night.'

'Err, Junie, I think I've already heard this before. It's because they are pollinated by moths, right? You're the science nerd, remember?' he whispered, trying to stop her.

But Junie was on a roll. 'People believe the sundal tree is haunted by the Pontianak. You know, ladies in white with long black hair who like to linger around the sweetly scented chempaka tree in full bloom and—'

Before she could finish the sentence, Souchong suddenly hissed and attempted to jump out of the knapsack. Nathan and Junie jumped with fright. Nathan pulled the knapsack to the front and attempted to calm the cat down, 'Shh . . . Souchong, it's okay!

You're safe in the knapsack.' But the cat became increasingly agitated. A sudden gust of wind blew through the trees making the leaves shiver. Dark shadows with long stick-like fingers seemed to move towards them. The fragrance of the flowers became stronger, and Nathan could have sworn the claw-like stick fingers were reaching out towards them.

Junie yelled, 'Run!' and sprinted away as fast as she could.

Gripping the knapsack tightly, Nathan ran behind her. They ran all the way to Junie's house. Souchong had stopped struggling when he sensed that Nathan was running. Nathan managed to catch up with Junie and they only stopped when they were in front of the gate of her house, gasping for breath. When she had recovered her breath, Junie asked Nathan if he wanted to come in for a cup of hot chocolate to recover from the fright. Nathan was about to agree to this suggestion when he saw his mother's BMW coming towards them. He waved at her to stop and decided to ride home with his mother. He waved and said, 'See you tomorrow, Junie!' And shut the car door, relieved that he had a ride home.

* * *

The next morning, Junie's mother dropped Junie and Nathan at the Subang Jaya train station at 10.30 a.m. on the dot. Sachin's mother dropped him off a minute later and they waited for a few minutes for Aida to arrive. She came in a chauffeur-driven Mercedes Benz. The car stopped and the driver, who was dressed in uniform, got out to open the door for her. The people who were waiting for the train were staring at her—Mercedes Benzes were common enough in Subang Jaya but very few had uniformed chauffeurs to drive them around.

Aida was dressed in a black knit top from GAP and a denim jacket and fitted jeans with machine embroidery along the two side pockets. Junie noticed the brand—True Religion. It was unfamiliar to her, but she thought it looked cool. A pair of black leather gladiator sandals completed her look. Junie herself was wearing black leggings paired with a white cotton shirt dress from Forever 21, grey and silver Converse sneakers, and a grey faux leather Guess handbag with silver trimmings completed her look. She wanted to look smart and still be comfortable. Surya KLCC was one of the largest malls in Malaysia and required a great deal of walking. Junie felt gratified by the approving look Aida gave her. The boys were in ubiquitous jeans, T-shirts, and sneakers.

They greeted each other cheerfully. Sachin said, 'We're taking the Kelana Jaya line. If we are lucky, we get to try the new coaches!'

When the next train arrived, they all climbed on board. Sachin was thrilled at being able to try out the new high-speed train. Everyone was impressed by the brand-new, sparkly clean interior of the coach. The ride was fun, although they felt a little uncomfortable being stared at by some of the passengers; but most people minded their own business. Junie reminded Aida to keep an eye on her purse and she quickly checked to make sure it was in her pocket. But this watchfulness lasted only for a moment, as she soon became absorbed in watching the scenery. The view was very different from what she usually saw from sitting in a car as the train tracks faced the back of buildings, which looked less well-kept as compared to the front façade.

Nathan and Junie recounted their adventure the night before, to while away time. Aida listened with rapt attention, while Sachin looked confused, 'Where did you say you were walking last night? I don't ever remember seeing a lane like that.'

'Chempaka Lane, I remember seeing the sign,' Nathan replied.

'Nate, there is no such place called Chempaka Lane in Kota Kemuning! All the roads and lanes are named after orchids as in Jalan Aranda!' Sachin exclaimed.

'Yes, Sachin, it was Chempaka Lane! I remember seeing the sign as well and it did feel . . . well, it felt a bit haunted,'

Junie insisted. Sachin decided not to pursue the matter further and changed the subject.

When the train finally stopped at KLCC, it was close to noon. Sachin suggested that they have lunch first, because, 'Once Junie enters a bookstore, you can't expect her to leave in less than two hours!'

KLCC was a huge mall, and it took the four of them several minutes of walking along brightly lit corridors that overlooked the vast central atrium and ascending a series of escalators before they reached the fifth floor where the food court was. The two boys secured a table while Aida and Junie bought lunch for themselves. They both decided on Japanese-style ramen. Nathan and Sachin chose sizzling mushroom noodles and side dishes of roti canai. While they were munching away, the four of them saw two women they knew by sight, walking along the corridor outside. Junie exclaimed, 'Look! It's Minji's mother and Maiandra's mother. Whoa, what a contrast!'

Minji's mother was dressed in an elegant knee-length jade green dress with a black lace inset at the front. A lacy green cardigan, an expensive-looking black leather handbag, and black leather high-heeled shoes completed her look. Maiandra's mother, on the other hand, was dressed in a white top and a grey tracksuit with a matching jacket. A pink leather backpack and a pair of pink leather sneakers completed her look. Sachin said aloud, 'Posh Spice meets Sporty Spice,' and all of them burst out laughing.

'I guess the super-rich can only relate to other super-rich,' said Junie.

To their surprise, Aida said, 'Urm, I think only one of them is super rich. The woman with the black leather handbag is carrying what looks like an original Chanel, while the woman with the pink backpack is carrying an MCM. MCM is flashy and expensive but not a top-end luxury brand, like Chanel and LV.'

'My mother has an LV so I know what that is, but what's MCM?' Nathan asked. He had heard of Chanel before, from his mother who was debating whether she should get one. She was bemoaning the fact that even their plainest handbag was so outrageously expensive. In the end, she had settled for an LV. Everyone knew what LV stood for and she felt less guilty about buying it.

Aida said, 'It used to stand for Michael Cromer Munchen, but a Korean company, Sungjoo Group, bought over the brand. Some people think it stands for Modern Creations Munchen or even Monster Creations Munchen, now.' She giggled a little.

Junie stared at her. 'Wow! You've profiled people based on their fashion!' She understood that Maiandra's family was probably in the same situation as her own family—struggling to pay for a child in private school and trying to keep up with wealthy friends. 'I guess you would know, being one of the people who could actually afford designer stuff,' Junie added, with a tinge of envy in her voice.

'Oh no!' laughed Aida. 'My mother used to carry a Guess handbag until I had to point out to her that only junior diplomats carry Guess. In the end, she bought a Coach, which is even more affordable than an LV.'

'Yes, but you get to travel all over the world. I mean you see so much more than we do,' Sachin pointed out.

'I guess it's true that I get to live in other countries and learn about different cultures, and ways of life, and eat all kinds of food. You really learn to appreciate a country for its food!' She replied with a broad grin.

'And attend glitzy parties, and mingle with diplomats from all over the world, and be driven around in a black Merc by a chauffeur!' Sachin continued for her.

Aida blushed slightly, 'The car actually belongs to the government and the chauffeur is paid for by our government as well. Even the house we live in belongs to the government. Back home, we do have a Honda SUV, but my mother and father have to drive it themselves. In Astana, we live just like everyone else.'

Junie felt her envy fade away and noticed that Aida was feeling self-conscious. Sachin had a sharp tongue at times. She decided to change the subject. 'The food is getting cold, so let's eat up!'

Nathan nodded, 'Your sizzling noodle has stopped sizzling, and I noticed you've still got a plate of *roti chanai* to finish, Sachin!'

They were all eager to visit the bookstore and finished their lunch as quickly as they could. They picked up their phones and got up and did a bit more walking to the escalator, which led them to the entrance of Kinokuniya, on the top floor. Sachin whispered reverently, 'Ladies and gentlemen, we have finally arrived at the sanctum!' And gestured at the store with a flourish. Aida smiled and looked at the signage and door admiringly. She said, 'It's huge! It's even bigger and better than I had imagined.'

'Yes! It's so cool, isn't it? According to legend, they opened the Kinokuniya Kuala Lumpur flagship store ten years ago, and it went on to become the top Kino bookstore in the Asia Pacific region.'

'And I've read that they get over 100K visitors a month who buy over 100K books!' Junie added with a beam.

'Wow! That's mind-boggling,' Aida said in open-mouthed surprise.

'It turns out that Malaysians are actually serious readers,' said Nathan thoughtfully.

They waited for Aida to enter the store first and followed suit. Junie knew exactly where she wanted to go and made a beeline for the manga shelves. She scanned the rows of manga, spotted what she wanted, *Fruits Basket No. 25*, quickly picked it up and held on to it carefully. She was now free to browse the shelves for new manga releases and Young Adult books which were trending. She was only allowed one book per month and had chosen to collect the entire *Fruits Basket* series. Some of the girls she knew at school had started raving about *Twilight* so she flipped through a copy but decided that she didn't like the style.

Aida wandered around the store as though she was under a spell. She looked slightly dazed to the three friends. Apparently, Kinokuniya had managed to sweep her off her feet. Nathan, on the other hand, knew what he wanted as well and picked up *Charles and Emma: The Darwins' Leap of Faith*. He tucked it under his arm before turning his attention to other books. He thought *The Evolution of Calpurnia Tate* sounded interesting but wondered if he would be teased by the other students for reading a book with a girl on the cover. Sachin picked up *Full Metal Alchemist No. 21* and then decided to look at music CDs.

After about an hour of wandering around, Aida spotted Junie and decided to join her. She had picked up a book on Malaysian folktales and said she wanted to find out more about local culture. Junie nodded and showed her a copy of *Fruits Basket*. Aida said, 'Cool! I don't read manga but I love anime. My favourite is *Inuyasha*, have you seen it?'

Junie exclaimed, 'I love *Inuyasha* too. The series has the best storylines. I only wish his "girlfriend" Kagome was less annoying! All she does is wail, "Inuyasha! Inuyashaaa!"'

Aida agreed, 'Kagome Higurashi, the annoying air-head. As the keeper of the Shikon Jewel, you would think she would be a lot smarter. I mean, if our school uniforms were as short as hers, we would be sent home instantly!'

Junie gave a muffled laugh and said, 'It's hard to believe that Kagome is the reincarnation of Kikyo, the Shinto priestess who was the original keeper. I mean Kikyo is so self-composed and cool. I guess Kagome became the keeper of *Shikon no Tama* by default.'

'*Shikon no Tama*, the "Jewel of the Four Souls", it sounds so mysterious and creepy.' Aida gave a little shiver. 'But the best part of the series is of course Sesshomaru . . . he's so gorgeous!' She added with a sigh. Junie sighed in agreement. They were both silent for a while, conjuring the icy beauty of Inuyasha's demon brother, with his long flowing platinum blond hair and piercing blue eyes, in their mind's eyes.

Junie snapped out of the spell first and continued their conversation about Kagome, 'It's also amazing that she has an ancestral shrine in her backyard, right in the middle of Tokyo, with a well which is actually a time portal!'

Aida nodded. 'I looked it up—all the action takes place during the Sengoku Period—the Warring States Era. I guess many Japanese families go back a long way—hundreds of years.'

Junie replied thoughtfully, 'Actually, all of us go back a long way, it's just that we don't live in our ancestral land any more. We have a new ancestral land now. My family goes back six generations because we are members of the Baba and Nyonya community. But most Malaysian-Chinese have only been in this country for three or four generations.'

Aida looked puzzled and asked, 'Who are the Baba and Nyonya?'

Junie explained, 'They are the people who settled in this country before the nineteenth century and adopted local culture. The earliest came during the Malacca Sultanate in the fifteenth century, from Ming Dynasty China. Many came later. There are also Baba and Nyonya in Penang, but they probably came later during the eighteenth or nineteenth century. My father and Nathan's father, are Baba from Malacca.'

'That's really interesting. You mean all Chinese in Malaysia are not Baba?'

'Umm no. In fact, the Baba are sort of a minority. They speak a type of Malay and have their own cuisine, which is quite spicy, unlike normal Chinese food. They also have their own traditional costumes, songs, and dances. During Chinese New Year, we always visit the ancestral house in Melaka,' Junie explained. She felt a bit awkward saying this because she had never seen herself as a minority before.

'What about you? What's your life like in Kazakhstan? Do you have an ancestral home?' Junie asked.

'Our ancestral home is in Almaty, which is where my grandparents live. We live in Astana of course, because my parents work for the government. But the house in Almaty is not that old either. Some of the people in Kazakhstan used to be nomadic and roamed around Central Asia, we really only settled down sometime in the last century, although a few of the cities along the Silk Road are really ancient,'

'Yes, you mentioned Almaty being the ancestral birthplace of the apple. Nathan and I looked it up. It seemed that Genghis Khan destroyed the city at the end of the twelfth century,' said Junie.

Aida nodded. 'Almaty was already ancient when it was destroyed by the Mongols. It dates back to around 700 BC.'

'Wow! With a history that old, I guess, you might have a chance of finding a centuries-old ancestral shrine in your backyard!' said Junie with a wistful smile.

'I doubt it. Is *Fruits Basket* a bit like *Inuyasha*?' Aida asked curiously.

'Umm . . . no. *Inuyasha* is a shonen manga, written mainly for boys. It's got a lot more action, like sword fights, magic, and adventure, I guess. *Fruits Basket* is shojo manga, written mainly for girls. There's more emotional stuff—interpersonal relations, family conflicts and, romance.'

'I didn't know you were such an expert on relationships and conflicts, Junie,' a cool voice interrupted her. Junie and Aida turned around and came face to face with Minji. She was standing behind them with Maiandra beside her. As always, they looked stunning with perfectly groomed hair and flawlessly made-up faces. Junie was about to reply but Minji ignored her, turned towards Aida and said, 'You must be the new girl from Kazakhstan, we've heard so much about.'

Aida smiled and said, 'Yes, I'm Aida Anargul. It's a pleasure to meet you!'

Minji said with superficial politeness, 'Hi Aida, the pleasure is all mine. I'm Minji Lee and this is Maiandra de Souza.'

Maiandra smiled and said pointedly to Aida, 'I never figured you for a bookworm, you don't look like one of them . . . '

Junie tensed. She'd always felt intimidated by the two girls, but Aida responded cheerfully, 'Oh, I've always loved books. I think bookstores and libraries are the best places to visit on a rainy day.'

'Oh reeaally? Who knew under the skin, you're just like Junie, only somewhat prettier,' said Maiandra.

Aida looked slightly taken aback. Then she replied, 'Have you heard of the expression, "Don't judge a book by its cover"?'

Minji snapped, 'Apparently, the Kazakh girl prefers to hang out with the nerd herd. Do they still ride on camels over there?'

Aida gasped. She was speechless.

Junie snapped back, 'The people of Kazakhstan are the Cassocks, known throughout history for their horsemanship. They do not ride camels . . . although that's perfectly okay, I mean riding camels . . .'

Before she could complete her sentence, Maiandra interjected, 'Where's your Chindian cousin? I heard he's crying over dead birds. Some of us think he needs to see a shrink.' Her voice dripped with venom.

Junie turned pale and clenched her fists in fury. She didn't mind being called a nerd but had always been protective of Nathan. Before she could say anything, Sachin was standing beside her. He exclaimed, 'Oh look, the terrible twins M & M are here! You do realize you're actually in a bookstore . . . *the* bookstore, the Mothership of the Nerds?'

Junie recovered her tongue, 'Yes, did you lose your way, Mini and Mai? I think the over-priced cosmetics store is just around the corner.'

'GPS malfunction, perhaps?' added Sachin. Junie smiled, even though she did not really know what GPS meant.

Minji and Maiandra gave them a withering look. Minji said, 'Whatever! Who wants to hang out with a bunch of boring bookworms anyway! Go choke on a book!' They tossed their shiny, perfectly groomed hair, turned around and left.

Nathan who had just noticed what was going on from afar, walked swiftly towards his friends. He asked, 'What did those two want?' He looked at Junie and Aida thoughtfully and realized that the encounter must have been intense. Junie looked tensed and Aida was actually shaking.

'Apparently, my intervention had the desired effect; they ran out of here like bats out of hell,' Sachin said nonchalantly.

Nathan said, 'Bats from hell? That pretty much describes them. Anyway, I've found what I was looking for. Do you want to stay on a bit longer, Junie?'

Junie shook her head. The encounter with Minji and Maiandra had spoilt her mood and even the normally effervescent Aida looked pale with shock. Junie replied, 'No, I'd rather go home early and think of ways of getting even with those two. Let's pay for the books and leave.'

After paying for their purchases, they took the escalators down to the lower level. However, Nathan spotted a stall selling cupcakes and exclaimed, 'Oh look! Vanilla butter-cream cupcakes! Why should we let those two girls spoil our mood? I think we should have tea and cupcakes while we go through our stuff. I want to know what everyone bought.'

Vanilla butter-cream cupcakes were Junie's favourite dessert and she paused to consider. Should she or shouldn't she? Before she could make up her mind, Aida exclaimed, 'They even have salted caramel cupcakes! I love them! Let's forget about those mean girls and have some tea!'

Sachin did not object and Junie decided Nathan was right, they should make full use of their time there. They sat down and had tea with cupcakes. Junie and Aida ordered their favourites, while Nathan had strawberry cream and Sachin had chocolate cream. Nathan showed his book to Junie, 'It's about Charles Darwin and his life with his wife, Emma, who was supposed to be quite religious—I mean his wife was. I also came across another book you might be interested in, Junie. *The Evolution of Calpurnia Tate*, it's historical fiction and might be even more interesting than *Charles and Emma*.'

Junie nodded, 'This is the last issue for *Fruits Basket* so I'll be able to buy that book next month.'

Aida noticed Sachin's purchase, which had a fiercely confident blond boy with a metal arm on the cover and said, 'Must be a shonen manga!'

Sachin beamed, 'Yup! *Full Metal Alchemist* is action-packed. But it's the premise that is very fascinating—it's set in a dystopian steampunk world that resembles World War II Germany, but their main weapons are state alchemists with incredible powers. These alchemists are like mutants with magic.'

'Why Full Metal?' asked Aida.

Sachin answered, 'Erm, well, the main character, Ed Elric, has a metal arm and leg, and his brother, Al, is actually an empty suit of armour. Al's soul is tied to the armour, which I suppose makes it a Horcrux. Oh, I forgot to mention that Ed is a state alchemist, he is, in fact, the youngest person to ever become one.'

Aida looked puzzled, so Nathan chipped in, 'Al doesn't have a physical body so his older brother, Ed, tied his soul to the armour to keep him in this world. Ed used his own blood to draw the magical symbols on the inside of the armour.'

Aida looked slightly stunned at this so Junie said, '*Full Metal Alchemist* is really thought-provoking—if you can stand the violence. It's about Ed's quest for the Philosopher's Stone. He thinks the Stone will restore his brother's body, which is trapped in another dimension.'

After a long pause, where she pondered over the story, Aida said, 'The first Harry Potter book is also about the Philosopher's Stone.'

Nathan replied, 'I guess the first HP and FMA have something in common, but the HP Philosopher's Stone is way less sinister than the FMA stone. And the entire FMA series is about Ed's quest for the Stone. Ed and all the other state alchemists, and scary evil creatures called Homunculi. Of course, when he finds out what it takes to create the Stone—'

'Spoiler alert! Spoiler alert!' interjected Sachin, silencing Nathan.

'Well, there are references to the Holocaust in an updated version, or at least to a group of minority people who are clearly different from the White people who hold all the power and wealth in the State,' Nathan added.

'You can borrow the old issues, if you are interested. I have the entire series,' continued Sachin.

Aida nodded, 'Thanks, Sachin. I'm really interested in reading them now.'

Nathan said, 'Now that everyone has calmed down, can someone tell me what happened back then at the bookstore?'

Junie filled him in as calmly as she could, although she could not keep herself from calling the two girls some vile names.

Aida nodded vigorously and added her own angry comments, 'Apparently, they were keen for me to join them even though they thought I'm a camel rider! Anyway, they made themselves look older with way too much makeup . . . And those skanky clothes! So last season! Imagine dressing up for a cocktail party while in a shopping complex!'

Junie could not help bursting out into laughter. 'You sound like one of those characters in *The Devil Wears Prada*!'

Aida burst out laughing too. 'That's one of my favourite books! Although I think, Prada is overrated, I mean their designs are so plain and their products have no second-hand value. It should have been, *The Devil Wears Hermes!*'

'What do you mean by no second-hand value?' asked Junie, intrigued. She had no idea what 'Ermehz' was either but didn't want to reveal her ignorance. She felt slightly relieved when Sachin asked, 'What's Ermehz?'

'Hermes, named after the Greek messenger god. It's probably the most expensive brand of accessories in the world. And no second-hand value means no one would pay you close to the original price, if you decided to resell your item,' Aida replied.

Seeing their dazed look, she added, 'I know stuff like this because I intend to be a fashion writer, you know get to attend New York fashion week, Paris fashion week, and all the cool events with fab, free swag.'

Junie nodded. 'I've read that Paris, New York and Milan are the fashion capitals of the world.'

'Oh, there's also London and Tokyo, and I wouldn't count Shanghai out, either,' said Aida with a smile.

Nathan and Sachin looked bemused by the new direction taken by the conversation. They were surprised that Junie understood what Aida was talking about. They had always assumed that she was a science nerd who took the occasional foray into history and manga. She never talked about clothes or fashion, at least not when she was with them. Nathan decided to change the subject, 'I wonder what drives them to behave this way? According to my Mom, those who bully are just as unhappy as those who get bullied.'

Junie looked confused, and then she said, 'You're talking about Minji and Mai? You really think they are unhappy?'

Sachin said, 'I wouldn't count on that; some people are plain nasty and enjoy picking on people. Bullies get high on putting people down.'

'I wonder . . . Nathan may have a point. Jin once mentioned that Minji was always worried about her grades and Maiandra was unhappy with herself about something, although he wouldn't say what,' Junie added.

Sachin snorted, 'Nah, that would require sensitivity on their part. Basically, they are determined to maintain their position as the Queen Bees of Noble Hall.'

A slightly glum look descended on all their faces at the thought.

'If it's any consolation, my mother said that being popular in school does not guarantee success in adult life. In fact, she mentioned that the most popular boy in her class is now selling shoes in a store!' Aida said.

Nathan, Junie and Sachin looked thoughtfully at her. They tried to imagine Minji and Maiandra selling shoes at a shoe store but somehow the idea seemed incongruous, until Junie said, 'Well, maybe Jimmy Choos!' And they burst out laughing.

They decided to change the subject and switched back to talking about the books they were reading. The encounter with Minji and Maiandra had brought them closer together and they felt a deeper sense of camaraderie with Aida, almost as if they had gone through a trial by fire to prove their loyalty to each other. After the cupcakes and the tea, they all felt uncomfortably full but cheerful.

At this point, Nathan felt comfortable enough to ask Aida, 'You remember the Silk Road project I mentioned before? I've almost completed the part about the trading routes and settlements through Central Asia.'

Aida turned towards Nathan, smiled and nodded when she heard Silk Road being mentioned. 'Ms Jones asked me about my history project as well and she suggested that we collaborate since I might not have enough time to come up with something new.'

Nathan looked pleased. He nodded in turn and added, 'That's great! I'm really interested in the stuff you mentioned about apples originating in Kazakhstan. Maybe we could include the possibility of plants and seeds being moved around the route.'

Junie interrupted the conversation, 'That's cool! But I think it's time we made a move cause it's getting late. My mother doesn't like being kept waiting!'

They walked through the underground tunnel to The Avenue Mall, where the train station was located and made the journey back home. Some of the seats were occupied and Aida sat beside Junie, while the boys sat a few rows away. During the journey, she remarked, 'It's not true, what they said about you.'

'What's not true about me?' Junie asked, puzzled.

'What Maiandra said about you being plain and nerdy. You're cute; you have fine features, and your hairstyle is sharp. It's just that you haven't fully grown yet.'

Junie felt flattered and unexpectedly shy. Since she could remember, she was used to being overlooked most of the time and was not used to being complimented. She blushed slightly and mumbled, 'Thanks, Aida. I guess, I'm developmentally slow, at least physically.'

'The thing is to accept what's happening to you as natural,' Aida continued.

Junie looked at her in surprise, Aida noticed more than she let on. It's true that she had started to feel self-conscious of her body and had started hunching a little and wearing loose clothes because she felt self-conscious of her developing figure. She never admitted the fact that she disliked the Jin Jeanies not just because they were mean and arrogant, but also because she felt disadvantaged by the fact that they seemed so at ease with themselves and the way they looked. It was hard for her to admit this to herself. She was about to say something when Aida suddenly burped. Everyone laughed.

Aida groaned aloud, 'I feel so full now! Why did I eat the entire cupcake? I think I've exceeded my calorie allowance for the day. I'll have to skip dinner, tonight.'

Junie said cheerfully, 'It was delicious though and worth eating every crumb!'

When the train arrived at the Subang Jaya station and they all got up, Aida suddenly exclaimed, 'You know what?'

'What?' her three friends exclaimed.

'I've just got an idea! But I can't tell you what it is yet! If it works out, you'll get something in the mail next week!' she said with a wide smile on her face.

They got out of the train and said their farewells before returning home.

4

The Diplomatic Party

On Monday, Aida did not mention anything to them about the surprise she was planning, even when they had time to chat during the lunch break. She clearly did not want to talk about it so they did not bring it up, whatever it was. Sometimes, things did not always work out the way you want them to. When Nathan returned home after school, Souchong came out to greet him at the door. Nathan bent down to stroke his soft fur and fed him some cat treats he always carried in his bag. Nathan was about to climb up the stairs when Kak Yam stopped him, 'Nathan *tunggu dulu! Ada surat untuk awak!*'

She handed him a white envelope. Nathan's heart missed a beat, was this what Aida was hinting at? He took the envelope from Kak Yam and peered at it closely. The envelope had his name and a crest printed on it—two winged horses flanking a gold ring; upon closer examination, he decided the horses were in fact, unicorns. He whispered to himself, 'Cool!'

Kak Yam, who was hovering around him said, '*Dari mana ini? Nampak macam dari orang besar!*'

Nathan said, '*Dari* Kazakhstan!'

He ran up the stairs to his room, followed closely by Souchong. He carefully opened the envelope with a letter opener and pulled out the thick white card inside. It was an invitation to The Constitution Day of the Republic of Kazakhstan on 30

August 2010. It was the first time in his life he had received an official invitation card with his name printed on it. Normally, his invitations came in the form of text messages. His phone pinged. He sat down on the bed to check his messages. Souchong jumped onto the bed and sniffed at his phone. Nathan ignored him. Then the cat sat on the laptop that was lying on the bed. Normally, this was enough to draw Nathan's attention, but he was too intent on the phone to pay Souchong any attention.

It was Junie.

> Did you get it? So posh!

Another message popped up, this one from Sachin.

> Mad cool invite from Aida!

Nathan replied promptly.

> From her parents, you mean! I'm looking at it now! 'Mr Turan Anargul and H.E. Mrs Adina Anargul have pleasure in inviting Mr Nathan Kwan to the Constitution Day of the Republic of Kazakhstan.'

By this time, Souchong decided the laptop was too hard and uncomfortable, and got up. He bumped his head against Nathan, who allowed him to snuggle up against him. Content, Souchang settled down to take a nap.

Sachin

> What's Constitution Day? Shouldn't it be National or Independence Day?

Nathan

It's the day their Constitution was first promulgated. They also have a National Day

Sachin

You learn something new every day

Junie

It's only for us though, no parents are invited!

Nathan

Cool! We'll have to ask our parents to drop us off though

Junie

I would ask my Mum but I think we need a posher car than a Toyota SUV

Nathan

Well, I guess I could ask my mother to drive us there but she usually works quite late

Junie

Maybe Uncle KC can drive your mother's car?

Nathan

Yeah! My mother won't mind exchanging cars with my Dad for a day, I guess

Sachin

Glad that's fixed! Did you guys notice they have a dress code? It says Black Tie/National Costume

Junie

I noticed that. Why would they ask all the men to wear a black tie?

Nathan

LOL! Black Tie is the code for very formal evening dress attire. As in a black jacket, silk bow tie on those high collar white shirts, and tight black sash around the waist! I heard my mother mentioning it before

Sachin

Oho! You mean those black & white penguin suits! I don't think even my father has one!

Junie

LOL! Penguin suits! Actually, it's what James Bond wears when he goes to posh places for dinner

Sachin

Cool! I wouldn't mind wearing a James Bond suit!

Junie

Probably cost a bomb $$$

Nathan

More like $$$$, I think

Sachin

Hell no! How much does James Bond earn? Looks like we'll have to fall back on national costume . . .

Nathan

I don't think I have any national costumes to wear either . . .

Junie

I do! I'm going to wear the silk batik *baju kebaya* my mother gave me. My mother was quite slim when she was young and we are almost the same height now

Nathan

Hmm . . . I'm going to have to ask Dad about this

Sachin

Well, I'm going to talk about this Invite to a Diplomatic Party all week at school!

Nathan heard a car enter the driveway; he knew it was his father; his mother would come in later at night. Kak Yam called out to him, '*Bapa sudah pulang*!' His father was home early, something which was becoming more frequent now, and would check up on him about homework. It was time to take a bath, change, and complete his assignments.

Nathan texted his friends.

> I can hardly wait! My Dad's back so I got to go. See you guys tomorrow!

When he came downstairs a few hours later—bathed, changed and with all his assignments complete—followed by Souchong at his heels, his father was already seated at the dining room table and about to have his dinner. 'Hello, Nate! How was your day? Any new friends?'

While Souchong darted into the kitchen for his food, Nathan sat in the chair opposite his father and said excitedly, 'Dad, guess what? I've got an invitation to a Diplomatic Party!' He waved his invitation card in the air.

His father's dark eyebrows shot up in surprise. He reached out to take the card from Nathan and examined it. 'Wow! This is impressive! I didn't know you had friends in the Kazakhstan Embassy.'

Nathan said, 'There is a new student in my class whose mother is the Ambassador of Kazakhstan.'

His father's eyebrows rose even higher. 'Even more impressive! So you do have a new friend at school . . . well, never too early to start networking.'

Nathan had heard the word 'networking' since he was in kindergarten. His father was a firm believer that networking and hard work, and of course a bit of brains, were essential to achieve success in life.

Nathan decided to press his advantage, 'Junie and Sachin are going as well. Dad, can you drive us there?'

'Sure, it's on the 30th. As Merdeka is the next day, I could come home earlier and pick everyone up,' his father replied.

Nathan nodded and started eating his dinner in silence.

'What are you going to wear? Constitution Day sounds like a formal event so you can't wear your usual jeans and shirt,' his father added, reaching out for his glass of mineral water. He took a sip and put it down.

'Umm...Sachin and I have been discussing that. The invitation said either Black Tie or national costume,' Nathan replied.

His father raised his eyebrows again. 'Whoa! Black Tie is expensive for a one-off event. Besides you're still growing and won't be able to wear it when you're older, maybe even by next year!'

'I know, Dad. But I don't have a *baju melayu* with a *samping* either,' Nathan pointed out. The *samping*—a hand-brocaded cloth using gold or silver threads, wrapped around the waist over a plain matching tunic and trousers—was the most expensive part of the ensemble.

His father looked up, 'Oh, you don't need *baju melayu* for this, Nate! Not about to meet royalty after all. Actually, a *batik* shirt also counts as a national costume.'

A look of relief appeared on Nathan's face. He put down his spoon, whipped out his phone, and said, 'Sorry, Dad, but I have to tell Sachin about this,' and texted Sachin.

> According to my Dad, a batik shirt counts as national costume!

He put his phone away, even though it pinged a few times, and they continued their dinner in companionable silence. His mother arrived home just as they were about to start dessert, consisting of yoghurt with cut fruits. Nathan called out, 'Hi, Ma!'

'Hi, Nathan! How was school?' She tossed her briefcase on the sofa, walked to the dining table and sat down, with a sigh of relief. 'I'm starving! I hope there is some food left.'

His father said, 'Sounds like you had a tough day . . .'

'Every day is a tough day. Something always turns up . . . I have no choice but to deal with it, if I want to make it as partner,' his mother replied with a sigh.

Nathan poured her a glass of ice-cold water and said, 'Kak Yam made rice, fish curry, and cabbage fried with prawns. Quite good!'

His mother brightened up, she took the glass of water from Nathan and drank all of it. Her husband picked up an empty plate, scooped some rice, fish curry, and cabbage on it and passed it to her. Nathan got up and took his glass and plate, as well as his father's plate to the kitchen. He deposited them on the kitchen sink for Kak Yam to wash up. Souchong ran to him and rubbed against his leg. Nathan picked him up to take him upstairs with him. He paused at the foot of the stairs and called out to his mother, 'Ma! Can Dad use your car to drive Junie, Sachin, and me to a party on the 30th?'

His mother looked surprised. She replied, 'Sure, Nathan! But why do you need my car?'

'It's a Diplomatic Party and Junie said we need a posh car!' Nathan replied.

His mother looked quizzically at his father. He replied, 'Long story about a black-tie dinner, but this event could be good for networking . . . and you're never too young to start networking, you know.' Nathan ran up the stairs, walked to his room, sat on the bed and texted Sachin. Junie joined the conversation later. When he heard his parents walk up the staircase, he put his phone away. His father opened the door and said, 'Goodnight, Nate! Time to go to bed!'

Nathan wished him goodnight cheerfully. Then he went to the bathroom to brush his teeth and rest for the night.

* * *

On the day of the party, Nathan got into the car with his father, promptly at 6 p.m., and they drove to Junie's house to pick her up. She came out of the door the minute the car stopped outside her gate. Her mother appeared behind her to see her off. Nathan was surprised to see how different Junie looked—she was dressed in a black silk *baju kebaya* with hand-painted pale-yellow orchids, blue pea flowers, and green leaves scattered across the fabric. The *kebaya*—a long fitted tunic—was held together at the front by three matching ornate gold brooches, called *kerosong*. The gorgeous outfit was completed by an antique gold necklace around her neck, which matched the brooches perfectly. He thought she looked grown up and oddly, prettier. He himself was wearing a cotton *batik* shirt with prints of hibiscus flowers in red and white on a black background.

Junie greeted them cheerfully, 'Hi, Uncle KC! Hi, Nathan!' And took her seat at the back. She breathed in deeply; the seats were leather upholstered and smelt plush and expensive.

Nathan's Dad said cheerfully, 'Hi, Junie! You look amazing in that outfit. You'll fit right in with the black-tie crowd!'

'Thanks, Uncle KC!' Junie beamed. She was fond of her uncle, and he never failed to compliment her.

Junie's mother waved at them as they drove away to pick Sachin up. 'Enjoy yourself but not too much and remember to come home by 10 p.m.!'

They drove to Sachin's condo complex; he was already waiting for them outside the lobby with his mother. Everyone greeted each other. Sachin got into the car and whistled under his breath. This was the first time he had a ride in Nathan's mother's car. He sat down beside Junie, but wisely refrained from making any comments. Sachin wore a *batik* shirt that was almost identical to Nathan's, except the hibiscus prints were in burnt orange and white. They drove off in good spirits.

Nathan's father had no trouble locating the residence in the nearby township of Putra Heights. Aida's place was an impressive two-and-a-half storey building in glass, steel, and concrete, located in the exclusive area of Putra Heights, known as 'the Glades'. It was in the vicinity of a lake, which at one time used to be an abandoned mining pool but now served as an attractive and desirable feature in a very exclusive residential area. There was a much larger lake and park near Nathan's and Junie's place in Kota Kemuning, but their neighbourhood was not nearly as posh as the Glades. As their car approached, the gate opened into a driveway which led to a porch. They could see Aida standing at the front door with her parents. She was dressed in a peach silk evening gown with white lace covering the shoulders and the sleeves. There was a string of pearls around her neck. Junie unconsciously touched the gold necklace she was wearing.

Nathan's father drove to the porch, and two men dressed in sharp black suits came on either side of the black BMW and opened the door smartly for the three of them. They got out and tried to look as cool, composed, and as smart as possible—which was not easy when even the car attendants are in black tie! Aida walked towards her friends to welcome them, 'Sachin, Junie, and Nathan! I'm so happy to see you! Come and meet my parents.'

When Nathan turned around to wave at his father, Aida's father walked towards the car and said, 'Please join us for the celebration! I will ask the attendants to park your car!'

Mr Kwan said, 'Oh no, please. Thank you. I have something else I must attend to.'

Mr Anargul said, 'Please, please, I insist! I am very keen to meet more Malaysians, especially the parents of Aida's friends. After all, we are new in this country and it is not easy to meet people when you are a foreigner.'

Nathan's father realized that he was not just being polite and really wanted to get to know him better. *Aida's father is obviously a networker as well*, he thought. So he agreed to join the party. He handed the car keys to one of the attendants, introduced himself to Aida's parents and walked in with them. Nathan, Junie, and Sachin walked ahead with Aida. 'It's not actually a formal dinner, more of a cocktail and buffet, because we can't seat that many people.'

Sachin quipped, 'Oh that's okay, we've never been to a cocktail either!' And he felt an irresistible urge to give Nathan a high five.

Aida took them through the small anteroom and into a large and breathtaking drawing room. Half of the room had a high ceiling reaching all the way up to the second floor, with a glittering crystal chandelier hanging midway as a centrepiece. The sense of space was amplified by the floor-to-ceiling glass windows facing the garden. The three friends paused to admire the room for a while. Then they switched their attention from the room to the guests. They noticed that the men were mainly dressed in black suits while the women were dressed in national costumes—a colourful melange of traditional *kebaya* and *baju kurong*, rustling silk *sarees*, and a distinguished-looking older woman even wore a colourful *hanbok*, with sleeves sewn from ribbons in every colour of the rainbow. Some of the women, clearly from the West, also wore evening dresses. Junie noted that black tie did not mean black evening gowns when it came to women.

Smartly dressed waiters served them drinks—Aida and Junie chose orange juice, while the boys picked colas—alternating with canapes. These were mainly thinly sliced toasted French baguettes with various toppings. Some had cream cheese with smoked oysters while others had mashed hard-boiled eggs sprinkled with what looked like tiny black seeds. Aida told them these were caviar. The boys eagerly gobbled them up while Junie held back before finally giving in and trying one of each; she reasoned they were equivalent to anchovies. Someone rang a bell—a small one made of crystal and everyone turned to face the hosts. The national anthem was played, followed by a short speech by Mrs Adina Anargul about the Constitution Day. During this time, the waiters stopped serving canapes and weaved among the guests, handing out fluted glasses filled with champagne. They looked longingly at the champagne-filled glasses and Nathan said aloud, 'Would it be okay if we tried a glass, just this once?'

Aida was about to reply, 'Sure!' But Junie reminded them, 'We're not allowed to drink alcohol, you know!' Although she secretly wanted to try a glass as well, she felt they should not break this rule; and it was not just a family rule, it was the law as well. As for Aida, she decided it was not diplomatic to allow herself a glass of champagne if her friends were not allowed to.

The speech was followed by a toast to the Republic of Kazakhstan, and after that, the guests continued with their conversation. Nathan noticed that his father was talking to Mr Anargul. They seemed to have made friends quite quickly.

Aida said excitedly, 'Follow me, the food and drinks are in the garden.' The three friends brightened up—they were wondering if cocktails meant only canapes would be served. They exited the room through the glass doors leading into the large garden at the side of the house. There were two tables arranged into an L-shape. The longer table had large serving trays filled with food, while the other had a bewildering array of drinks.

Their hearts lifted when they saw the amazing variety of food—including grilled tiger prawns, chicken casserole, roast lamb and potatoes, another side of roasted peppers, button mushrooms and sliced zucchini, a large plate of *mendi* rice with raisins and almonds, two types of pasta, and dessert. Led by Aida, they each took a plate and helped themselves to the food and a glass of fresh apple juice. Junie had a more limited selection, but she was keen on the pasta. Aida explained that the one with black sauce had squid ink in it while the creamy mushroom pasta had truffle oil and minced truffles as ingredients. Both were delicious. Junie was happy with the truffle pasta, and also took some roasted vegetables and a generous helping of salad. She was excited that apart from the usual sliced hard-boiled eggs and lettuce leaves, the salad had her favourite salad ingredients—rocket leaves, dried cranberries, and roasted pine nuts. Nathan helped himself to chicken and *mendi* rice, with grilled vegetables, while Sachin took a generous helping of roast lamb and potatoes, and as an afterthought, after noting Junie's enthusiasm, some salad as well. Aida had the pasta in squid sauce accompanied by grilled prawns and salad.

Aida led them to a small pergola at the back of the garden. It was hexagonal in shape, with cross-hatched lattice walls made of thin strips of wood along five sides, the sixth one was the entrance. The five enclosed walls had wooden benches lined along their side. The four of them sat on the benches and munched away happily at their food. Junie enthused, 'OMG! The truffle mushroom pasta is so amazing! It's rich and creamy, with a subtle smoky flavour! I've always wanted to try pasta with truffle sauce and now I have!'

Sachin nodded enthusiastically, 'I'm going to try the pasta later . . . but this is the best lamb and rice I've had in, like a decade!'

Nathan added, 'I'd like to try some later. The grilled vegs are pretty rad too. This might be the first time I feel like taking a second helping of vegs!'

Aida beamed at them, 'My mother and father went all out to get the right caterer for this event, trying out food at many different places before choosing them. They will be thrilled to know that you loved the food!'

Sachin added, 'Indeed! No doubt that the unerring taste buds of Junie, Nathan, and Sachin would reflect that of the rest of the guests!'

At that moment, three fabulously dressed young people, led by Aida's mother appeared at the entrance of the pergola. Nathan, Junie, Sachin, and Aida stared at the two gorgeous young women in silk cocktail dresses and the handsome young man in Black Tie; momentarily bedazzled before it dawned on them that they knew them. 'Aida, Junie, Nathan, and Sachin, I have some surprise guests for you! This is Minji Lee from Singapore, and her friends, Maiandra, and Hafiz. They are from Noble Hall as well!'

Nathan and Sachin's jaw dropped in shock and Junie and Aida froze in horror. It can't be true! Aida stared at her mother, who was smiling cheerfully at her. It took her so long to respond that her mother's smile slowly turned into a puzzled frown. One of the rules Aida had been taught was that one must never be rude to guests—no matter how badly they behaved or how much you disliked them.

Aida quickly stood up and said, 'Erm . . . yes! Hello, Minji, Mai and err . . . Hafiz! What a surprise to meet you all here!'

Mrs Anargul smiled again, 'Since Minji's parents were attending, we thought it might be a good idea to invite more young people to our celebration! They always say: the more, the merrier!'

Minji and Maiandra had frozen smiles on their faces. Hafiz said cheerfully, 'Hi Aida! We've never met, so allow me to introduce myself, I'm Syed Hafiz, a classmate of Minji and Maiandra.'

He turned to Nathan, Junie, and Sachin and said, 'Hi guys! Nice to meet you too!' Nathan, Junie, and Sachin were sure that he did not recognize them, but they all knew him by sight. Syed Hafiz Hisham was tall and athletic and one of the coolest, most popular students in the school. In fact, one of the hot topics of discussion among the girls of Noble Hall was—who was the handsomer one, Syed Hafiz or Jin Kwan? He was also the captain of the rugby team and had a legion of star-struck followers.

Since Nathan and Junie remained silent, Sachin got up and said with a slight flourish, 'Hello Hafiz, Minji and Mai! I'm actually really delighted to meet all of you here! This party is turning into a real opportunity for diplomatic exchange!'

Hafiz shook his hand, but Minji and Maiandra remained silent. Mrs Anargul said, 'Aida, why don't you show your friends around? I'm sure Minji, Mai . . . and Hafiz would like some food? And Junie, Nathan and Sachin would like second helpings?'

Hafiz said cheerfully, 'Oh yes, please! I'm starving!'

Aida forced herself to smile and said stiffly, 'Sure! I'll take you to the food and drinks table, please follow me.'

Nathan, Junie, and Sachin regretfully decided not to take seconds, so Mrs Anargul and Aida left the pergola, accompanied by Minji, Maiandra, and Hafiz to the food and drinks. When they were out of earshot, Sachin said, 'Awkward! And we were having such a great time too!'

Nathan said, 'We can't pick a fight with them here, this is actually a diplomatic party where people are supposed to be on their best behaviour.'

Junie nodded, 'Right. We can't let Aida down, this must be so much harder for her.'

Sachin sighed, 'And we are going to miss seconds! Good thing I took enough lamb and rice! There is a lesson here—always take enough in the first round because there might not be a second!'

Junie could not help laughing. She admitted, 'I didn't want to take seconds in case I slip up and drop my food on my lap, and the news goes all around the school!'

Sachin said in an imitation of Minji's 'popular girl' American accent, 'Rumour has it, Junie Kwan took third helpings at a diplomatic party and spilt her salad all over her antique silk *kebaya*!'

They all laughed. Then Nathan said in a more serious tone, 'I never knew Minji's parents were diplomats from Singapore!'

'Probably an ambassador as well,' said Junie.

'High Commissioner; ambassadors from the British Commonwealth are known as High Commissioners,' Nathan corrected her.

'Thanks, Nathan, I really needed to know that,' Junie said with a sigh.

'Well, that explains her entitled attitude,' Sachin remarked.

'Hello! Aida's mother is an ambassador and she's not entitled at all!' Junie snapped back.

'Point taken! But I'm actually glad the Popular Posse is here. Not, M&M of course, but Syed Hafiz actually seemed friendly. I mean you'd never get another chance to talk to him, man to man, and he might be in a good mood after all that food,' Sachin said. Both Nathan and Junie were about to ask him what he meant when they heard voices approaching. Aida had returned. She was walking with Hafiz, while Minji and Maiandra followed a few steps behind.

Hafiz was carrying a plate piled with both chicken and lamb, and roast potatoes and rice while Minji and Maiandra had taken a small helping of chicken and rice, with a huge side of salad. Aida was carrying a large plate of pastries and cakes. She sat next to Junie, so that the four of them occupied two of the benches. 'I brought some dessert for us to share, since no one went for seconds,' and passed the plate around.

Minji, Maiandra, and Hafiz sat on two of the benches facing Nathan, Sachin, Junie, and Aida. The fifth bench between Aida and Minji was empty. For a while, everyone was silent as they focused on eating their food, until Hafiz said, 'The lamb is fantastic, Aida! I never get to eat roast lamb with potatoes any more. What a great spread!'

Aida smiled, genuinely pleased. 'Thank you, Hafiz! My parents will be happy to hear that!'

There was another silence until Minji cleared her throat and said, 'Erm . . . Aida, I think we kind of started on the wrong foot at Kino last week. We kind of got carried away in the heat of the moment.'

Nathan, Junie, and Aida looked up at her, clearly surprised, while Sachin sniggered. Minji glared at him, and Junie nudged him.

Maiandra continued where Minji left off, 'As Minji said, we sometimes get a bit carried away, due to our erm . . . extremely competitive nature, being in the rhythmic gymnastics team and the cheerleading team. We expect everyone to fall in line and be single-mindedly dedicated.'

'Yes, as I was saying, we are naturally competitive and tend to be hard on people because we are hard on ourselves. We didn't actually mean anything by the things that we said,' Minji concluded.

This time it was Hafiz's turn to be surprised when he finally caught on that they had met before and must have had a spat. He commented, 'You all went to Kino? Looks like I missed some heated discussions! I kind of agree about the rhythmic gymnastics team being competitive. Their training must be punishing—I mean Minji and Maiandra here, are fitter than maybe all of the rugby players! I mean those flying leaps, mid-air twists are positively gravity-defying!'

Junie said grudgingly, 'The coordination of the dance moves is impressive too. I've always been struck by the way the whole team seems to move as a single entity.'

'Since rhythmic gymnastics is so specialized, Minji and I started the cheerleading team three years ago, to get students with less training into the sport. Our cheerleading team plays a supportive role and is not competitive—we don't do the pyramid formation, stunts or tumbles, because we don't want to risk injuries performing in the field. We stick to RG dance moves, leaps and jumps, and the occasional mid-air spins, and of course, cheers!' Maiandra explained enthusiastically.

Minji nodded, 'That's true, our cheerleading team is really popular but non-competitive. But we are competitive when it comes to RG. We are now the top RG team among all the private schools and we are even ahead of some of the government ones,' Minji said proudly.

'There are over forty students in the school who take RG as a sport, only twelve are in the cheerleading team, and only three of us compete against other schools—Minji, Zara and I,' added Maiandra.

Hafiz added, 'I've heard that you're trying for the national RG team, Minji?'

Minji looked pleased and nodded, 'Our coach at the Holiday Villa Club thinks I have a chance of qualifying. She used to coach the National Team and one of her students won five gold medals at the SEA Games!'

The four friends were momentarily silent and realized that perhaps their tendency to be dismissive of the cheerleading team's accomplishments as compared to the more traditional sports, was perhaps biased and ill-informed. It was difficult to do those moves, nearly impossible in fact. They probably spent hours in practice, and sometimes didn't do so well academically. But still, Nathan thought, they were bullies . . . and he remembered being tripped by one of the athletes. It had sent him sprawling on the floor and had scattered his books everywhere. Maiandra and Minji had called him a clumsy nerd for not paying attention to where he was going. He felt conflicted.

Aida spoke up, 'We all may have overreacted a bit at the store. And of course, I, just like everyone else, did not mean anything I said.' Her voice was slightly stiff.

Junie silently continued eating her food, she didn't feel like apologizing to them, after all, she was not obliged to.

Minji added, 'And Aida . . . there is a vacancy in the cheerleading team, and we want you to try out . . . only if you are interested of course.'

Aida felt flattered, in spite of herself. She knew it was almost impossible to get into the cheerleading team at Noble Hall, not unless the Jin Jeanies wanted you in. She hesitated before saying, 'Thanks, Minji. But I'm not that athletic and erm . . . I don't think I will even qualify.'

Minji said quickly, 'That's okay. Although our team is non-competitive—no precarious pyramids and tumbles—members need to be committed. Physical strength, coordination, flexibility, and grace are necessities and not everyone is suited for it.' She sounded relieved.

Junie breathed out a sigh of relief as well. Clearly, it was just a goodwill gesture; not a genuine desire to include Aida in the team. She had felt a tinge of envy when Minji had invited Aida to join the team and clearly had no intention of asking her, Junie.

There was another silence before Sachin unexpectedly chipped in, 'I heard that the rugby team won the National Schools Rugby Tournament against the Agnes Jones school last week; an incredible feat as AJ's supposed to be the top sports school. And you scored the try in the last minute, Hafiz!'

Hafiz looked pleased, 'Well, they say that, when one person scores that try the whole team takes the glory. But yes, we did! We beat the All Jocks school with a try! I'm surprised you know about rugby, thought you spent all your time in the computer lab, erm . . . not that that's a bad thing!'

Nathan, who was feeling bemused by Sachin's sudden interest in school rugby decided to play on a hunch, 'Wait! Sachin, are you confessing to being a secret rugby stalker?'

Junie jumped in, 'What! You don't actually want to try out for the rugby team, do you, Sachin?'

Nathan added, 'You know, you actually have to run around the field carrying a ball, while being chased by a bunch of crazed guys intent on bringing you down!'

Junie and Aida burst out laughing at this description of the game.

But Sachin was unfazed. He replied, 'Famous rugby quote— "Strength doesn't come from what you can do, it comes from overcoming the things you once thought you couldn't".'

Junie added, 'Well, if you can handle those huddles and head butting . . .'

This time, everyone burst out laughing, apart from Sachin and Hafiz.

Hafiz ate the last piece of roast lamb, looked up and replied, 'Scrum, not huddle, Junie. We scrum for possession of the ball.'

But Hafiz was in a good mood after the fabulous meal. He added, 'As a matter of fact, tall skinny players make good flankers. If you are serious about playing rugby, Sachin, I mean in real life and not a virtual game, why don't you try out during the practice, next Saturday?'

Sachin leapt at the chance, 'Done deal! I wouldn't miss this for the world!' To seal the deal, he jumped to his feet and gave Hafiz a high-five.

Minji and Maiandra looked amused, while Nathan, Junie, and Aida, looked bemused. This was totally unexpected. The idea of their lanky friend playing rugby seemed incongruous, but Sachin seemed fired up about being given a chance to try out for rugby. However, in the end, his three friends were happy for him. Perhaps it was worthwhile putting up with people you didn't like, if it meant one of them getting a chance at something they really wanted.

Sachin said, 'And just to show that I read up on the sport, the game of rugby was named after a school in England, Rugby School.'

Maiandra burst out, 'OMG! Why must you be such an annoying know-it-all!' Noticing the surprised look on everyone's face, including even Minji, she quickly corrected herself, 'No offence intended!'

Sachin replied quickly, 'None taken.'

Hafiz nodded, 'Yup. Rugby was born in that school and the game was mentioned in the now-classic book, *Tom Brown's School Days.*'

After that, they chatted amicably about school, and their projects and interests, and even about their past while they finished every morsel of food remaining on their plates. The four friends managed to find out that both Hafiz and Minji had actually studied at UNIS before, and had known each other even before they had enrolled in Noble Hall. However, they left New York a few months after Aida arrived. This information was as much a surprise to Aida as it was to her three friends. Minji said that her parents had mentioned meeting Aida's parents at Diplomatic parties in New York. They also became friends with Hafiz's parents in New York.

Junie said, 'I didn't know you were Singaporean, Hafiz!'

Hafiz laughed and replied, 'I'm actually Malaysian. My father was posted to New York as well. He works for Wisma Putra—that's what our Ministry of Foreign Affairs is called; named after our first Prime Minister, Tunku Abdul Rahman Putra Al-Haj.'

At that moment, both Nathan's father and Minji's father turned up to take them home. Everyone got up and walked back into the house.

They said farewell to Aida and thanked Aida's parents on the way out. Minji's father's car, a gleaming black Mercedes Benz driven by a chauffeur, pulled up first. Minji, Maiandra, and Hafiz said goodbye to everyone, got into the car and drove away. Then their BMW arrived at the driveway. Nathan's father took the keys from the car jockey, and they all got into the car and drove away. His father was in surprisingly good spirits.

They were all silent for some minutes, as if each was processing what had happened that evening. Finally, Mr Kwan broke the silence, 'So how did it go? I noticed that you all seemed to be enjoying yourselves, at least based on my casual observation.'

Nathan replied, 'I never would have believed that we would actually spend an entire evening talking to the Noble Hall Popular Posse . . . I mean it was quite weird to find out that they are actual human beings behind those scary masks.'

Junie agreed, 'I didn't want to be in the same place with them at first, but the conversation turned out to be quite interesting. Who would have known that Hafiz and Minji went to the same school as Aida in New York?'

'But only get to meet her here, in a school in Subang Jaya? It's like living in an alternate reality!' Sachin added.

Mr Kwan interjected, 'It sounds like you all did some serious networking there! That's actually the point of parties—to network. Not just to eat, drink, and have a good time, although that's important as well.'

'Yes, Dad, we see what you mean. People like Hafiz, Minji, and Maiandra wouldn't give us the time of day if we didn't get to meet them at this party.'

Nathan paused and added, 'Do you think they will actually start talking to us now? I mean start being nice to us in school?' Nathan wondered aloud.

'No way! There is no reality alternate enough for those two to be nice to us!' Junie declared.

They all burst out laughing. Sachin said, 'I don't really care. I get to try out for the rugby team and that counts as a huge win for me. I'll put up with any number of catty people for that.'

Junie said loudly, 'Catty? Ahemmm . . .'

Sachin replied, 'Sorry, Siamese cats are excluded from the catty label, because they are almost dog-like in their devotion to their humans.'

Nathan suddenly remembered that his father had been talking to Mr Anargul at the party too. 'What about you, Dad? Did you get to do any networking at the party?'

His father nodded and replied, 'Oh yes, it was quite an eye-opening experience for me. I realized there is a lot going on in my field, which we don't get to read about in the newspapers. In fact, according to Mr Anargul, there are some exciting developments in Kazakhstan now.'

Sachin perked up on hearing this. 'I didn't think they would be so far ahead, I mean innovations are coming in so quickly, even China has difficulty catching up with Silicon Valley.'

'South Korea might,' Mr Kwan said. 'But I'm talking about more basic stuff such as making high-end microchips and even nanochips.'

The conversation came to a halt as they arrived at Sachin's place. The next stop was for Junie and finally, Nathan and his father arrived home. When they entered the house, Lapsang Souchong, who had been napping on a comfortable velvet cushion, jumped down from his perch and ran towards them to greet them. He weaved himself around Nathan's legs before giving his father the same warm welcome. Mr Kwan picked the cat up and stroked his head before handing him to Nathan. They retired for the night.

* * *

When they returned to school on Monday, they were eager to meet up with Aida again to talk about the party. During the lunch break, Nathan and Sachin gave her a high-five in turn and Junie burst out laughing and hugged her. They talked animatedly about the party and Sachin thanked her again, 'Thanks for inviting us to your glitzy party, Aida. I could never have gotten a chance to talk to Hafiz about trying out for rugby, not even till graduation.'

Nathan nodded, 'And the food and drinks were beyond any *atas* standard! Even my Dad had a great time.'

Junie did not notice that Zara, who was sitting at the front of the class looked upset and angry. Her face was red, and she looked tense. Junie called out to her when they were walking to the canteen, 'Hi Zara! Do you want to join us for lunch today?'

But Zara ignored Junie and walked straight ahead to meet up with Jin and the Jin Jeanies. Junie frowned slightly, and said to her friends, 'I guess she didn't hear me call her.'

'Don't worry about it, you've got us,' Nathan said. Junie sighed, but she soon cheered up. She was too preoccupied with Aida and still basking in the afterglow of the party to worry about Zara.

When it was time to return to the classroom, Junie went into the washroom to wash her hands. She always did that after lunch at school, even though they had all washed their hands at the washbasins in the canteen. She was surprised to see Zara in the washroom as well.

Zara walked up to her, her face flushed in anger and said, 'So all of a sudden, I'm not good enough to be your friend!'

Junie was confused, 'What do you mean, Zara?'

'How is it all of you got invited to Aida's party except for me?!' Her fists were clenched but she kept her voice low in spite of her fury.

Junie was stunned. She said, 'But, but . . . it was Aida who invited us! I mean we didn't have a say about who got invited.'

'What about Minji, Mai, and Hafiz? I mean they don't even talk to any of you, not even Aida! They wouldn't even give you the time of day! At least I talk to you. I thought we were friends!'

'I'm sorry, Zara! We didn't even know they were going to be invited, not even Aida! She said she was only allowed to invite a few friends. It was her parents who decided to invite them,' Junie said, looking upset.

'Well, I know who my friends are now, and you're not one of them. Apparently, you're the shallow type who will dump her old friends the minute someone new comes into your life,' her voice was harsh and cold.

Junie's face flushed red. Zara's words really stung her. The one thing she hated was to be called shallow and small-minded. She protested, 'But I'm not like that! You know I'm not.'

She added, 'Too little, too late! I'm not talking to you any more, Junie Kwan!' She turned around and walked out of the washroom.

Junie was too upset to say anything. She felt tears pooling in her eyes. She washed her face as well as her hands and had to spend a few more minutes composing herself before returning to her class. Since she was almost never late for any class, Ms Jones let her off with a light reprimand before continuing with the class.

For the rest of the week, Zara did not talk to Junie. Junie did not tell any of her friends what Zara had said to her, she couldn't bring herself to tell them that Zara no longer wanted to talk to her. In any case, they did not seem to notice what was going on. Junie realized that they did not share her friendship with Zara. Although she had Aida to talk to her now, she still felt upset about losing Zara's friendship. She had known Zara a lot longer than she knew Aida; although they rarely spent time together now, they were closer before Zara joined the cheerleading team and started wearing make-up. Zara was her first cool friend.

As predicted by Junie, they were all ignored by the Jin Jeanies. It was as if the party at Aida's house had never taken place. However, the sense of hostility was gone. Nathan, Junie and Sachin no longer felt intimidated by them, and they sensed that the rest of the popular posse was no longer actively bullying them. The shoving and 'accidental' tripping had stopped. The other reason Nathan did not notice the tension between Junie and Zara, was the upcoming rugby practice on Saturday. Throughout the week, Nathan and Sachin, and even Aida, obsessed about Sachin's try-out with the school rugby team. Their enthusiasm finally infected Junie and she decided not to dampen her friends' mood by worrying about Zara.

Saturday morning dawned bright and clear, with only a few wisps of cloud in the blue sky. Nathan, Junie, and Aida had arrived early to secure the best seats to watch the rugby match in comfort. Members of the cheerleading team were there as well, including Minji, Maiandra, and Zara. Junie and Aida made an attempt to be friendly and waved at them, but the cheerleaders ignored them. As they waited, more students started trickling in to watch the match.

Finally, the members of the rugby team ran onto the field, led by Hafiz, who wore jersey number ten. He was the outside half, the player who orchestrates the attack and defence of the team. The cheerleaders went into formation to cheer them on. Sachin came last and both Nathan and Junie gasped in shock. Sachin was dressed in a dazzling white long-sleeved cotton shirt and long white pants. The rest of the team wore dark khaki shorts and black T-shirts. A ripple of laughter broke out among some of the onlookers, while others looked mystified.

Nathan stared in stunned silence before remarking, 'Why is Sachin dressed in a white shirt and pants for a rugby match?'

Aida said, 'It looks like Ralph Lauren's Polo collection!'

Junie said, 'Well, that doesn't explain anything . . .'

Nathan burst out laughing and so did Aida.

When they were in the field, Hafiz yelled, 'Are we ready to play rugby?'

The rest of the team yelled, 'Yes!' and punched the air with their fists.

Hafiz signalled to Sachin and said, 'Flanker!'

Sachin lifted his clenched fist in the air to show he understood.

They started with a scrum and Nathan, Junie, and Aida were relieved that Sachin was not a part of the scrum and had positioned himself at a distance in the back. The game seemed to be going well apart for the fact that none of the players passed Sachin the ball, even though he was the flanker. In fact, whenever he tried to go anywhere near the ball, another player would trip him or tackle him to the ground. Nathan, Junie, and Aida cringed at each fall, while a ripple of laughter ran through the crowd. Nathan muttered under his breath, 'Sachin is not going to come out of this alive.'

Junie overheard him and said, 'Just pray that he doesn't get squashed flat by all the players.'

After about an hour of rugby, Sachin's crisp white clothes were an unrecognizably muddy brown. Finally, Hafiz passed the ball to Sachin, and he ran with it. Nathan, Junie, and Aida were too shocked to cheer him and watched in jaw-dropping suspense as Sachin ran with the ball. They were too afraid to even breathe. Somehow Sachin managed to outrun the crazed mob following him and actually scored a try! His three friends finally exhaled to cheer him on; together with the crowd who broke into wild clapping and cheering, including the cheerleaders!

Hafiz blew the whistle to signify that the game was over. The team ran to the boy's games locker room, with Sachin following in the back. Hafiz turned around and yelled at him, 'Yo Sachin, practice same time next Saturday. You wear jersey number seven and this time dress for rugby, not the catwalk!'

Sachin brightened up visibly, jumped with his fist in the air and said, 'Right, Number 10!'

Nathan, Junie, and Aida jumped up and down in delight. He had made it, he was in the rugby team. When the cheerleaders passed them, Junie called out, 'Hi Zara!' but Zara just gave her a cold stare and walked off. Junie sighed but that slight could not dampen her mood. They were all elated. Who knew Sachin could outrun all the other rugby players? They waited impatiently for him to emerge from the boy's locker room.

When Sachin finally emerged, he had changed into his regular street clothes. Junie impatiently asked him, 'Why would you dress in white for a rugby match? And in long sleeves and pants?'

'My mother bought them for me because she thought I was trying out for the cricket team . . .'

'But we don't have a cricket team!' Nathan interjected.

'Well, duh! But she doesn't know that and I didn't want to disappoint her. So, I decided to wear them at least once . . . and it turned out okay, right? Maybe the clothes were lucky,' he replied.

Nathan clapped him on the back, 'Idiotic but lucky!'

They walked to the car park together, feeling a sense of camaraderie. Their parents came to pick them up; with Nathan and Junie sharing a car. Junie got out at Nathan's place for lunch and to help him with his homework. This arrangement actually suited her because she hated working alone and she always got more done when there was someone to discuss her ideas with.

Nathan asked her casually, during lunch, 'I noticed that Zara gave you the cold shoulder after the match. Are you guys not talking any more?'

Junie put her fork down and sighed. They were having stir-fried noodles with egg, finely sliced bean curd, and French beans. She said, 'She's angry because she wasn't invited to Aida's party. I think she blames us, me especially.'

'What! She can't blame you for that! I mean it's not even our party!' Nathan protested.

'I know. But she felt left out because Minji and Maiandra were invited, and she wasn't. You know she is the only one who actually talks to us . . . sometimes,' Junie said in a resigned voice.

'But that had nothing to do with us, I mean even Aida didn't know they were coming . . .'

'I know, but I guess she can't help feeling left out,' said Junie.

'You know what? This is so unfair of her! I mean she gets invited to loads of parties that we don't get invited to. And we don't hold it against her!' Nathan said in a surprisingly fierce voice.

'Well, she is popular, you know . . . and Aida's party was kind of extra-special, it's posh and for diplomats,' Junie said hesitantly.

'Well, so what? It's like she thinks we don't have the right to attend cool parties or be special or be happy,' Nathan said indignantly.

His voice was loud enough to attract Kak Yam's attention. She ran out of the kitchen to check on Nathan and Junie. The two of them almost never quarrelled, and it was rare for Nathan to raise his voice. Nathan waved at her to show that everything was okay.

Junie stared at him in surprise and realized that he was right. Her friend was holding her happiness against her instead of being happy for her. She said, 'I didn't think of it that way.'

'Zara thinks we're nerds and therefore we don't deserve better things than her. That's not how a true friend behaves. And remember Aida, who is just as cool as Zara, accepts us for what we are,' Nathan said emphatically.

Junie looked him in the eye and nodded. She said, 'You're right Nathan. I won't allow this to bother me any more. We are all cool in our own way and I guess it's time to move on . . . but you don't have to be so smug about it.'

Nathan grinned and nodded, pleased that he had managed to change her perception of Zara. The two of them turned their attention to finishing their lunch. Kak Yam didn't approve of good food going to waste.

However, their euphoria over Sachin joining the rugby team faded somewhat in the coming days. They hadn't realized that this meant that he had less time for them; and Nathan, Junie, and Aida found themselves having lunch without him on more than one occasion. Sometimes, even Aida could not join them because she had extra music lessons.

Exactly a week later, Junie could not resist asking Nathan casually, during lunch, 'So how are things going on with Sachin. I don't see him hanging out with you as often as he used to. I mean he didn't even visit last weekend.'

Nathan said reluctantly, 'He's been kind of busy since he got into the rugby team, you know. He has to hang out with Hafiz and the other teammates, even after practice. Apparently, team spirit is vital in rugby.'

'You mean, hang out with the Popular Posse?' Junie asked in an innocent voice.

Nathan sighed before replying, 'Well he still eats lunch with us, you know . . . sometimes . . . and so does Aida. I mean they actually like being with us and treat us like friends, not like we're social pariahs!'

Junie relented. It was true that they were still friends when it mattered. She said, 'Looks like we're the only two still in the Nerd Herd while Sachin and Aida are one of the Cool Crowd. And I guess I'm kind of happy for them, in a way.'

Nathan agreed. 'The boys in the lower form follow Sachin around after Rugby practice and ask for his autograph!'

Junie nodded. She said, 'I heard some of the girls discussing him and they actually think he is good-looking!'

They both burst out laughing and felt better.

They cleared the dishes and took out their books to start their homework.

5

The Kwan Family Dinner

It was time for the 'Kwan Family Dinner' at Nathan's home. He had done well enough after the first school term to warrant a small celebration. When the children were younger and still in primary school, the two families took turns hosting a dinner every month so that the adults could catch up with one another and the three cousins could spend some time together with their parents and uncles. These get-togethers became increasingly rare when the children grew older and work responsibilities increased for their parents.

Although he saw his cousins, Junie and Jin, at school every weekday, Nathan still enjoyed these cozy get-togethers. He decided to invite his best friend, Sachin, over for dinner as well, so that he could spend the weekend at Nathan's place to work on a science project.

The menu that evening was simple but satisfying—a starter of Chinese-style vegetarian spring rolls, followed by the main course of fragrant steamed rice and chicken *rendang*, accompanied by prawn *sambal*, sliced cucumber, and *chap choy* (stir-fried mixed vegetables). They decided to have the dessert—*bubur cha cha*—in the large living room. Bubur cha cha was a simple concoction of cubed yam, tapioca, and sweet potatoes boiled in coconut milk and sweetened with brown sugar. Mr KB Kwan occupied a large comfortable armchair while Jin sat on the sofa. They both looked bored and took out their handphones to check messages and text people. But it was perfect for Nathan, apart from the fact that his father could not turn up. His mother told him that he was held up at work.

Nathan's mother and Auntie Fei helped Kak Yam to clear up the dishes and spoon out the *bubur cha cha* into bowls, while Nathan, Junie, and Sachin chatted away in one corner of the living room. At that moment, Lapsang Souchong sauntered into the room and stretched himself luxuriously on the carpet. Junie settled down on the carpet beside the cat to stroke his fur. She loved to hear him purr. He sounded like a little engine.

Jin looked up and remarked, 'Cute cat! What's his name? Lapsong Sue Chong?'

'It's Lapsang Souchong,' Junie corrected him.

'Why give him such a complicated name, Nathan? Sounds quite girly. You should have just called him Garfield or Sagwa, something like that. You know . . . easy to remember!' Jin remarked. He stretched himself on the sofa. His skin was tanned, and his muscle-T shirt showed his 'ripped' torso from countless hours of swimming practice.

'Lapsang Souchong is a type of tea. He was given this name because of his points . . .' Nathan replied.

Jin looked at Nathan, genuinely bemused. He said, 'Points? Your cat has points?'

'His points are his ears, muzzle, paws, and tail, which are darker than the rest of his body, like all Siamese cats.' Nathan explained, his voice raised slightly in irritation. As if sensing his annoyance, Souchong looked up at Nathan. The dark, almost perfect diamond-shaped mask on his face began at a point at the centre of his forehead, stretched outwards covering both eyes and then swept downwards, covering his muzzle towards a point below his chin. Nathan forgot his annoyance with Jin. He was startled by how blue Souchong's eyes looked, the dark mask made them stand out even more. As always, he felt a wave of love wash over him, and he thought again about how lucky he was to have this extraordinary being as his friend.

Jin continued, 'Oohkaay . . . so your cat has points. But why name him Lapsong Suechong? Why name a cat after an exotic tea? Why not call him Lord Dark Face?'

Nathan looked even more annoyed, so Junie cut in, good-humouredly, 'Oh, Souchong has points which are almost black with a hint of red, just like the famous tea. I helped to name him as well . . . aaand both Nathan and I love that name.' Then she tickled him on the tummy murmuring, 'Who's the cutie pie, now?' Souchong got up and rubbed himself against Junie, purring contentedly.

Nathan recovered his humour and added, 'And also because lapsang souchong was Sherlock Holmes' favourite tea. Actually, it's the only type of tea he ever drank.'

To everyone's surprise, Mr Kwan chipped in unexpectedly, 'Yes, lapsang souchong is very special, this tea made black tea popular in the UK because of its smoky flavour. Tea farmers learnt that when they dried the tea leaves over slow-burning pinecones, the smoke gives the tea the aroma of smoky pine. The name "lapsang souchong" also comes from the fact that the tea is made from the fourth and fifth leaves at the tip, which is called the souchong.'

Jin and Junie stared at their father in surprise. He had never shown any interest in any subject, apart from how much money his business was bringing in. He sold commodities imported from China and Junie realized that that must include tea. Then she had a vague recollection of seeing boxes of tea at home in the past, but she never paid any attention to them.

Seeing that he had everyone's undivided attention, Mr Kwan continued, 'I visited the place where the tea originated from in China. It's called Tongmu Village, in Fujian Province. Very beautiful place, we should all visit one day.'

Junie spoke up, 'But you only bring in green tea into Malaysia, I don't remember any lapsang souchong tea at home.'

Her father replied, 'That is because most Malaysians are not interested in this type of tea, they prefer Ceylon tea, grown in Cameron Highlands, and Darjeeling tea from India. The popular teas from China are black teas such as oolong, Tie Guanyin, and Pu Er; and the green teas such as jasmine and chrysanthemum tea. Yes, India and China are the two major tea producers in the world.'

Nathan, who had been listening to his uncle with keen interest, nodded in agreement. He said, 'And there are only two words for "tea" in the world. People who use the word "tea" or "*teh*" in Malay, "*te*" in Spanish, got their tea over the sea. Dutch traders brought tea leaves to Southeast Asia and Europe by sea, during the seventeenth century. But "*cha*" or "*chai*", was brought overland on the Silk Road to India, Russia and Persia much, much earlier.'

Junie nodded, 'Yes! "Tea" if by the sea, "*cha*" if by land. You've really been doing your research, Nathan. And a new girl in our class, who is from Kazakhstan, said that apples may have come to Europe by the Silk Road as well.'

But Jin was not going to give up so easily. He said, 'Hmm . . . interesting. But are you sure souchong is a pure-bred Siamese cat? I mean he doesn't look like those Siamese cats with triangular faces, slanted eyes, and pointy ears, which are always winning prizes on TV?'

As if sensing that he had been insulted, Lapsang Souchong stared haughtily at Jin. Sachin muttered 'Blockhead!' under his breath.

Jin gave him a sidelong look and said, 'Shouldn't you be home, watching cricket and Bollywood movies like *Slumdog Millionaire*, Sachin Sundara?'

He knew Sachin's cricket-mad father had named him after Sachin Tendulkar, the greatest batsman in the history of cricket. Sachin again felt grateful to his father for shortening the family name from Sundararamamurthi to Sundara. He could imagine the hazing he would get from people like Jin.

Sachin replied off-handedly, 'Actually we are more interested in rugby now and *Slumdog Millionaire* is a British production and not even a Bollywood movie.'

Junie interrupted them, she didn't want the argument between her brother and Sachin to continue. She said enthusiastically, 'I love *Slumdog Millionaire*! Guess what? Zara and the . . . err . . . Minji and Maiandra are going to sing *Jai Ho* for the school talent contest!'

But Nathan was not bothered by Jin's statement. In fact, he was thankful that his pet Siamese did not have the triangular wedge-shaped head, enormous bat-like ears and fragile long bodies of the Siamese cats featured on fancy cat shows on TV. He said nonchalantly, 'To return to Siamese cats—those weird-looking cats on TV are not traditional Siamese cats. Anyway, an old friend from Bangkok gave Souchong to Dad. He said that Souchong's dam and sire came from the Thai royal palace so he's a pure-bred Siamese for sure.'

Everyone looked up when they heard the words 'Thai royal palace'. Junie interrupted him, 'You never told us that! I always thought you got him from a pet shop, no wonder he looks so regal! Imagine, a cat from a royal bloodline . . . we kowtow to you, O Prince Lapsang Souchong!' Junie clasped her hands together and bowed to the cat, who gazed at her quizzically with its huge sapphire blue eyes and then turned away, looking bored.

Nathan replied, 'Err . . . sorry I forgot . . . anyway, among the Thais, being given a cat, especially a Siamese cat is a sign of high esteem. Cats were kept in Buddhist temples because they were supposed to guard ancient texts from being eaten by mice, but Siamese cats were kept in palaces. They were first mentioned in texts in the fourteenth century and Souchong is close to what original Siamese cats look like. He is a *"wichien-maat"* in Thai.'

This time it was Sachin who gasped, 'Witch and mutt what?'

Nathan corrected him, 'Wichien-maat, it means "moon diamond". The Siamese cats on shows on TV have been selectively bred for some features to make them look more "Oriental"!'

Sachin said, 'Woo hoo! Moon diamond cats—that's way cooler than Siamese cats! Anyway, the prize-winning cats are gross; they look like aliens, not Orientals . . .'

Junie interjected, 'It's ridiculous to try to make cats look like people! Have you seen Persian cats now? They have squashed faces, which makes it hard for them to breathe and their eyes water all the time! I've seen old pictures of Persian and Siamese cats, they used to look like normal cats before.' Then she turned to Souchong and tickled him under the chin, 'You may not win any prizes at cat shows, but you're still the handsomest cat in the world!'

Jin remarked with a slight hint of sarcasm, 'Luckily for humanity, just in case the alien Siamese cats decide to take over the world, we can still find normal Siamese cats in Thailand to fight them!'

Sachin couldn't help agreeing with him. He said with a grin, 'Yup, in the movie, *Cats vs Dogs*, the cats were trying to take over the world and for some reason, cats are always depicted as the bad guys.'

Mr Kwan looked up from his handphone and interrupted their discussion again. He said, 'Did you know that of all the domesticated animals, the cat is not included in the Chinese Zodiac? All the other common animals, even the rat, the tiger, and the snake are in!'

'Not forgetting the mythical dragon,' added Jin.

'Yes, I always wondered about that,' said Nathan thoughtfully. 'Maybe, they didn't like cats in China,' he added.

Mr Kwan explained to him, 'One of the stories of the Chinese Zodiac is that Rat tricked Cat—'

Junie interrupted her father, 'Yes, we know, Dad!' She recited from memory, 'Once upon a time, the Jade Emperor invited all the animals in the world to a race. He wanted to name the years after the first twelve animals to win the race.'

'All the animals listened very carefully to what the Jade Emperor was saying, except for Cat, who decided to take a nap while the Emperor was talking.

'Rat told Cat that the race would only start in the afternoon. So, Cat slept while Rat slipped out at dawn. All the animals were racing furiously. Clever Rat knew that he could not win the race, so he jumped on the back of Ox. Close to the end of the race, Rat jumped off Ox and crossed the finishing line first!'

'So, the first year of the Chinese Zodiac is the Year of the Rat!' Jin capped the story.

His father added, 'It seems you all can remember everything I ever said! Anyway, in the other version of the story, Rat also tricked Cat and told him that the banquet by the Buddha was the day after tomorrow so Cat missed the banquet.'

Jin stroked his chin and said, 'Rat used strategy to win the Zodiac Race. But you can't always use strategy to win a race in real life. You really got to practise your ass off.'

'Jin!' His mother, who was sitting in a corner of the room with Nathan's mother, cut him off with a warning tone. The two women had quietly joined the little group and were listening in on their conversation, unobserved for some time.

Jin rolled his eyes and sighed, 'Yes, Ma! I hear and obey! Anyway, it's weird that you all are obsessed with cats when you were born in the Year of the Dog!'

Junie smiled. 'Actually, I'm reading a really interesting manga series called *Fruits Basket*,' Junie said brightly. 'It's about a powerful clan in Tokyo called the Sohma. But they all carry a curse. In every generation, some of them are possessed by the spirits of the Zodiac animals and will transform into a Zodiac animal if they get stressed, or come into contact with the opposite sex.'

Sachin looked confused, 'You mean they all turn into animals whenever they bump into someone?'

'Errm . . . in a way. If they hug or kiss a member of the opposite gender who is not a Sohma. Anyway, each Sohma child represents an animal of the Zodiac. One of the main characters, called Yuki turns into a rat whenever he's overly stressed or if a girl hugs him. A little girl called Kisa turns into a tiger cub and a cute boy called Momiji turns into a rabbit. But the point is there are thirteen of them, not twelve, because one of them is actually a cat! In fact, he is the one who is really cursed because he is not supposed to even exist,' she added.

Jin gave a mock sigh and said, 'Yeah, poor Kyo Sohma, the cat-boy! I've read a few issues of *Fruits Basket* and he always gets beaten by Yuki, the cool and popular rat-boy. Cats are always the unlucky guys who never get invited to the banquet.'

'You mean the super athlete Jin actually reads girly *shojo* manga?' Sachin asked slyly.

Jin looked annoyed and snapped, 'Can I help it when all the girls in school talk about nothing else? You have to know what is going on or be left out!'

Sachin made an unexpected confession, 'I'm actually quite intrigued now with *Fruits Baskets*. So, Junie, what happened in the last few books you bought from Kino?'

'Well, it turned out that the cruel and vicious Akito, the head of the Sohma family, whom we all thought was a man, is actually a woman and he/she plays the role of god in the story!'

'Woah! Akito Sohma is a cross-dressing woman playing god! I didn't see that coming!' Jin exclaimed.

'But it was a huge letdown for me. The person everyone was terrified of turned out to be a spiteful coward who was jealous of Tohru Honda because of her bonding with all the Zodiac kids,' Junie said with a sigh.

Nathan added, 'Bullies usually turn out to be cowards. Akito always wanted to get rid of Kyo for being the cursed cat, you know lock him up forever, but it never happened. If *Fruits Basket* was a Hollywood movie, they would have wanted to sacrifice him to break the curse!'

Junie said thoughtfully, 'Well, Tohru did manage to break the curse in the end . . . I think. And Cat got his revenge in real life.

In the game of Cat and Mouse slash Rat, who do you think is the predator and who is the prey?'

Nathan's mother interrupted them, 'Actually, Cat is not in the Chinese Zodiac because cats are not native to ancient China. They were introduced in China much later by Buddhist monks from India. But by that time, the animals of the Twelve-Year Chinese Zodiac, the *Sheng Xiao*, were already fixed in stone.'

Junie sat up and looked at Nathan's mother with interest. 'I never knew that, Auntie Nalini, but it makes sense. Imagine, a country without cats!'

Nathan chipped in, 'So the cat must have travelled over the Silk Road from India to China? This is interesting . . . traders brought silk, tea, and apples from China to the West, and brought back cotton, gold, and cats back to China.'

Junie, Sachin, and Jin burst out laughing.

Nathan's mother actually rolled her eyes. She said, 'Probably. Some cats could have been transported in ships over the maritime Spice Route. The Chinese Zodiac story is spot on in a way . . . the poor cat literally missed the race.'

Junie pondered over this, it felt unfair that the cat should be excluded from the Zodiac just for taking a nap. She felt compelled to point out, 'But Auntie Nalini, there is a Year of the Tiger, and a tiger is technically a cat!'

Nathan's mother said, 'You're right Junie and I believe we are in the Year of the Tiger. I guess the Tiger represents all cats . . . Anyone want some tea? We may even have lapsang souchong, although I personally prefer Ceylon tea.'

But everyone declined so she turned to continue her discussion with Auntie Fei and they both walked into the study.

They continued their discussion of cats until Nathan said, 'Hmm, wait, I think I've got pictures of Souchong from when he first arrived.'

He got up and walked towards the staircase. His mother was talking to Auntie Fei in low voices. Nathan stopped in his tracks when he heard his mother say, 'KC should be back by now . . . maybe something happened to him.'

Auntie Fei replied, 'Don't worry, maybe KC went on a business trip, maybe he's very busy with his new project, *lah*.'

His mother said anxiously, 'But he hasn't called the whole day . . .'

Nathan felt his heart go cold and he turned slightly pale—so that was the secret his mother was keeping from him. He had suspected that something was not right; his mother had been tense the entire evening. And it was unlike his father not to call or even email them, no matter how busy he was. He walked sombrely up the stairs into his room and sat on his bed. He was surprised when Souchong slipped in through the half-open door. The cat meowed, rubbed himself against Nathan's leg and jumped onto the bed. Nathan absentmindedly picked the cat up in his arms and stroked him. Junie and Sachin appeared a few minutes later. Sachin said, 'Did you have temporary amnesia or something? You left us alone with Jin downstairs!'

Nathan looked up, startled, and said, 'Ummh . . . sorry, I forgot . . . here take my laptop downstairs, I'll carry Souchong with me.'

They all trooped downstairs. Although he pretended to be cheerful, Nathan felt tense and anxious, and his mind was in turmoil. Souchong rubbed his head against his chest and Nathan felt slightly comforted. He rubbed his face against the cat's soft furry head. However, everyone perked up when Kak Yam brought out an unexpected plate of curry puffs. Junie and Sachin were soon helping themselves to the savoury treat of buttery pastry filled with spicy potatoes, chopped onions, carrots, and green peas. Jin asked to be served a cup of lapsang souchong tea but Kak Yam told him, 'Souchong *nama kuching lah, di rumah ini ada* Boh tea *saja*.'

The three friends exchanged glances and even Nathan found himself grinning. Kak Yam didn't like him, either. Soon, both Auntie Fei and Nathan's mother joined them in the sitting room. Nathan noticed that his mother seemed more relaxed now, at least her face had lost that tense preoccupied look. It seemed that Auntie Fei had managed to reassure her.

It was close to midnight when Auntie Fei said, 'KB, I think it's time for us to go home already. Thanks for the dinner, Nalini, we all really enjoyed Kak Yam's chicken *rendang*! Next time, our place and I will make my special spiced chicken rice.'

Everyone said goodnight and slowly walked out of the door. Unnoticed by anyone, Lapsang Souchong slipped out of the door, behind Uncle KB. He padded silently into the bushes, which lined the garden at one side of the porch. Nathan and Sachin opened the large main gate to let the visitors out. When everyone had walked out, Nathan was about to close the gate when Souchong quickly dashed out. He was astonishingly fast and bolted out of the gate before Nathan could stop him.

Nathan called out desperately, 'No Souchong! Come back here!' but Souchong was already running across the road. Nathan and Sachin dashed out of the gate and ran after the cat.

Junie was equally aghast at the prospect of losing Souchong and she ran after the two boys. She did not even hear her mother calling after her, 'Junie, don't follow them! Nathan and Sachin can catch the cat!'

Her father called out, 'Junie, come back! Come back home! Girls are not supposed to go out at night!' but Junie seemed oblivious to them. Finally, Jin decided that he couldn't allow his sister to be out so late at night and decided to join the three of them. He sprinted as fast as he could and caught up with his sister and Sachin. Nathan was running ahead as fast as he could to catch up with the retreating cat. He couldn't understand it, why was he running away? He called out to the cat, 'Souchong! Souchong! Come here! Souchong!'

It was to no avail. The cat seemed to be chasing an invisible person or object and paid no heed to Nathan. They chased the cat for several minutes as he ran down one lane after another and then broke into the green belt which surrounded the cluster of terrace houses on Aranda Lane. They had to run through wooded terrain before they entered into another cluster of terrace houses. Then the cat turned into a quiet lane and seemed to disappear into thin air!

Junie noticed the name of the lane again—Chempaka Lane— the one Sachin said he had never seen before. Sachin commented, 'I don't think this lane was here before during the day!'

Nathan, Sachin, Junie, and Jin walked up and down the lane, calling out for Souchong. Mysterious cats started coming out to look at them, but none looked like Souchong. Finally, Jin said, 'It's close to midnight. I think we should go home, before someone calls the police.'

Nathan protested, 'We can't leave now! What if Souchong turns up and he can't find his way home?'

For once, Sachin decided that Jin was right. He said, 'It looked to me like he knew where he was going. Why don't we rest for the night and look for Souchong tomorrow?'

Nathan insisted, 'Sachin, it will be too late tomorrow! What if he gets lost and can't find his way back? What if someone finds him and decides to lock him up in a cage?' He sounded distressed and close to tears.

Junie had an idea, 'We could print out posters with his picture on it and offer a reward for his return tomorrow. People will want to return him if they get some money in return.'

Nathan considered looking for Souchong on his own but in the end, decided that perhaps they were right. Besides he was beginning to feel tired. They slowly walked back home in silence. When they finally went to bed, it was almost 1 a.m. in the morning.

Nathan woke up at 7 a.m. sharp the next morning and started designing a poster on his laptop. He was glad that he had a good picture of his cat on file and immediately pasted Souchong's picture on it. The text ran:

I'M LOST!

Reward for lost Cat

Answers to the name:
Souchong (Sue Chong)

Please call Nat at: 017 567 123

RM 800 reward
for the return of the cat (alive and unharmed)

Once the poster was complete, Nathan started printing out copies. He had printed out about twenty copies before the ink ran out but he decided it might be enough. By the time Sachin woke up an hour later, Nathan had already changed to his day clothes. The two of them ran downstairs for breakfast. Nathan called Junie during breakfast and was relieved to find out that she was already awake. In fact, she was already on the way to his place.

When Junie arrived, they were examining the posters. Sachin was surprised at the amount of the reward and asked Nathan, 'Wow, dude! Do you actually have RM 800 to spend? That's my allowance for five whole months!'

Junie said with a sigh, 'I only get RM120 per month for pocket money. All the money goes to Jin because he's the oldest . . . and the favourite son.'

Nathan said, 'I've got about RM 500. I've been saving some pocket money since last year and Mom has agreed to give me RM 300 for the reward. I was going to replace my Nokia C5, which is really a kid's phone, with the HTC Droid, but Souchong is more important.'

'Yup, Android phones are the way to go. But do you really have to offer so much for a cat?' Sachin asked in disbelief.

'That's what it costs to buy a pure-bred Siamese cat. I don't want anyone to try to sell the cat to a pet shop,' Nathan replied firmly.

They set out, armed with the posters, masking tape, and a pair of scissors. They put the posters up along the route they took last night, plus some additional routes nearby. It was past noon when Junie said that she was beginning to feel dizzy from the heat and intense sunlight. Sachin agreed with her and even Nathan had to admit it was too hot to continue with the search. They decided to return home, drenched in sweat and exhausted.

On the way back, they passed a row of shophouses, and Sachin spotted a familiar bright red board with Japanese lettering and the number 100Y on it. He pointed at it, 'Look! We can get some shaved ice cream from the 100 Yen store!'

Junie perked up immediately, 'Let's go there! The strawberry-flavoured ice is yummy! And I'm going to ask for extra strawberry sauce!'

Nathan nodded enthusiastically, 'Best of all, the place is air-conditioned!'

They stopped for the flavoured shaved ice—Nathan and Junie chose strawberry-flavoured ice while Sachin had mango ice with extra toppings. The fruit-flavoured ice shavings, which were as soft and fluffy as cotton candy and deliciously sweet, worked its magic. They returned home in a much more cheerful mood.

Junie felt relieved that Nathan had recovered enough to enjoy his favourite shaved ice.

Nathan's mother was already home for lunch when he arrived. She looked up and called out cheerfully, 'Nathan, guess what?'

Nathan asked expectantly, 'What is it, Ma?' He pulled up a seat and sat down opposite her. It must be good news because she was no longer tense.

'Your father called me in the office, this morning. Apparently, he is in Kazakhstan!' his mother said.

'Kazakhstan? How come he went there without telling us? He didn't even come home to pack his bag!' Nathan was hugely relieved and actually felt happy momentarily. Then he felt puzzled and annoyed with his father.

'Oh! You know what your father is like . . . he said that when the call came from the Embassy, that there might be a project for him at Astana in Kazakhstan, there was only one flight available to Astana and it was leaving in less than three hours. He had to prepare all his documents and papers in less than an hour, and only took his laptop and briefcase with him,' his mother replied.

Nathan said, 'He could have called on the way to the airport!'

'He said he did, but no one picked up the phone. He only sent me a message that he might be away for a few days, early this morning after he landed. But it seems that the meeting went well, and he might be there for a few weeks . . . erm . . . maybe longer,' his mother continued.

Nathan nodded. His father was all right, he might even get a big job. Apparently, meeting people at parties can lead to work. He only had to look for Souchong now.

6

A Gathering of One Hundred Candles

The next few days, Nathan was in a pensive mood and had difficulty paying attention in class. As the days turned into weeks, he became even more despondent—the probability of finding Souchong became even less likely but he refused to accept that he had lost him forever. He was startled when he heard Miss Jones call his name one day, 'Nathan! What do you think the Albatross around the neck of the Ancient Mariner, signifies?'

Nathan was momentarily stumped. He sat up and replied, 'Err . . . that his men were angry with him?'

She nodded and said, 'What else?' but Nathan could not think of anything else.

Zara put up her hand and Ms Jones nodded at her. 'It's his punishment for killing an innocent creature and also a symbol of his guilt!'

Miss Jones said, 'Excellent answer, Zara! Nathan, can you stay back after class? There are a few things I would like to go over with you.'

Nathan sighed. Miss Jones was one of the nicer teachers in the school (she was not the nicest teacher because Junie had given that special spot to Mr Yeoh) and he considered himself lucky to have her as his homeroom teacher. But this would mean he would miss half his lunch break and probably have to listen to a long lecture. After the class, he sat pensively on a chair in front of her and tried to avoid looking into her piercing grey eyes. Miss Jones reprimanded him, 'I've noticed your lack of attention in class these last few weeks. Your marks are not going to improve if you don't pay attention in class, Nathan!'

Ms Jones continued her tirade, 'In the last class test, your average grade dropped from an A minus to a B minus. While you're maintaining your Biology and History grades, your English, Math and Geography grades are sliding. Math and English are compulsory subjects to get a full certificate for O Levels. You can't afford to do badly in either subject!'

Nathan looked downcast. Nothing Ms Jones said surprised him. He knew he was not working as hard as he should. He mumbled an apology, 'I'll try to pay more attention in class, Ms Jones . . . I'm just a bit um . . . pre-occupied now.'

However, she said in a less severe tone, 'I heard about your cat from Mr Yeoh. I understand that you feel upset about this, but you have to somehow find the resolve to work harder and pull up your grade. This year and next year are crucial in your schooling.'

Nathan was surprised to hear that Mr Yeoh and Ms Jones knew about him losing Souchong. He was also surprised to find out that they talked to each other, and that they talked to each other about him. Perhaps it was the poster, but he felt touched that his teachers actually cared a little, about what was happening to him. Tears started to pool in his eyes.

Ms Jones continued, 'You're a bright student, Nathan. We all have to deal with our losses in life and move on.'

But 'move on' was something Nathan did not want to hear or accept. He told himself mentally, 'No! *Souchong is not dead, he is just lost!*' but he forced himself to stay calm and said quietly, 'I'll try my best to move on, Ms Jones.'

After the thankfully short meeting, Nathan rushed to the canteen to join his friends for the rest of the lunch break. He even managed to grab a bite to eat. His friends did not bother to ask him about his meeting with Miss Jones, guessing that he wouldn't want to talk about it. Sachin asked him, 'Any luck with the posters?'

Nathan scowled and said, 'Gah! Just some stupid messages like "Why you so stupid and careless, *lah*?", "Why you don't take care of your cat? That's why your cat run away" or "Serves you right for being so careless!" or "I got nice cat look just like your cat. Can sell you for RM800"!'

Sachin couldn't help laughing but Aida said, 'That's so mean! It's weird how people judge you when they don't understand what happened.'

Junie agreed with her. She added, 'They even send spiteful SMS to parents who've lost a child.'

Sachin said, 'Yeah, but in some cases, the parents need to have their heads examined.'

After school that day, the four friends gathered at the walkway to the car park. Aida was the first one to leave. As always, the shiny black Mercedes with the chauffeur was already waiting for her at the car park. The next one to leave was Sachin. While Nathan and Junie waited for Junie's mother, they were surprised to see Zara walking towards them. She looked awkward and slightly shamefaced. She stopped in front of them and said to Nathan, 'I'm so sorry to hear that you've lost your cat, Nathan! I've got a Siamese too and I can't imagine losing her!'

Nathan was slightly stunned to hear Zara talking to him. He sometimes wondered if she knew his name or just that he was Junie's and Jin's cousin. He replied awkwardly, 'Thanks, Zara! I never knew that you had a cat . . .'

Zara replied, 'Yes, she's almost five now. A pure-bred Siamese but not as adorable as your cat! I really hope you find him! I'll help to post posters at our place.'

Nathan was touched by her unexpected kindness, 'Gosh, thanks again, Zara! I really appreciate that!'

Zara smiled and said to Nathan, 'You can pass me the posters tomorrow. According to my friends, cats have been known to turn up after going missing for months!'

Then she turned to Junie and said to her, 'My Mom's here but we'll catch up tomorrow!'

Junie was equally touched and relieved that Zara was talking to her again. She broke into a big smile and said to Zara as she walked to the waiting car, 'See you soon, Zara!'

For the rest of the week, Nathan had to force himself to pay attention and do his homework. His friends noticed that the only class he took an interest in now was Biology—Nathan was more determined than ever to go ahead with his Egyptology project. His mood improved considerably when Mr Yeoh told them that they could use the laboratory next week after school. Nathan had already done the research for the mummification process at home, and he wanted to discuss the next course of action with Junie.

He told Junie and Sachin after school, 'Souchong gave me the bird as a gift. I have to preserve it, it's the only thing I have to remind me of him.'

Junie and Sachin exchanged glances. They both knew he had plenty of photographs of his cat, but they decided not to mention it. Instead, she said, 'He's just lost, Nathan. I have a feeling that he's going to return when he's ready . . .'

Sachin nodded, 'Yup, he won't be able to give up Kak Yam's treats for long! My aunt once lost her cat for over a month and had practically given up hope when he walked into the kitchen one day and asked to be fed!'

Nathan brightened up a little after hearing that from Sachin. He said thoughtfully, 'It's true that most lost cats tend to make their way home safely . . . while it's not easy to recover lost dogs.'

Junie added, 'I guess it's because cats can climb over fences and trees and it's quite difficult for people to . . . err . . . catch them.' She was about to say 'abduct them' but decided not to.

Nathan changed the subject, 'I've already researched the subject on Wikipedia. Apparently, the Egyptians used salt, camphor, sandalwood, and oil in their mummification process. I'll have to get all the stuff ready first.'

'And where are you going to get those stuff? Salt is easy enough, but I don't think they sell camphor and sandalwood at Carrefour!' asked Junie.

'I have an idea where we can get all this stuff. Mom's going to Klang this weekend and I'm following her,' Nathan replied.

Junie perked up when she heard that Nathan was going to Klang. She asked, 'Can I come too? I love going to Klang! The Indian restaurants there serve the best *masala dosai*! And I also need to get a costume for Bollywood Night.'

'I forgot about that. I probably need to get a costume as well since my old kurta is getting too small,' Nathan added.

Next Saturday, Nathan and his mother picked Junie up from her home and drove to Klang. It was a pleasant drive, and the traffic on the highway was sparse. Nathan's mother parked the car in a parking lot behind a *Chettynad* restaurant. They were in the Little India enclave in Klang. The sun was already quite high in the sky when they got out of the car, and it was getting warm. The delicious aroma of spice and food became stronger when the three of them entered the restaurant. It was quite dimly lit, and had mounds of desserts displayed on counters right at the entrance to entice people. They sat down at an empty table and ordered lunch. Nathan had chicken *biryani* while his mother and Junie had a *masala dosai* each. Junie loved the savoury thin crispy pancake with curried potatoes, carrots, and peas inside. It was accompanied by *dhal, chutney*, and grated and creamed coconut that was spiced to perfection. Junie said after the meal, 'It's easy being vegetarian when you eat Indian food. I don't miss fish and meat at all.'

After lunch, they walked along Jalan Tengku Kelana, the main road which traversed the length of Little India. The shaded walkways along the rows of traditional shophouses protected pedestrians from the sun. Time seemed to have stood still in Klang. Nathan and Junie caught the scent of spice, incense, and perfumed oil. There were women selling flowers—masses of marigolds and chrysanthemums made into garlands and smaller posies of jasmines and the cheaper coral jasmines. Others were selling costume jewellery—bright and shiny fake gold necklaces and bracelets that were studded with red and white stones.

After a short walk, they came to the shops selling a bewildering assortment of colourful *sarees* and *salwar kameez*—all imported from India. Both Nathan and Junie walked into the most well-stocked one to purchase a costume each. Finally, they arrived at the row of goldsmith shops—all of which had counters with bars in front of them for safety.

Nathan's mother walked into a goldsmith store. A relative was getting married and she wanted to buy a matching pair of gold chains as a wedding gift for the bride and groom. While she negotiated the price, Nathan and Junie went to the store next door to purchase the supplies for their project. Nathan bought some camphor and incense, a packet of sandalwood shavings as well as rock salt and a bottle of oil. Junie was looking at some clay oil lamps but eventually settled for wax candles—small tea candles in round metal containers. Nathan was astonished to see her purchase over a hundred candles. There were six boxes with twenty candles in each. When they were about to pay, Nathan's mother walked into the store and asked them if they were ready to return home. Nathan had to help Junie carry two boxes of candles as well as his own purchases. He asked Junie, 'Why do you need so many candles?'

Junie replied cryptically, 'You'll see. I have a little paranormal experiment of my own in mind . . .'

Nathan and Junie did more research on the mummification of animals that weekend. Early Monday morning, Nathan placed the sealed container—where he kept the bird—in a small cooler that he sometimes used to carry his lunch in. He brought the cooler with him to school when Auntie Fei came to pick him up. The cooler was to ensure that the bird did not thaw too quickly. He impatiently waited for school to be over. Auntie Fei had agreed to pick them up two hours after school as Jin also had swimming practice on that day. When the bell rang, Nathan and Junie rushed to the biology lab as quickly as they could, carrying their school bags and the cooler with them.

They carefully put on their laboratory coats and disposable gloves. While Junie took out a set of dissection tools that Mr Yeoh kept in a cupboard, Nathan took out the container and unsealed it. The content inside was no longer frozen solid. They had both agreed that Junie would do the actual dissection and embalming work as she had the scientific skills; Nathan didn't want to admit that the idea of cutting open a dead bird or any animal for that matter made him feel sick. He said, 'According to some of the stuff I've read, we should only preserve the bird from the inside. There is no need to wrap it up in bandages like an actual mummy because we want to preserve all the bright feathers for display.'

Junie nodded in agreement. She said, 'It's so small that it should be quite easy to mummify.'

She took the bird from Nathan and placed it on a sterile wooden board. Junie carefully stretched out its wings and legs and pinned them on the board. Then she made an incision down the front. Nathan had to look away while she removed all the internal organs and placed them in a little jar. Then she cleaned the inside with cotton wool dipped in oil and packed the empty cavity with rock salt and camphor before carefully sewing it up again. She said, 'The rock salt will desiccate the body and prevent it from rotting. The camphor acts as a preservative as well.'

Nathan helped her unpin the bird and carefully placed it in a clean box. They stretched out its wings to pin it to the bottom of the box. Nathan filled the box with sandalwood shavings to absorb any moisture and neutralize any smell. Then they sealed the box and placed it in the special cabinet for biological specimens in the lab. He said, 'We can unseal it in a week's time when the bird is well and truly preserved.'

On the way out of the lab, Junie asked him, 'Is your father back yet?'

Nathan said shortly, 'No. Mum said that he sent an email saying that he has to stay away another week. He's never even telephoned . . . he just sends an email every day . . .' His voice trailed off despondently.

Junie tried to sound cheerful, 'At least you know that he's okay!'

Nathan nodded miserably. Junie's phone rang, it was time for them to return home. They walked to the car park where Junie's mother was waiting for them. Jin was in the car as well. Junie's mother dropped Nathan off at his home before driving the short distance to her home. Jin and Mrs Kwan finished their dinner quickly and returned to their respective rooms. Junie did not feel particularly hungry and had barely touched her dinner.

Her father came home while she was still lingering over her food and handed her a small box wrapped in expensive-looking patterned red paper, 'This is for you. A business friend of mine came to visit me today and brought this gift from the UK.'

'Thanks, Dad! What is it?' Junie asked curiously.

'Just unwrap it and you can find out for yourself!' her father replied cryptically.

Junie unwrapped the box very carefully, making sure that it did not tear. She liked to save wrapping paper to reuse them later and this one was lovely. She gasped when she saw the words 'Lapsang Souchong' written on the ornate box underneath the paper with the tagline, 'A Black Tea That Emerges From Fire'. Her heartbeat quickened. She looked up and was about to thank her father again, but he had already left the room. Her spirits lifted and she had an idea.

That evening, Junie decided to organize something special for the coming weekend to help Nathan come to terms with his loss.

She had read about an ancient Japanese parlour game and had bought the candles from Klang based on a whim and thought this might be the time to try it out. She also wanted to repair her relationship with Zara, who had started to talk to her again. She sent an SMS to Nathan, Sachin, Aida, and Zara to invite them to her place 'for dinner and to sample some Lapsang Souchong tea from London plus a small ceremonial get-together known as *Hyaku-monogatari Kaidankai.*' She knew her parents had a dinner to attend that evening and Jin was going to spend the weekend with his friend, so she had the entire house to herself. She also requested some food from Kak Yam and agreed to pay her for them. It was three simple dishes, which she knew complemented each other—Chinese-style mixed vegetables, tofu cooked in soy sauce and ginger, and egg fried rice for everyone.

At four o'clock in the afternoon on Saturday, Junie took out her mother's best Noritake dinner and tea set. Her mother had given her permission to use them for the first time ever. She arranged the dinner set carefully on the round dining room table—which seated exactly six people—and the tea set would be placed on the long coffee table in the drawing room. The tea was for later. There was an ornately carved four-panelled wooden screen, separating the dining room from the drawing room.

At five o'clock, Nathan brought the food Kak Yam had prepared, carefully packed in Tupperware containers, and helped Junie to lay them on the dining room table. Jin's laptop was on the dining room table, so Junie moved it to the sideboard.

At six o'clock, Sachin, Aida, and Zara arrived and everyone took their places around the dinner table and helped themselves to the food. By the time they had cleared up and washed up the dishes, it was almost dark. While Nathan and Sachin pulled away all the chairs and lined them up against the wall, Junie brought out the tea candles she had bought from Klang, and Aida and Zara helped her place them on top of the dining room table. They were arranged in five rows, each row with ten candles.

Zara walked around the room to admire Mrs Kwan's porcelain collection on the sideboard. She asked Junie, 'Whose laptop is this? It's pretty rad!'

'It's Jin's! You can always depend on him to leave his stuff all over the place!' Junie replied while she and Aida placed a small mirror on top of the dining room table. It was positioned to face the windows at the back of the room, while the tea candles were already positioned in rows in front of the mirror. A person would have to walk to the other side of the table with their back to the windows to look into the mirror. Junie switched off the dining room lights to test the candles.

Zara said, 'I think we need to light more candles, it's still too dim in the dining room. I'm going to stay here to light more tea candles, so that we have exactly one hundred candles on the table.'

Junie agreed with her. She and Aida went to the kitchen to prepare the tea while Zara lit up more candles in the dining room. Nathan and Sachin decided to join Junie and Aida in the kitchen. When the tea was ready, Aida carried the cups and saucers on a tray to the drawing room while Junie placed the tea pot on the coffee table and poured out the tea for everyone. Zara joined them to place twenty of the remaining lighted candles on the coffee table as well. Then Junie dimmed the light in the drawing room and called out to her friends solemnly, 'We shall all adjourn to the drawing room now in preparation for the *Hyaku-monogatari Kaidankai*.'

Nathan and Sachin walked to the drawing room, and everyone sat on cushions which had been laid out on the floor, around the coffee table. Junie said, 'I think we should sip some tea and sit silently for a few minutes. We should focus on Souchong, and those of us who have met him should try to remember everything we can about him.'

They all nodded, picked up their teacups and drank some tea. Tears were starting to form in Nathan's eyes. However, before they could proceed, the door opened and they were surprised to see Jin walking in. Jin looked astonished and exclaimed, 'What the . . . ? Junie, is that you? Why is it so dark? How come so many candles? Is there a blackout?'

Jin was about to turn on the lights when Junie shouted, 'Jin, please don't turn on the lights!'

'Hi, Jin! We're here!' Zara called out. Jin sounded surprised when he heard her voice. He replied, 'Oh . . . hi, Zara! Didn't see you in the dark . . .'

As his eyes grew used to the dim candlelight, he realized there were more people in the room. 'Why is everyone sitting on the floor? Is this some kind of séance?'

Junie said in an annoyed voice, 'We are in the midst of the *Hyaku-monogatari Kaidankai*. Anyway, aren't you supposed to go for swimming practice and have dinner with Steven tonight?'

Jin said, 'Change of plans. Steven's got an eye infection from the swimming pool. Anyway, what is *Haiku-mono*? Why do you and Nathan always speak in Japanese?'

'It means "a gathering of one hundred supernatural tales". It's an ancient Japanese parlour game to test a samurai's courage. But we are doing this for Nathan and Souchong. We want to share cat stories with each other so that we can come to terms with our loss,' Junie explained patiently.

'Well, I kind of miss Souchong too. Maybe I can help with the hundred tales gathering too?' replied Jin. He found the idea rather intriguing and sat down on the floor beside Zara. Jin noticed Aida for the first time and said, 'Hi, you must the new girl from Kazakhstan. I'm Jin, Junie's older brother.'

Aida said, 'Oh . . . I know. Hi, Jin, I'm Aida.' They leaned towards each other and shook hands politely.

Jin remarked, 'Wow! Your eyes really glow in the candle light, almost like a cat's!' He sounded sincere, not like his usual banter when he met pretty girls. Aida tried to look nonchalant, but Junie noticed that she was slightly flustered and her green-brown eyes did look unusually bright in the candlelight.

Jin suddenly noticed Nathan and Sachin sitting some distance away from the table beside the settee and said, 'Oh, hi, Nathan and Sachin! Couldn't see you two sitting in the dark! By the way, can I have some tea as well?'

Nathan scowled and Sachin looked annoyed, but they decided to shrug it off. This was Jin's house as well as Junie's and they didn't want to create a scene. Besides it was for Souchong, even if Jin didn't understand it.

Junie sighed in exasperation. But she didn't want to create a scene either and decided it was more important to start the ritual. She poured Jin some tea in the last remaining cup and thought that perhaps he was meant to be there. She said, 'During the *Kaidankai*, people normally tell scary ghost stories to test each other's courage. But here we are going to share fun information and stories about cats. Who's going to start first?'

Zara decided to be the first. She said, 'According to old Malay beliefs, cats are able to carry the souls of the dead. That's why during wakes in the past, people were not supposed to fall asleep at night. They had to stay awake to make sure that no cats were allowed to come anywhere near the departed person.'

'I think I've seen an old movie about this. People fell asleep during a wake in a *kampong* house and a black cat jumped over the body of the dead woman and err . . . the dead person came to life as a *Pontianak*,' whispered Junie.

Nathan and Sachin looked alarmed, and Aida looked puzzled. She was about say something, but Zara continued, 'I've heard that story too and some old folks in the *kampong* still believe in this superstition.'

Then she got up, walked around the wooden screen and entered the dining room. She heard Junie call out, 'Since there are only six of us, remember to blow out five candles!' Zara blew out five of the candles and she looked in the mirror. She was relieved to see only her own reflection looking back at her and calmly walked back into the drawing room.

When Zara had left the room, Aida whispered, 'What's a ponteeana?'

Junie said in a whisper, 'Women who die in childbirth, sometimes turn into a type of vampire known as a *Pontianak*.'

'Only if they are not given proper funeral rites,' Nathan added.

Aida picked up the thread. She said, 'Everyone knows that cats, especially black cats, have some kind of magic. In the West, black cats are the witches' familiars. Black cats are supposed to carry messages from the witch to . . . err . . . you know who . . . and back. The cats follow the witches everywhere they go, even sitting at the back of their broomsticks when they fly around at night!'

Then she got up and performed the same ritual that Zara had just carried out.

Junie sat up and said, 'Cats can hear sounds which are too faint or too high in frequency for human ears, such as those made by mice. That's why they are so good at catching mice and even rats.'

And she got up and walked into the dining room to carry out the same ritual.

It was Jin's turn. He said, 'The Egyptians were the first to tame cats, I think. Isn't there a cat goddess called "Bast" or something, whom they used to worship in some temple in ancient Egypt?'

Sachin jumped to his feet, raised his hand and said triumphantly, 'Wait! I know the answer to this one! It's Bastet . . . the goddess with the body of a woman and the head of a cat!' Jin looked irate as Sachin rushed into the dining room, blew out five candles, looked at his reflection nonchalantly, and strode back.

Nathan nodded at Sachin and said, 'My turn now! Bastet . . . her name means "she of the city of Bast". And you're kind of right, Jin, the Egyptians started worshipping cats over 5,000 years ago and the Egyptian Mau is the most ancient cat breed. They were first bred in the temple of Bast, and "*mau*" means cat. Plus, Bastet was the protector of cats and those who took care of cats.' Then Nathan got up, blew the candles out, looked at his own reflection and calmly walked back.

Everyone looked at Jin—he was the only one who had not performed the ritual. Jin said, 'Well, I can't help it if other people steal my ideas.' Finally he thought of something and said, 'The Japanese preferred cats with bobtails, which are supposed to be lucky. They were afraid of cats with long straight tails because they thought these cats could turn into fork-tailed demon cats.'

Aida and Zara looked at Jin with admiration while Junie, Nathan, and Sachin looked astonished that he actually knew something they didn't. Jin got up and confidently performed the ritual of blowing out candles and looking at his own reflection.

It was Zara's turn again and she turned out to be quite knowledgeable about cats. She said, 'In ancient Scotland—I know this because my Mum is Scottish—people believed that certain witches could turn into cats. They were called "Cat *Sith*" and they roam the Scottish Highlands. However, they had to be careful not to shapeshift into a cat more than nine times. After the ninth time, the witch will not be able to return to her human form. I think this is because cats are supposed to have nine lives.'

Nathan thought the idea of a Cat Witch sounded really cool. He asked, 'Is it Cat shee?'

Zara explained, 'No, it's spelt s-i-t-h. Some people think they are dark faeries.' Then she got up and walked swiftly into the dining room to complete the ritual.

When Zara returned and took her place in the circle, Nathan remarked, 'It's not my turn yet, but I think I have to say that although we think it's cool that witches have cats. Back in the Middle Ages, it wasn't cool. In fact, a woman could be condemned as a witch just for having a black cat, and at one time, thousands of cats were rounded up and killed.' He paused to collect his thoughts. Then he continued, 'In fact, some people think the plague also known as the Black Death happened because people killed all the cats out of superstition, and mice and rats exploded in numbers.'

Everyone was silent for a few moments, in fact they looked slightly shocked. Zara said, 'Thanks, Nathan. I guess the people in Europe paid a terrible price for being cruel and killing innocent cats for no good reason.'

Junie added, 'That was a great point, Nathan, but it's Aida's turn next so you have to wait your turn to blow out more candles.'

Aida, nodded, she already knew what to say. 'Although it is believed that the Russian Blue is descended from the pet cats of the Czars, it actually originates from the port of Arkhangelsk in Northern Russia. Sailors took cats from the Archangel Isles to England and Europe in the nineteenth century, which is why they are also known as Archangel cats.'

Jin looked at her admiringly and said, 'That's really cool, Aida! I never knew there were blue cats called Archangel cats. They must look amazing.'

Aida looked pleased at Jin's compliment and blushed. She said, 'Russian blues are actually blueish-grey.' She quickly got up to her feet and rushed to the dining room to hide her confusion. Her heart was beating unusually fast.

Junie could not help noticing that Zara looked upset, not like her usual poised, confident self. She worried that her brother's presence was causing tension within the group, and gave Jin a cold measured stare. This was meant to be a warning but Jin raised his eyebrows and shrugged. When Aida returned, she exchanged glances with Jin, and they smiled at each other.

Junie decided to continue the thread from Nathan about the Egyptians. She said, 'Unlike the people in Europe, the ancient Egyptians valued their cats and had good reasons to worship them. Cats protected their granaries from mice and also hunted rats and may have prevented diseases like the plague, as mentioned by Nathan. In fact, a human who killed a cat, even accidentally, could be put to death.' And she got up and blew out five more candles.

Sachin racked his head to come up with a cat factoid and groaned, 'Oh gosh! Why can't we tell each other stories about computers.' Then he finally recalled an email he had recently received which had a picture of an enormous cat. He said, 'The biggest cat in the world is the Maine Coon! Yay, Sachin scores again!'

Jin snorted and said, 'Oh please! That's pathetic! We all got that email with the picture of the giant Maine Coon!' But Sachin had already jumped to his feet and rushed into the dining room.

Nathan had no problem coming up with another cat factoid. He said, 'The oldest book about cats, the *Tamra Maew*, was written in Thailand. It means "The Cat Book of Poems" and was written during the Ayudhya Period. The book describes the seventeen "good luck" cats of Thailand, which includes the Siamese, of course.' He got up and walked slowly into the dining room. Although he tried to appear as nonchalant as Sachin, Nathan felt increasingly apprehensive. He noticed that the dining room was getting darker as each person had to blow out five candles in turn. Night had fallen and the streetlights had come on outside.

When he returned, he tried not to show how tense he felt. He looked at each of his friends and wondered if they could read his emotions. He realized that was unlikely as their faces were partly in shadow.

It was Jin's turn again. He announced, 'The scientific name for cat is *Felis sylvestris catus* and cats have retractable claws, just like tigers and leopards.'

Sachin said, 'Wow! I never knew I could be so underwhelmed!' Jin ignored him, got up and sauntered into the dining room.

When Jin returned, no one could think of a cat fact for a while so Jin decided to tell them a cat joke. He said, 'You know those local cats with a knot in their tail? A friend of mine from Canada was horrified when she saw one. She actually thought that someone had tied a knot in its tail when it was a kitten!'

Everyone sniggered except for Aida who looked mystified. She said, 'There are cats here with knots on their tail?'

Jin replied, 'Yes, but they were born that way. It's genetic and as far as I know, it doesn't cause them any pain.'

Zara suddenly said, 'Wait, I think I remember a story about how the cat got a knot in its tail. My grandmother told it to me a long time ago. It started with a cat called Besing who loved honey. But there was no way she could get honey from a beehive as she could never survive the bee stings. However, she knew a sun bear called Matahari, and used to stalk her. One day Matahari found a huge beehive hanging on a tree. Having a thick coat of fur, the bear managed to bring the beehive down in spite of the angry bees. She took the honeycomb with her and stored it in a hollow tree trunk, which was also her home. Matahari ate a small chunk of honeycomb before leaving the tree trunk the next day. The cat saw where the bear hid the honeycomb but she could not reach it because the entrance was blocked with a large stone. The cat tried to move the stone but she couldn't budge it. She walked all around the tree trunk until she saw a small hole on the other side. The cat looked in and saw the honeycomb. So, she slipped her tail in through the hole, dipped it in the honey and licked it.'

A ripple of laughter went through the group and Jin called out, 'Way to go, Besing!'

Zara paused for breath and then continued, 'When Matahari returned, she knew at once that someone had been stealing the honey. There was fur sticking all over the honeycomb! Matahari was really annoyed when the same thing happened the next day. She decided to ask her old friend, the mousedeer, for help. Sang Kanchil agreed to help her and hid in the tree trunk the next day. When the bear blocked the entrance and walked into the forest, Besing returned to steal the honey. The cat dipped its tail in the honeycomb again but Sang Kanchil grabbed the tail and tied a knot in it! Besing could not pull her tail out and became frantic! She clawed and scrabbled at the hole until she managed to pull her tail out just before Matahari returned. But the knot was permanent and since then, all her descendent were born with a knot in their tail and called Besing cats!'

When Zara finished her story everyone said that it was really interesting, cool and funny. Zara beamed, got up and bowed and walked into the dining room.

When Zara returned, Aida decided to tell a story as well. She said, 'This story is from seventeenth century Japan. Once a feudal lord called Ii Naotaka was on his way to Edo (which is the old name of Tokyo) when he was caught in a storm. He stopped for shelter under a tree near Gotoku-ji temple, when he saw a cat lift his paw at him from the door of the old run-down temple. The cat seemed to be waving at him! Lord Ii urged his horse towards the temple to take a closer look at the cat. At that moment, a bolt of lightning struck the tree under which he was just resting. Lord Ii realized that his life had just been saved by the cat! He became friends with the priest who owned the cat and the Gotoku-ji temple prospered after that. Since then, the beckoning cat has always been a symbol of good fortune!'

Junie nodded. She knew the story as well but had decided to let Aida tell it, since she was a guest. She said, 'That's a really nice story, Aida. I've seen porcelain figurines of those cats—they are known as *Maneki-neko*. They usually have a bell hanging on a red ribbon around their neck and are supposed to bring good luck.'

Aida looked pleased at Junie's compliment. She got up and walked to the dining room and blew out five candles before looking at herself in the mirror. When she returned, she said, 'The room is quite dark now. I wonder if we should continue playing until all the candles are out?'

Zara said, 'The last time I went into the dining room, it looked really spooky now that most of the candles are out. Anyway, we have to go home quite soon as it's almost eight o'clock. Maybe someone should have a last go?'

Junie agreed with her, 'It gets spookier each time we enter the room. The last time was positively creepy. Anyway, it's my turn! I just read that a cat with three colours, usually white, black, and orange, is called a calico! Calico cats are invariably female, in fact, only one in three thousand calico cats is male. And male calicos are erm . . . sterile. But the interesting thing is that the calico cat is not a cat breed, the rare colouring is due to random combination of genes. They are considered extremely lucky and will protect a house from harm. And the Maneki-neko that Aida talked about just now is actually a calico cat!'

Everyone clapped. Junie beamed and rushed into the room to blow out five candles.

It was Sachin's turn again and this time he remembered reading a story when he was young, 'The only cat story I know is that of Dick Whittington, but you all probably know it?'

Nathan knew the story, but the rest of them didn't so Sachin decided to recount it.

'Dick Whittington was a poor orphan boy, who decided to go to London for a better life. But he couldn't find any work and fell asleep, cold and starving, at the gate of the home of a rich merchant called Fitzwarin who gave him a place to stay. Fitzwarin hired him to be the scullion, which is like a dish-washer, in the kitchen.

'Dick had to sleep in a room in the attic, which was infested with mice. So poor Dick had to shine the shoes of rich folks when he was free, to buy a cat from an old woman who lived in a cottage some distance away. I'm pretty sure this woman was a witch and the cat was black as night. Anyway, the witchy cat killed all the mice in the attic, which made her Dick's best friend.

'Sadly, poor Dick had to give up his cat when the merchant organized a trade expedition. This was because Fitzwarin insisted that everyone in his household must contribute something of value on the venture, and the most valuable thing Dick had was the cat. I guess this was supposed to bring good luck.

'After giving up his cat, Dick was fed-up with his life as a scullion because the cook and the kitchen maid beat him up for the slightest mistake. So, he decided to run away. He ran as far as Bunhill when he heard the bells of a church ringing. To Dick, the ringing bells seemed to be telling him, "Turn again, Whittington, Lord Mayor of London" which made him change his mind, and he returned to the merchant's house.

'The ship was driven off course and ended up on the Barbary coast, where the Moorish Sultan purchased the entire cargo for a load of gold and insisted on entertaining the English traders with a feast. But the banquet was swarmed with rats and mice! Then the agent for the merchant had a lightbulb moment. He remembered that he had brought a cat with him. So, he informed the Sultan that they had a creature which could exterminate all these vermin.

'What happened next is history. Dick Whittington's cat was brought down from the ship and released in the main hall. The cat chased and demolished all the rodents. The Sultan, even more thrilled to learn that the cat was carrying kittens, paid more for the cat than the rest of the cargo combined. When the ship returned to London, Dick Whittington became a rich man and married Alice Fitzwarin, the merchant's daughter. And yes, Sir Richard Whittington eventually became Lord Mayor of London, not once but three times!'

Everyone clapped, and Jin even whistled in approval at the conclusion of Sachin's story. Sachin stood up, bowed to everyone, and went to blow out five more candles.

Nathan's turn was next. Sachin's story about Dick Whittington reminded him of something he had read. He said, 'Cats have always had a place at sea. They were treated with respect even on pirate ships. It was believed that they could whip up storms using the magic stored in their tails! And although pirates had no qualms about throwing people overboard, they would never do that to a cat. Because if a cat ever fell overboard, the ship would be cursed with nine years of bad luck!'

When his turn came up, Jin, surprisingly, had a cat fact to share with them, apparently all the cat stories had triggered his memory. He said, 'In the Vietnamese Zodiac, there is a cat!'

Nathan and Junie sat up when they heard this. This was interesting!

Jin continued, 'The Cat takes the place of the Rabbit in Vietnam, and shares the same traits as the Rabbit of the Chinese Zodiac. I'm not sure how they would square this with the *Sheng Ziao* legend . . . maybe in the Vietnamese version, when the Rat tried to trick the Cat, one of the animals must have warned the Cat to be on time. I'm guessing this is probably the Dog, because the Dog is actually the Rabbit's secret friend in the Chinese Zodiac!'

Nathan felt surprisingly gratified hearing this story. He even felt a grudging admiration for Jin, and he wondered if the 'I'm too cool to be interested in anything' attitude was just an act. He looked at Junie, who looked oddly conflicted, and knew that she probably felt the same.

Junie said, 'There are only ten candles left now. The last story is going to be by Nathan, because we organized this for Souchong but we still have a slot for another cat story . . .'

Since it was her turn again, Aida was the one who volunteered a story. Her story, called *The Bayun Cat*, originated from Russia and turned out to be the weirdest one they had ever heard.

Aida recounted from memory, '*Beyond the thrice nine lands, in the thrice tenth kingdom, in a silent forest where no bird songs or animal calls could be heard, there dwells a magical cat. Sitting high atop an iron pole, he spins his magical tales. His hypnotic voice spread its enchantment far and wide . . .*'

'According to legend, the Bayun Cat is a monstrous cat with a magical voice. When he spins his magical tales, travellers who hear him are lulled into a deep sleep. Those who do not have the will power to resist his magic or the strength to battle him, will be ruthlessly killed by the cat-sorcerer. But those who manage to capture a Bayun Cat will have a long and blessed life, for the voice and tales of the Bayun Cat has healing power.'

The five of them applauded spontaneously when Aida finished her story. She bowed graciously, walked into the dining room and blew out five of the candles. There were only five more lighted candles left and the room was dark and spooky. The candles threw shadows on the wall, dark shapes sliding across the wall as Aida walked towards the mirror. She held her breath and closed her eyes when she faced the mirror, knowing that the rest of them would not notice. Then she turned away, opened her eyes, and walked as calmly as she could back into the drawing room. She said, 'It's your turn, Nathan.'

Nathan felt slightly deflated after Aida's riveting story of the Bayun cat. He had planned to tell them the story of the *Sheng Xiao* but changed his mind; Sachin and his cousins knew the story and he was sure that both Aida and Zara would have heard of it in one form or other. He decided to tell them about the story of his own beloved cat, Lapsang Souchong instead.

How three years ago, his father had returned from a business trip to Bangkok and had brought home a three-month old Siamese kitten. 'My Dad said that it was a special gift from a friend who is a cat fancier with ties to the Thai Royal family . . . err . . . the more distant members, I mean.'

'Junie and I decided to name the kitten after an exotic tea, and I remembered reading that Sherlock Holmes drank lapsang souchong tea, so we decided that would be the best name for a cat . . .' Nathan felt a catch in his voice and could not go on. Sensing that he was overcome with emotion, Junie suggested brightly, 'How about the Rain Cloud Cats?'

Nathan took in a deep breath and pulled himself together. 'The cats which are sacred in Thailand are the Siamese and the Korat. And while the Siamese is posh and associated with royalty, the Korat belongs to the farmers. That's because in Thai villages, the Korat plays an important role in the rain ceremony. What happens is that the village shaman, a kind of witch-healer, places the cat in a basket, which is tied to a pole. Then the cat is carried to each house in the village where the owner splashes some water on the cat. It's a kind of reverse magic because cats hate water so much. The Korat is supposed to be the most effective for bringing rain because of their bluish-grey colour, just like storm clouds.'

Aida nodded, 'The Korat probably looks a bit like the Archangel cat, which is also blueish-grey in colour with bright blue-green eyes!'

Everyone nodded and clapped when Nathan got up to his feet and walked into the dining room. As he performed the ritual, he understood why this was a test of courage. It must have been so much creepier when performed centuries ago in Japan, in a large old wooden house where there were no such things as streetlights or electricity. The dining room was much darker now as only five flickering candles were left, and each was casting its own shadows on all four walls of the room. As he looked into the mirror, he was startled because the face looking back at him looked different, with dark shadows under his eyes. But there was something else . . . something in the background. As he backed away from the mirror, he was startled to see another reflection in the mirror. Nathan yelled out in fright.

Junie turned pale and gasped, and everyone in the drawing room jumped to their feet. But before they could move Nathan came running into the room. He gasped, 'It's Souchong! I saw his reflection in the mirror! He's outside the window!' He rushed out of the front door to the side of the house. Sachin and Jin ran out after him. Junie turned on the lights and rushed to the door with Aida and Zara. At that moment, a familiar car pulled up outside the gate. It was Aida's chauffeur, he had come to take her home. Aida was also giving Zara a lift so they said goodbye to Junie and left with the car.

Junie went back inside the house to tidy up when something caught her eyes. She picked it up and frowned. It was a hand-rolled cigarette; tobacco wrapped in dried leaf. It had fallen where Jin had been sitting. She hid it in her pocket.

Jin re-entered the house. He said, 'Nathan and Sachin are off on a wild goose chase again and it looks like it's going to rain. I guess cats can really bring down the rain after all.'

Outside, Nathan and Sachin made another sweep of the neighbourhood, but to no avail. Dark clouds were gathering in the sky and ominous flashes of lightning lit up the night sky in the distance. Sachin said, 'I think its best we go indoors. We're not going to be able to do anything for Souchong if we get struck by lightning or catch pneumonia.'

A sudden gust of wind blew at them, and large drops of rain started to fall. Nathan felt his heart sink. He knew it would be a matter of minutes before it turned into a downpour. Nathan said with a catch in his voice, 'I was sure it was Souchong. I feel like I've let him down again. Maybe it's too late . . .' He felt his tears falling and was glad that Sachin couldn't see him crying because of the rain.

'I've read that cats can take care of themselves for weeks and even months. They are natural born hunters . . . and your Mum will get worried if we stay out too late.' Sachin put his arm around Nathan's shoulders and tried to comfort him.

Nathan felt comforted. He also became aware that he was soaked to the skin and shivered. He said, 'You're right, let's go home. I'm feeling cold all of a sudden. Maybe we can make some hot Milo.'

When they returned to Nathan's place, they were already drenched from the sudden downpour and had to bathe and change. Sachin wore Nathan's pyjamas, they fitted perfectly except for the fact that they were a little too short for him, causing his arms and legs to stick out a bit. They ran downstairs for dinner. Nathan's mother had already made two mugs of hot Milo and two steaming bowls of instant noodles with hard boiled eggs and *bak choi* sautéed with garlic, as side dishes. It was after 9 p.m. and Kak

Yam was resting for the night. Nathan was allowed to eat instant noodles on those days.

Nathan's mother sat down at the table with them, holding a mug of milk tea in her hands which she forgot to drink. She looked thoughtful and worried. She asked Sachin the usual questions about how his parents were doing and how he was progressing with his schoolwork. He answered politely that his grades seldom varied from their usual 'As' and the occasional 'Bs'; somewhat similar to Nathan's. Every parent in their grade knew Junie and Alex were the top students.

She suddenly switched the topic with a sigh. 'I might as well share this with the two of you. I just got another email from your father, and he said that he might have to stay longer in Astana. When I told him that Souchong was missing, he said that he had placed a tracking device on Souchong.'

'What does it mean, Mom? That Souchong has a tracking device?' asked Nathan, looking puzzled.

His mother said with a frown, 'I have no idea. As far as I know, there was no device stuck to him or anything.'

But Sachin interjected excitedly, 'Since your Dad is in IT, it's possible that he placed a microchip on Souchong, probably in his collar. I've heard that some chips are really cutting edge.'

Both Nathan and his mother stared at Sachin. Nathan's mother said, 'That's really insightful, Sachin. Something like this would never occur to me.'

Sachin actually blushed, 'Thanks, Auntie Nalini. It was in a movie I saw where a cat wore an entire galaxy . . . well never mind.'

'Oh, you mean, *Men in Black*? Yes, I remember that the cat wore a pendant which turned out to be an entire galaxy. We older people watch science fiction movies too.' She said with a smile. She continued, 'But upon reflection, I remember that Souchong had a pendant around his neck and your father had bought it for him.'

Nathan replied excitedly, 'If the pendant really had a tracking device, maybe we can use it to locate Souchong.'

'I forgot to mention, there were a series of numbers on the email as well. I've written them down somewhere.' His mother walked to the sideboard and picked up a piece of paper with the words, 'Here it is. It says, "These may help you to locate LS 103.5467354.954303".'

'Auntie, do you think the numbers stand for a safety deposit box number?' asked Sachin, excitedly.

Nathan's mother sighed, 'I really don't think so. We have one safety deposit box and I know the number. Also, most safety deposit boxes have only six-digit numbers. Besides, there are dots among the numbers.'

'Then I guess, we have to figure out what the numbers mean to track down Souchong,' said Nathan. But this time he felt oddly hopeful, even though they were no closer to tracking down his cat.

After finishing their mugs of hot chocolate, they decided to retire for the night.

That night, Nathan had a strange dream about a magnificent cat which looked like Souchong except that it was not really Souchong. It was the Zodiac Cat, a story his father had told him since he was young, but it was mashed up with his Silk Road project with Aida. His research and the stories Aida had told him about the ancient cities and places which had arisen along the crossroads of the many routes of the Great Silk Road came to life vividly in his dream.

7

The Zodiac Cat

'Is it morning already?' asked a sleepy voice. It came from a handsome cat who stretched out its limbs and yawned. He lived in a large barn that was dry and comfortable with plenty of hay to nestle in, even during cold winter nights. The cat shared the barn with a rat, a rooster, a dog, a goat, an ox, and a horse. He was best friends with the rat. He really had no choice, because the rooster, dog, goat, ox, and horse ignored both the cat and the rat and regarded them as lesser animals. They were known simply as: Cat, Rat, Rooster, Dog, Goat, Ox, and Horse.

The other animals looked down on Cat and Rat because they were the least favourite of their master, Farmer Wu. The farmer was fond of the brightly feathered Rooster who never failed to wake him up at the crack of dawn. He was also fond of loyal Dog who always kept watch at night when the other animals slept, and who seemed to be aware of the slightest sound which was out of place. Goat gave him milk, Ox ploughed his rice fields, and Horse carried him to the market every week. As for Rat, nobody knew what he did because he hid in the shadows most of the time.

Cat once asked, 'Everyone says I'm handsome! So why does the Master always ignore me?'

The other animals kept quiet, but Dog felt a little sorry for him and replied, 'Your good looks could have made you popular with the Master but you are lazy and you sleep all the time!'

'But you sleep all the time too,' retorted Cat.

Dog bristled a bit at this perceived insult. 'It's true that I like to sleep, but at least I wake up and bark whenever a stranger enters the farm at night!' retorted Dog.

'Dog is right! Cat, you are the only one who never wakes up when I crow every morning,' said Rooster in a disappointed voice. Cat did not reply because he knew that Rooster was right. All the other animals, apart from Rat and himself, had a special talent. He wondered what his special talent was.

Apart from telling the time, Rooster had another gift. He also gathered news from the other roosters when they crowed to each other every morning.

One morning, he ran into the barn, puffed himself up and strutted around. Then he crowed loudly, 'Wake up, friends! I have momentous news! The Jade Emperor has summoned all the animals in the kingdom to his palace tomorrow to make an important announcement!'

Cat, who was asleep, jumped up in fright at the loud crowing. Rat ran out of his hole, sat up and squeaked, 'All the animals in the kingdom? That means Cat and I are invited as well?'

'Yes, all the animals in the kingdom, which I suppose also includes the two of you,' sniffed Rooster disdainfully.

So the next day, all the animals in the barn walked to the palace of the Jade Emperor. They were joined by many animals from other farms, including an enthusiastic pig and an inquisitive rabbit. And from a nearby forest came a playful monkey, a regal tiger, and a shiny snake. Everyone was surprised and slightly awed when a fabulous blue dragon emerged from a cave in the mountains. Other animals appeared from all over the world, most of which the farm animals could not even name.

The animals were allowed to enter the palace grounds through a towering gate which led into a wonderful garden. When all the animals had gathered, they were ushered into a courtyard, where the Jade Emperor himself was waiting to greet them. The animals bowed down to him and sat on the ground.

The Emperor said, 'Welcome to the Jade Palace, my dear animals! Now listen, we have decided to create a calendar called the *Sheng Xiao* to mark the years. The *Sheng Xiao* will have twelve years and each year will be named after an animal. As there are so many of you, in order to choose the twelve most deserving animals, I have decided to hold a race.'

As he went on to explain the calendar to them, Cat who was tired after the journey, fell asleep in a secluded corner of the palace courtyard. He did not hear the Jade Emperor explain, 'Tomorrow, before dawn, all the animals who wish to take part in this race are to gather at the Eastern Meridian Gate. The race starts when the sun's rays lights the Eastern Gate. You are to race through the entire Middle Kingdom in one day. The first twelve animals to reach the Western Meridian Gate before the sun sets will be declared the winners. They will also dine with me at a special banquet in the Jade Palace.'

Cat missed all this. He only woke up when the animals were about to return home. Cat asked his friend Rat what the Jade Emperor said when he was sleeping. Rat told him, 'Don't worry you have plenty of time to sleep. The race starts at noon tomorrow at the Eastern Meridian Gate.'

The next day, Rooster crowed even earlier than usual. He only crowed once, instead of his usual three times, because he wanted to rush off to the Eastern Gate. One by one, all the animals, except for Cat woke up and quietly walked to the Eastern Meridian Gate. The other animals were already waiting there, and they had to hurry to reach the Gate before sunrise. All the animals rushed off at the exact moment when the golden rays of the morning sun set the Gate alight.

When Cat woke up, he found that the barn was deserted. 'Where were the other animals?' he wondered. Panic stricken,

Cat rushed to the Eastern Meridian Gate, which was deserted by now. As he wandered around at a loss, an old gardener told him, 'The race started at dawn. All the animals have already left.'

'But . . . but Rat said that it would start at noon,' he wailed in despair. His heart sank when he realized he had missed the race and even more so when he realized that Rat, his only friend, had lied to him. Cat sat down, too upset to do anything. Tears fell down from his blue eyes. The old gardener felt sorry for him. He said kindly, 'Don't be too disappointed, sometimes things don't work out the way we expect them to.'

Cat jumped up and said, 'If I ran as fast as I could, maybe I can catch up with them?'

The old gardener shook his head and said, 'It's too late. They are already halfway around the country by now.'

Cat wailed, 'I've been betrayed by my friend! Why did I sleep when the Emperor was speaking?'

The old gardener nodded wisely. He said, 'Sometimes, we have to watch out for ourselves, not all friends can be trusted. Why don't you walk to the Western Meridian Gate and watch the outcome of the race?'

Cat did not like the idea, but he walked miserably to the Western Gate and sat in the shadows. He consoled himself with the thought, 'It's not likely that a tiny animal like Rat will be able to complete the race, let alone be among the first twelve.'

During the race, all the animals were racing furiously. Wily Rat knew that he could never catch up with them, so he jumped on the back of Ox, who was the strongest runner among them. When the first twelve animals had almost reached the finishing line, the ox was leading. But Rat, which was sitting on the head of Ox, jumped off to cross the finishing line first!

Cat was devastated. He stayed long enough to watch the twelve animals of the Zodiac enter the Jade Palace to dine with the Jade Emperor. Then he sadly turned away and walked into the countryside. He felt too sad and ashamed to return to the barn. He thought, 'They are all going to jeer and laugh at me.'

So, Cat ran away. He slept in barns and ate whatever scraps of food people left behind. In that way, he travelled far from his home in the countryside, until he reached Xian, the ancient capital of the Middle Kingdom. He stood outside the Great Wall, which encircled the city. It had been built to protect Xian. Cat waited, wondering what to do until a caravan appeared out of one of the Gates. This was a long line of strange looking animals with humps on their back. They were accompanied by men in long, loose colourful robes. Some wore turbans, and others wore embroidered square caps on their heads. They spoke loudly and cheerfully in strange tongues. Some of the animals carried loads on their back while the others carried people.

A young man at the end of the caravan spotted Cat and said in surprise, 'Hello, what do we have here? A handsome cat! The only one in the city of Xian, I bet. Come join us on the Great Silk Road! There is always room on my camel for a fine cat!'

The friendly young man had twinkling brown eyes and he held a bowl and poured some milk into it. Cat ran to him. It was the most delicious milk he had ever had. After he had licked the bowl clean, the man picked up the bowl and tucked it into his belt. Then he picked up the cat and placed him on the camel. They travelled for many days and night, following the Great Wall which seemed to go on as far as the eyes can see, going ever westward. Fortunately, the weather was mild, with the occasional brisk wind blowing from the north.

Finally, they came to Nanshan, a long row of mountains covered with lush vegetation. It was cool and green here. The young man told Cat, 'There are wonderful animals living in the mountains—golden monkeys, and fat black and white bears—but I have never seen them. Nanshan is said to be the vein of the Dragon but I think it is the spine of the Dragon.'

Further on, the landscape became arid. Carved into the rock faces were grottos and statues of gods. The young man told Cat that this was one of the crossroads of the Silk Road—where the route from Bharat in the south met the one from Persia in the west. They stopped at the nearest town and trading post to rest and restock, trading goods for food and water. All the traders had a good meal before heading further West over the dry, rugged landscape where the days were hot and the nights bone-chilling cold. But Cat didn't mind. He had milk to drink, dried meat to chew, and he didn't have to walk.

Finally, after many more days of travelling, they came to the great fortress of Jiyaguan. The young man told Cat, 'Jiyaguan was built to keep out fierce invaders from the west. This is the westernmost post of the Middle Kingdom and the last gate of the Great Wall. We will rest here for the night, and if we are lucky, even obtain food and water from the Commander of the Fortress.'

The Silk Road traders woke up early the next morning and set out for their journey as the sun was rising on the East. They had to go through the Western Gate into the barren desert. The massive gate doors were opened only after the sentries had reported that there were no enemies in sight. The young man whispered to Cat, 'They call this gate the "Gate of Demons" because traitors and wrong-doers who have been banished are forced to go through this gate. Most will not survive, but don't worry, my friend, we will!'

After they left the Middle Kingdom, they had to cross the Gobi Desert. What seemed like endless days of travelling finally ended when they came to a sparkling blue-green jewel in the desert—the Crescent Spring Oasis. The traders broke into smiles and some even started singing. They set up tents to rest and replenish their water supply with sparkling clear spring water. The young man told Cat, 'Legend has it that this is the first spring under the sun!'

That night, Cat came to look at the lake under the light of the full moon. The desert sky, which was the clearest brightest blue during the day, had turned velvety black with the light of thousands of stars at night. An old monk, who was standing by the lake spoke to Cat, 'Beneath the waters of the lake lies the seven-star grass and the iron backed fish. If you eat both, you will be immortal!'

Cat looked up at him, quizzically. The monk reminded him of the old gardener at the Jade Emperor's Palace. Cat stretched out his paw towards the water, but he was too timid to jump into the lake. He was afraid of water.

After the Crescent Spring Oasis, they passed through trading cities, with legendary names—Kashgar, Samarkand, Bukhara, and Almaty—where the men stopped for food and water and traded their goods. These were walled cities, some of them built around the oasis. Inside the walls, were buildings made of cool white or pink stone and circled by winding streets. There were also grand bazaars where dried fruits and nuts, silk, carpets, musical instruments, bronze and silverware, and coloured glassware were sold. Finally, when they reached the port of Basra in Persia, the young man told Cat that that was their final stop.

Cat entered the city of Basra, where people were always rushing around carrying large crates and rolling barrels around. It was windy there and the air tasted salty and smelt of fish and something else. He saw a huge body of water with large wooden houses floating on it. Some had large pieces of cloth—mostly coloured white but a few in bright red—flapping in the wind. He didn't know they were ships. Suddenly, a strange creature approached him. Cat was alarmed and hissed.

The creature backed away in surprise. Then she said, 'Can't you tell I'm a cat, just like you?'

Cat said, 'You're a cat too? I thought I was the only Cat in the world.'

The other cat said, 'You're not that special. Anyway, where are you from?'

Cat replied, 'The Middle Kingdom.'

'You may be right. You might be the only cat in the Middle Kingdom because you're the first cat I've come across from there. But where I come from, cats are found everywhere.'

Cat did not reply. He was too confused by what he was hearing. The other cat continued, 'By the way, my name is Black, the beloved protector of the boy called Dick Whittington. What's your name?'

Cat said, 'Everyone calls me Cat.'

'Hmm . . . Cat. That's interesting.' Black looked at Cat and felt a little sorry for him. He looked thin and his fur which must have been smooth and shiny once, looked ragged. She asked, 'Have you had anything to eat? You look hungry.'

'I haven't eaten in days,' he said sadly.

'Then let's go and catch us some food,' said Black.

Cat was confused but he was too hungry to ask any questions and followed her obediently. She soon dived into an alleyway and pounced on something. She brought back a rat and lay it at his feet. 'Here, eat this,' she said.

Cat was horrified. He said, 'But . . . but . . . that's a rat!'

'Of course, it's a rat! Cats hunt and kill rats and mice. That's our main role in life. When we have nothing else to eat, we even have to eat them!' She said.

Finally, Cat was so hungry that he ate the rat. He felt a bit sick but the miserable meal filled his stomach. He followed Black everywhere and learnt how to catch rats and find food for himself. He soon became as fast, strong and as skilful a rat catcher as Black herself. However, in a few weeks' time, Black told him that she had to leave because her ship was sailing away. She said, 'You can come with me, if you like. There are plenty of rats and mice on board ships and cats like us are always welcome.'

But Cat said that he missed his farm and had to return home. Somehow, learning how to catch his own food made him feel better about himself, he felt strong and oddly unafraid. So, Cat waited at the Eastern Gate of the city of Basra, where he met the friendly man on the caravan again and joined him on the journey back to the Middle Kingdom. When they reached the Crescent Spring Oasis again, Cat waited by the side of the lake that night. When he saw a fish swim to the edge of the lake, he pounced on it and caught the fish in his jaws. Cat brought the fish back to the shore. He noticed that the fish had some grass in its mouth, so he ate the grass as well as the fish. Then he returned to the young man's tent.

They entered the Middle Kingdom, through the same Western Gate into Jiyaguan. From there, the journey to Xian, was relatively easy as they walked in the shadow of the Great Wall. Cat said goodbye to the man at Xian and continued his journey home. The journey back was much easier for him because he had become self-reliant and no longer needed to beg for food from humans. When he finally reached his farm, he went into the barn.

A rat came out and Cat pounced on it. At that moment the Farmer entered the barn and Cat guiltily dropped the rat. But the farmer said, 'So you're back, Cat! And you've learnt a new skill, I see!'

The farmer patted Cat on the head fondly and said, 'Well done, Cat! I was wondering when you were going to return home because the farm is overrun with rats now!'

Then he picked him up and took him home. He placed the cat on a rug near the hearth and gave him a small bowl of rice with roasted fish. Cat purred and ate contentedly before settling down on the rug to take a nap.

So, although Cat failed to be included in the *Sheng Xiao*, he became one of the favourite animals of all humans.

Nathan heard a loud meowing outside his window and woke up from sleep with a gasp. He sat up and stared at the window and thought he saw the silhouette of a cat, but it vanished when he called out to it.

* * *

Meanwhile, in her room, Aida dreamt about a cat with a musical and hypnotic voice which lulled her into a deep sleep. In her sleep, she heard a voice reciting a story to her. It was a story she thought she knew well, but not quite this version.

Once upon a time, a young prince called Ivan Tsarevich was tasked to capture a Bayun Cat by the Voivode of his kingdom—the second most powerful man in the kingdom, who was also in charge of the army. Ivan Tsarevich's father, the Tsar, was deathly ill. According to the Royal Physician, the Tsar's illness was the result of a curse and the only thing which can cure him was the song of a Bayun Cat. The Voivode, who wanted to rule the kingdom for himself, knew that attempting to capture this bloodthirsty beast meant inevitable death. No one ever came back alive with the Bayun Cat.

Ivan Tsarevich had no choice but to obey the Voivode, but he did not mind because he was determined to save his father. He journeyed far and wide, through the twenty-nine kingdoms, until he came to the thirtieth one. When he finally came across a silent and desolate forest, he knew that he had found the lifeless forest—a forest with tall, brooding, trees devoid of birds, insects, and animals. He felt all alone and fearful, and was relieved when he came across a beautiful young girl walking by herself in the forest.

He hailed her and asked, 'Fair maiden, allow me to introduce myself. I am Ivan Tsarevich from a faraway kingdom. Will you do me the kindness of giving me your name? And why do you walk alone in this lifeless forest?'

The maiden was surprised to see him, no one ever came into the lifeless forest. But Ivan Tsarevich was young and handsome, and she could not help liking him. So, she gave him her name. 'I am Vasilisa of the woods. I live in this forest with my aunt, Baba Yaga.'

Even Ivan Tsarevich had heard of Baba Yaga, the fearsome witch whose favourite food was young children, and he caught his breath. The young maiden asked him, 'But why do you journey through the lifeless forest? Even the most desperate people avoid this forest because it is haunted by death.'

Ivan replied, 'I am looking for the Bayun Cat, and I have been told that he lives in this forest!'

This time it was Vasilisa's turn to catch her breath. She said, 'The Bayun Cat is the reason why the forest is known as the lifeless forest. Why would you risk your life to search out the Bayun Cat?'

'My father is dying and the only thing which will cure him is the magical song of the Bayun Cat . . . and I have no one to help me,' Ivan said sadly.

Vasilisa felt sorry for him. She had lost her father a few years ago and had been forced to live with Baba Yaga since then. She said, 'The Bayun Cat belongs to Baba Yaga, the fearsome witch. I can give you something to resist his magical voice, but you have to rely on your own courage and strength to overcome him. Come follow me . . .'

Ivan followed Vasilisa to Baba Yaga's dwelling, a quaint wooden cottage which seemed to be alive and spun around on its own. Since it was still daytime, Baba Yaga was away. Vasilisa ran into the cottage and came out with an iron helmet, an iron chain, and a pair of iron mittens—that actually looked like gauntlets. She put the helmet on his head and said that although he will still be able to hear the cat spinning his magical tales, the helmet will impede the magic and Ivan will be able to stay awake. The iron gauntlets will help him to capture the cat and he needed the chain to bind the cat, 'Iron will defeat his magic.' She attached one end of the chain to one of the gauntlet while the other end was left loose.

Vasilisa also gave him a ball of herbs—which was, in fact, catnip—and told him they would calm the cat down. She also told him that he needed to capture the Bayun Cat before dark or Baba Yaga will return. Ivan thanked her and promised that he would return to take her with him to his kingdom. He knew Baba Yaga would punish Vasilisa for giving him the helmet and gauntlets.

Ivan travelled deeper into the forest until he heard the cat singing. He dismounted and tied his horse to a tree, and walked towards the iron pole where the cat was perched. It was striped in black, grey, and white, and looked both beautiful and terrifying. Ivan pretended to fall asleep near the pole.

The Bayun Cat jumped down to the ground and approached Ivan. The fabulous beast was the size of a Russian bear-dog. The cat crouched and sniffed at him and then opened his mouth to bite his throat. But when the cat's jaw came close enough, Ivan grabbed his throat with his hands and held fast. The cat gasped for breath and could only meow for mercy. Ivan wound the iron chain around the cat's neck and secured it with a lock. Once the cat was tied up, Ivan gave him some of the catnip. The cat was defeated by iron and followed him meekly to where his horse was tied. With the cat running behind the horse, Ivan rode back as quickly as he could to Baba Yaga's cottage. The sun was just beginning to set, and Vasilisa was waiting for him outside the cottage. Ivan pulled her up onto his horse and they rode away just before Baba Yaga arrived.

Ivan, Vasilisa, and the Bayun Cat travelled as quickly as they could through the lifeless forest because they knew Baba Yaga would be trying to track them. They could even hear her muttering and cursing at them in the distance. After a wild chase, they finally managed to escape the lifeless forest. It was already night when they finally managed to get some rest at a barn.

After a few days journey, Ivan, Vasilisa, and the Bayun Cat reached his kingdom. He went straight to his father's chamber with the Bayun Cat in tow. The Voivode tried to stop them, but the Bayun Cat snarled at him and he fled the palace. The cat, which was now almost tame due to a constant supply of delicious food and catnip, spun his most magical tale and the Tsar's health was restored. The delighted Tsar thanked his son, welcomed Vasilisa to the palace and arranged for them to be married the very next day.

The next day, the entire palace had been decked out for the wedding—all the maids in waiting, serving maids, kitchen hands, cooks, and footmen had been busy the entire night, preparing for this momentous event. However, before the actual ceremony could take place, Baba Yaga appeared in court. She grabbed Vasilisa and dragged her away out of the hall before anyone could do anything. She had cast a spell over the entire court so that everyone was frozen to the spot, everyone except for the Bayun Cat.

The cat sang his hypnotic magical song and everyone fell asleep, even Baba Yaga, who no longer had her metal helmet to protect her. The Bayun Cat pounced on Baba Yaga and devoured her. Then he turned to the sleeping Vasilisa, who now looked a lot like Aida, and told her, 'She was mean and horrid to me, she kept me chained up all the time. But you were nice . . . so I saved you and those you love.'

The Bayun Cat bounded out of the palace and disappeared into the thick forest surrounding the palace grounds.

8

The 'Shisha' Incident

A few weeks earlier, Jin and Steven were walking in the urban park, which surrounded the Kuala Lumpur City Centre. It was an oasis of green in the heart of the city.

'Are you looking for something interesting?' A young man, possibly of West Asian descent, accosted Jin and Steven. Jin was about to walk away when Steven asked him, 'Do you have any *beedi*?'

'*Beedi*? I have more than *beedi*, more strong and . . . spicy! Help you with homework, even make you smarter!'

Both boys perked up at the word 'homework,' the bane of their existence at the moment. Anything that can help them with their homework was worth investigating.

The young man opened a briefcase and showed them its content—rolls of what looked like *beedi*, 'I'm from Afghanistan and this is special from my country.'

'It looks like *beedi* to me,' replied Steven, sounding doubtful.

'No, not *beedi*! This is special . . . try one,' he said and lit one and passed it to Steven. Steven took in few puffs and passed it to Jin, who drew in the smoke cautiously. It was true, it was stronger than *beedi* and had a spicy, rather pleasant aroma. It was the scent of cloves and cinnamon, but the boys failed to recognize it.

Steven asked, 'What is it called?'

'What is it called? . . . *Shisha*! We call this shisha in my country,' the young man said enthusiastically.

'I've never heard of shisha, sounds quite exotic,' Jin remarked.

'Shisha very strong and spicy, make you very active!'

'How much is it?' asked Steven.

'Only two ringgits per stick! Very cheap!' The young man replied.

It was almost four times the cost of a normal *beedi*, but he was a very convincing salesman. Steven and Jin bought twenty-five sticks each and carried it with them, carefully concealed in sandwich bags. As they walked away, the young man called out, 'Remember, shisha very spicy! You can buy more from me!'

Soon rumours began to circulate in Noble Hall of a select group of students who smoked shisha, and whose identities were a carefully guarded secret.

* * *

Jin woke up early the next day to go for swimming practice—the swim team met every Saturday and Sunday morning and practised until lunch time. As usual, his mother drove him to the Club to drop him off. The school did not have an Olympic-sized pool, so the team preferred to practice at the Kota Kemuning Golf Club. The team usually stopped for lunch after practice and Steven's mother would drive them home after that.

As soon as their mother had driven the car away, Junie took the opportunity to sneak into Jin's room and systematically searched the place. She was extremely meticulous, making full use of her training in the laboratory to ensure that no nook, cranny, cupboard, or drawer was unsearched and at the same carefully replacing everything where she found it. She sighed in disappointment, ran her fingers through her hair, and sat resignedly on the floor. Apart from some girly magazines hidden at the bottom of a drawer crammed with clothes, she had uncovered nothing of interest. She decided to scan the room again from her vantage point on the floor and noticed that one side of his bed seemed higher than the other. Junie got up to her feet and quickly walked to the bed. She lifted the corner of the mattress which seemed higher with some difficulty. Her heart leaped with excitement when she saw a hard plastic casing—it had been taped on the underside of the mattress! She pulled the casing out and opened it. There were at least fifty rolls of *beedi* inside. Junie smiled to herself and said, 'I've got you, sucker!' Junie took seven of the rolls out and placed the plastic container on the floor, this time just underneath the bed.

Junie placed three of the *beedi* rolls in the room, arranging them to make it seem random while at the same time making sure they led from the door to the box under the bed. Then she placed the other four outside Jin's room, apparently in random order.

When her mother returned home, she stood outside her room and called her mother, 'Mom! I can't find my laptop! Did Jin take it last night?'

Her mother said, 'Jin got his own laptop, why would he take yours?'

Junie yelled back, 'I don't know! But I need my laptop now or I won't be able to complete my science assignment by Monday!'

Junie's mom walked up the stairs and found Junie standing agitatedly on the landing. She said, 'Come, I'll help you to look for it,' and walked towards Jin's room.

She stepped on one of the *beedi* rolls and Junie exclaimed, 'Mom! You stepped on something on the carpet!'

Her mother looked down and saw the crushed *beedi* roll. She picked it up and said, 'What is this? Your father never smokes!' Then she saw another roll on the floor just outside the door to Jin's room. Junie's mother picked up the roll and opened the door. She had no problem spotting the *beedi* rolls Junie had left lying on the floor. When she bent down to pick the last one, her eye fell on the plastic container carefully hidden under the bed. Junie's mother pulled it out and opened the plastic container with nervous hands.

Junie felt almost sorry for what she had done. She had expected her mother to be angry, but her mother seemed fearful, almost panic stricken. Her hands were shaking but there was no turning back now. Junie said, 'What is it, Mom? What did you find?'

Her mother did not reply for a while. Then she took a deep breath to compose herself, got up to her feet and turned around to face Junie. Junie noticed that her mother's face had turned pale and she felt even more contrite. Her mother said, 'Oh never mind . . . you use Jin's laptop first, okay? We will ask him about . . . it . . . when he returns home.' Then she quickly walked into her own room, holding the plastic container tightly in her hand.

Junie quickly ran into her own room and locked the door from the inside. While waiting for the fallout when Jin returned, she forced herself to calm down and read a book, but she was too nervous to do any real work. She jumped to her feet and paced the room. She dared not even call Nathan in case her mother overheard her. The house seemed uncannily silent.

When Jin finally came home, his mother was waiting for him on the landing. Her face was livid with fury and she was holding the offending plastic container in her hand. His mother practically shouted at him, 'JIN! What is this I found in your room? Are you stupid or what? You can go to jail for keeping these kinds of things in the house!'

Jin turned pale when he saw the plastic container. But he pulled himself together and protested, 'It's only shisha! It's not against the law to smoke shisha!'

His mother shouted, 'What shisha? Don't lie to me! Shisha is hashish spelt backwards! And do you know what hashish is? Hashish is *ganja*! You want us all to go to jail, is it?'

'Mom! Shisha is not ganja! It's just tobacco rolled in dried leaf! Everyone knows that! It's not just me, many of the students at school smoke shisha and no one's been arrested!' Jin protested. But he was beginning to realize that his mother was not going to listen to any reasons he had to offer, she was convinced he was smoking ganja.

Mrs Kwan had worked herself into a frenzy. She was unwilling to listen to any reasons that Jin had to offer. She almost screamed, 'I'm not going to listen to any of your excuses! I'm cutting your allowance. And you are grounded for a month! Do you hear me? You are GROUNDED! You are only allowed to go to school. No more hanging out with your friends, even on weekends!'

Jin actually turned pale. He protested, 'Mom, I have to go for swim practice! I'm representing the school in the state finals!'

His mother was about to shout, 'I don't care!' but managed to stop herself on time. She was after all, a 'Tiger Mother.' Jin was her eldest child and only son, his success was paramount. And the coach had said that he was likely to win the State Championship, and perhaps even represent the country next year. She paused for a moment, took a deep breath, and managed to calm down. Finally, she said, 'Okay, you can go to school and for swim practice, but that's all. Your father or I will wait for you during your practice and drive you home straight away! We will do this, until we are sure you are not smoking any shisha any more!'

Jin was dismayed but he knew better than to argue with his mother. At least he could hang out with his friend at school and during swim practice. It could have been much worse. Everyone in school knew that Alex's mother stopped him from extracurricular activities for a term just for failing to get an A in English. But then Jin remembered Bollywood Night was in a fortnight's time, and it would be staged after school, and he would have to miss it. He would not be able to watch Minji, Maiandra, and Zara perform 'Jai ho'.

In her room, Junie was torn between a mixture of alarm and amusement. Her mother's reaction was far beyond what she had anticipated. She had never heard her mother scream like this.

She was not just angry, she sounded frenzied, almost hysterical. Junie had expected Jin to be reprimanded and given a stern warning never to smoke again, and perhaps even have his allowance cut; but it never occurred to her that he would be grounded! Her little scheme had gone out of hand and made her feel slightly ashamed of herself so, she decided to keep her subterfuge a secret for the moment.

On the way to school on Monday, Junie put on her most guileless look while Jin glowered in the car. Nathan sensed something was amiss from his aunt's stony silence and Jin's irate look, but since Junie seemed unaffected, he didn't give it much thought. Junie held her peace until they met up with Sachin, and then she burst out, 'Guess who's been grounded for a whole month!' And she gave a detailed account of what happened during the weekend, but she left her role in exposing his secret.

Sachin said with a broad grin on his face, 'So, Jin's been grounded for a whole month! No more hanging out with the swim team! No more allowance! Best news so far!'

Nathan remarked, 'This seems a bit harsh for just smoking shisha, although I'm not complaining. I mean, I never thought Auntie Fei could ever find fault with her favourite over-achieving first-born child.'

'That's because Mum doesn't know that what we call shisha is actually *beedi*. She thinks shisha is hashish pronounced backwards ... you know ... ganja,' she said with a suppressed laugh.

Nathan and Sachin gasped and then burst out laughing. Sachin sniggered, 'Poor Jin! I almost feel sorry for him . . . not!'

Nathan asked curiously, 'How did she find out anyway? I mean even we didn't know he smoked *beedi*.'

'That's on a need-to-know basis only,' she said mysteriously.

'Wait, you had something to do with it! But why?' Nathan asked, and added, 'Again, not that I'm complaining.'

'For getting even . . .' Junie briefly told them what she had done but before she could describe her mother's reaction, she saw

Aida walking towards them. She cut short her sentence and gave both boys warning looks. Although she liked Aida and regarded her as a friend and member of the group now, Junie still didn't want to share certain things with her. The *Kaidankai* had shown her that, despite being well read and level-headed, Aida was as susceptible to Jin's charms as most of the girls in school. She would get in trouble if Jin found out that she had set him up. In school, there were few friends you could trust with family secrets.

Aida greeted them, 'Hi, Junie! Hi, Nathan and Sachin! How was your weekend? I kept on thinking about the *Kaidankai* and had bad dreams. I saw all kinds of cats surrounding my bed and meowing at me. And worst of all, I felt as if the Bayun Cat was staring at me from outside the window.' She shivered slightly.

Junie looked guilty because it had been her idea to organize the event. But before she could say anything, Nathan replied, 'Yeah, me too. I kept on dreaming about Souchong. He came to the window, and I felt like he was trying to tell me something . . . but when I woke up, there was nothing.'

Junie felt even worse than before. She had never expected the *Kaidankai* to get so intense—just as she never expected her brother to be at home during the event. What if Nathan had had a breakdown? She tried to apologize, 'Guys, I'm really sorry. I wish I'd never organized the *Kaidankai*.'

But Nathan said, 'It's all right, Junie, it was . . . the most interesting event you've organized so far and it made me face my worst fear.'

He paused and added, 'I also dreamt of the Sheng Xiao cat and I think cats really do have nine lives. Souchong is out there in the world having a great time.'

Junie looked at Nathan, relieved. She thought to herself, maybe what Marie Curie said is true, 'Nothing in life is to be feared. It is only to be understood.'

Sachin decided to change the subject by announcing, 'Guys, time to get real! I love ancient folklore and all that, but this is 2010!

There's something new on the World Wide Web! Ever heard of Facebook? Some tech-geeks, supposedly from Harvard, started it in the US some years ago. The worldwide launch was in 2006 but it's only taking off in a big way now. They say it's the new MySpace.'

'What's MySpace?' asked Nathan and Junie.

Aida said, 'I've heard of MySpace. Some of my friends in New York have MySpace accounts but I've never heard of Facebook.'

'Okay, allow me to explain. MySpace is the top social networking site, or it used to be, like the year before. You know, it's where you connect with long distance friends and long-lost relatives. Anyway, the new kid on the block, Facebook, managed to grab the lead and is gaining traction.'

Realizing that he had their undivided attention, Sachin pressed on, 'So why did MySpace sink like the Titanic or is about to? Well, it could be because MySpace was bought over by Rupert Murdoch and is run by news people, not by tech gurus. Instead of innovating to compete with Facebook, they spent their time selling ad space.'

'I've heard of Rupert Murdoch,' said Nathan. 'He goes around the world buying newspapers and TV stations.'

'Exactly! You can't run a high-tech online portal like a newspaper. Anyway, MySpace is unheard of in Malaysia; that should tell you something. My theory is, if something doesn't take hold in Malaysia, it's doomed anyway!'

'So, what makes you think, Facebook is going to be big?' asked Junie.

'Facebook is simpler, you only need a valid email address to join. But you have to add other friends who are on Facebook, otherwise you'll be "talking" to yourself in cyberspace. You can do cool stuff, like write status updates, and also upload pictures,' Sachin explained. He felt pleased that a part of his obsession with computers and the Internet was finally of interest to his friends.

Nathan said, sounding surprisingly excited, 'Wait, I think this Facebook might be quite useful for us. I was thinking that if we post Souchong's picture on Facebook, together with a contact number, more people might get to see it and call us.'

'You're right, Nathan. The Internet may be more effective, instead of handing out flyers which people throw away, anyway,' added Junie, enthusiastically.

'This is cool! Let's all join Facebook!' added Aida. The bell for class rang.

Sachin said, 'No time now, but we can meet up during break.'

While Nathan, Junie, and Sachin walked in the direction of their classroom, Aida walked towards another building. Nathan turned around and called out to her, 'Aida! We have history class now!'

Aida waved at them cheerfully. 'I have permission to skip history today. I'm seeing Ms Rosela in the music room to discuss something.'

'Okay! See you at the computer lab during break!' Sachin reminded her.

As they approached the classroom, Nathan remarked, 'I guess she intends to audition for Bollywood Night.'

'It's a bit too late for that, I mean Bollywood Night is in a few weeks' time. She could be trying for the year-end choir,' Sachin replied.

'Anyway, we don't even know if Aida can sing. I know that Zara, and Minji, Maiandra and probably all the other popular students practised really hard to get into Bollywood Night. It's weird but the competition is really fierce this year, like there is some kind of big prize involved,' Junie replied as they entered their classroom.

Nathan said as an afterthought, 'It's going to make some people really mad, if it turns out that Aida can actually sing.'

* * *

Aida hurried to the music room and entered slightly out of breath. An attractive woman in her forties, elegantly dressed in a pale pink and grey chiffon *baju kurong* with her hair pulled back in a neat bun, was seated at the baby grand piano. She looked up at Aida and smiled. 'Good morning, Aida! I'm glad to see that you are right on time for your audition.'

'Thank you for giving me this chance, Ms Rosela! I'm really keen to take part in Bollywood Night,' Aida replied eagerly.

'It would have been better if you had informed me earlier about this and you could have practised with the rest of the students. But I've decided to give you a last-minute audition since someone has pulled out. Anyway, you joined the school quite late this year so I'm giving you some leeway, and I really liked the Kazakh folksong recording you sent me.'

Aida said fervently, 'I'm truly grateful and I'm going to do my best, Ms Rosela!'

Ms Rosela replied, 'I'm sure of that. Many students are competing to be in this show, so you have to show everyone that you deserve to be in the show. Now where shall we start?'

Aida nervously took out a few sheets of music from her school satchel and handed them to the music teacher. 'Ms Rosela, instead of the Kazakh folk song, I thought of singing a classical Italian song called "Nella Fantasia" and perhaps a pop song as well . . . erm . . . because I don't think the students would be keen on folk songs,' she said tentatively.

Ms Rosela took the music sheets from her and studied them. She said, 'All right then. I'm familiar with the Bruno Mars song, and also with "Nella Fantasia". It's not exactly a classical song, but I'm sure it will reach classical status in time. Both songs require quite a wide vocal range, but we shall rise to the challenge and try our best. Shall we begin with "Nella Fantasia"?'

Aida sang the expressive and poignant song from start to finish. Ms Rosela said, 'Interesting interpretation and your diction in Italian is wonderful! Perhaps you could sing the introduction with a much slower tempo, breathe, and take your time to build up to the middle verse with a brighter tone to the vibrato.'

In the dance studio, next to the music room, Zara was practicing her dance moves for the Bollywood Night concert. She had come to school early to practise and had already put in more than an hour, dancing to a CD of 'Jai Ho'. She was almost finished and turned off the tape to return to class. She could hear the faint sound of singing coming through from the next room, even though the rooms were sound-proofed.

Zara opened the door connecting the two rooms to eavesdrop on whoever was singing. She was stunned to see Aida singing an Italian song, accompanied by Ms Rosela. The song moved her and she realized that Aida was a gifted singer, but she also felt a stab of envy. How could she be able to sing like that on top of all her other gifts? It was so unfair! And Ms Rosela was helping her! They all had had to audition on stage and had received very little instruction. Zara closed the door and ran to gather all her things. Her mind was in turmoil, and she felt so much resentment, it was almost a physical pain deep in her stomach.

* * *

Aida was absent from class until the lunch break. When she joined her friends at the canteen, she seemed excited but did not tell them the outcome of her music lesson with Ms Rosela. They gobbled down their lunch and rushed to the computer lab, led by Sachin. In the next half an hour, Nathan, Junie, and Aida joined Facebook. Sachin added them to his network and they added each other. They were surprised and excited to find that a number of their friends and 'enemies' were also on the site.

Sachin helped Nathan upload Souchong's picture on Facebook, together with a description and also his mobile number. Everyone shared the picture and the information. Throughout that week, they spent a lot of their spare time on Facebook, competing with one another to see who could amass the largest number of contacts. Surprisingly, Aida beat everyone and emerged as the one with the highest number of contacts. 500 people—including many students from the school—added her the first week itself. Sachin and Nathan were baffled. Nathan remarked, 'Aida's got even more friends than the Jin Jeanies! Does that mean she's actually more popular than them?'

Junie said, 'I'm guessing that it's partly her worldwide contacts and students in school want to add her because of her background and looks.'

Sachin said, 'Yes, a perfect combination of East and West!'

Junie gave him a sidelong look, *Was Sachin falling under her spell as well?* Junie also noticed that Jin had added Aida as a friend, while ignoring the rest of them. On the other hand, Zara had added Nathan, Sachin, and herself as friends, but not Aida.

However, despite all the time they spent on Facebook, it failed to yield any information about Souchong. Instead, Nathan was spammed with nasty messages. He felt disheartened and commented to his friends, 'You never realize how mean people can be, until you get on the World Wide Web.'

Junie pointed out, 'Not all the messages are mean; some students we've never even met said that they would look out for Souchong.'

The group decided to continue sharing the post in case someone spotted Souchong.

One day, when Nathan opened his Facebook account, he saw a picture of a dead Siamese cat pasted on his wall. The cat was laying on his side on the ground, and looked bloodied and mangled, as if it had been hit by a car. Nathan turned pale with shock, he stood up so quickly, his chair fell backwards as he gasped out, 'No!'

Junie turned to look at him and noticed that he looked like he was about to cry.

'Nate, what is it?' Junie asked him, turning pale herself.

He managed to stammer, 'It's Souchong . . .' while pointing at the computer.

'Wait, let me take a look!' She quickly took his laptop away and studied the picture carefully. She pointed out that the markings of the cat were different. 'This cat has dark grey points, while Souchong has dark reddish points. Besides only the area around its muzzle is dark, whereas Souchong's mask extends all the way up his face and around his eyes, and Souchong's socks extend all the way up to his knees.'

Nathan forced himself to look at the ghastly image again. He still couldn't bear to look at the cat's head, but he knew at once that Junie was right—the dark socks on this cat only covered its paws. He felt a huge sense of relief flooding over him and sat on a nearby chair for a while to recover his composure. Then he slammed his fist furiously on his desk, muttering, 'I hate them! I hate them! I hope they all get knocked down by lorries and buses and—'

Sachin told him calmly to ignore the message and delete it, 'Trolls and hacklers are everywhere; you just have to shake them off and continue with what you were doing. Getting upset is equivalent of giving them power over you.'

Nathan was about to delete the post when Sachin stopped him. 'Wait! Don't delete it yet. Let me look at the address. Maybe we should note it, in case, it's connected somehow.' Sachin carefully wrote down the IP address in his notebook.

However, as the days passed, everyone forgot about Facebook and only had one thing on their mind—Bollywood Night! Excitement reached a fever pitch when a rumour started circulating about talent scouts attending the show. Sachin was the first one to break the news to his friends, 'Guys, some talent scouts from Korea may be attending Bollywood Night!'

'We all heard about the talent scouts, but how would you know that they are from Korea?' Nathan asked, sounding slightly sceptical.

'It's from the rugby team and we always get the latest and hottest news, you know! They may pick someone from this school to join a K-Pop group!' Sachin replied, sounding absolutely sure of himself.

'Oh my god! This is too amazing to be true!' Aida gasped. Nathan, Junie, and Sachin looked at her in surprise. Aida appeared ecstatic.

Junie agreed, 'This is amazing news, all right but I guess one of the popular students would be the lucky one.'

Aida did not reply but her eyes sparkled with excitement.

However, Bollywood Night had to take a back seat when Mr Yeoh reminded Nathan and Junie about their year-end science project. Mr Yeoh called them up after class and told them, 'I think we can set aside the biology lab class next week, for the two of you to talk about the ruby-cheeked sunbird. I'm quite curious myself about how well the ancient preservation method will work in a humid climate.'

Nathan and Junie had forgotten all about the bird that they had undertaken to preserve and memorialize! They both looked slightly shocked and looked at each other, guiltily. Junie recovered first and said, 'We'll be ready to give a talk next week, Mr Yeoh!'

Nathan nodded his head vigorously, 'Yes, we'll be prepared for it!'

Mr Yeoh nodded and walked out of the classroom. Junie whispered, 'It's been like weeks since we preserved the bird. What if all that's left of Ruby Cheeks is a pile of feathers and bones?'

Nathan replied, sounding sombre, 'We'll just have to admit that our experiment failed.'

'Yes, but that might affect my grades,' Junie said, sounding upset. She almost regretted agreeing to help Nathan but decided not to mention it. You had to make sacrifices for friends . . . and relatives.

After school, the two of them rushed to the lab to prepare the specimen before the talk. They held their breath when they opened the cabinet to take the specimen out and gave a huge sigh of relief to find out that the ancient Egyptian preservation method had worked. The bird was intact, if a little shrivelled up. Most importantly, the feathers looked as shiny as ever. The two of them mounted it on a cardboard and placed it in a small glass case. Nathan had prepared a note for the bird:

Chalcoparia singalensis also known as the ruby-cheeked sunbird. Totally protected,

Found in both Malaysia and Singapore

When the day for the talk arrived, they were surprised to find that the lab was packed with students. Mr Yeoh had decided to allow younger students from the Form Four classes who were interested in Biology to attend the talk.

Mr Yeoh did the introductions and explained to the students gathered, 'The ruby-cheeked sunbird is totally protected and the only reason we have a specimen was because the bird was the victim of a predatory cat's hunting instinct. To be fair to the cat, it is probable that cats are as much a victim of their killer instinct.'

Junie was up first since she did the actual dissection and the mummification process. Her explanation was clear and concise, and she backed it up with some slide displays of the process.

Nathan came up next and explained about the important role of sunbirds in the ecosystem—just like bees, they helped to pollinate flowers. He pointed out that they occupied the same niche as the hummingbird did in the Caribbean and Central America. He also took the opportunity to talk about the Temple of Bastet and the important role of cats in Ancient Egypt and how cats may have evolved there. He also gave additional information about the mummification of cats.

Mr Yeoh ended by explaining the devastation domestic cats and feral cats can inflict on small birds and mammals and the importance of belling and neutering them.

The students present gave both Nathan and Junie an enthusiastic round of applause before leaving the lab. Nathan and Junie cleared up the lab and placed the bird, now mounted in the little glass case, into the permanent display case in the lab. Before they left, Mr Yeoh told them, 'That was an excellent presentation, Nathan and Junie. It will not affect Junie's grade of course, since you can't get more than an A+, but Nathan's grade has improved to a B plus.'

They both thanked him and rushed out of the class, with wide grins on their faces.

9

Bollywood Night

Excitement and anticipation had reached a fever pitch when Bollywood Night finally arrived. That Friday afternoon, almost all the students had decided to stay back after school. School ended after lunch time to give the students and staff time to set up the stage and do some last-minute rehearsals.

Minji, Maiandra, and Zara—and all the students who were performing in the show—were there to practice their act, accompanied by members of the orchestra. There were a few others who were setting up the props and sound system, and for work behind the stage. The rest of the students chose to chat with their friends or work on their class assignments in the library, computer laboratory, or canteen. Nathan, Junie, and Sachin had brought their costumes for the evening along with them, but they had decided to change later. They were surprised when Aida turned up in a gorgeous black Kazakhstani costume, with red and gold embroidery.

Nathan and Sachin said, 'Wow!'

Junie said, 'Aida, you look amazing! But we're only changing just before the concert!'

Aida flashed them a smile. She said with suppressed excitement, 'Guys, guess what? I'm in the show!'

'What do you mean, "in the show"?' asked Nathan.

'I mean Bollywood Night! Ms Rosela, picked me to open the show as a solo singer!'

'What? But you never even auditioned!' Junie gasped.

'But I did, for Ms Rosela. I just never told you all about it. I wasn't sure I would actually get to participate,' said Aida with a wide grin.

'Yay for you!' said Sachin. 'Slay them all!'

'Slay all the mean girls!' said Nathan.

Aida beamed. 'See, you guy's later!' And she ran towards the hall for the dress rehearsal. The three friends had a leisurely lunch and spent time in the computer laboratory before they changed into their costumes for Bollywood Night.

They went into the hall early to book the best seats and found out that the first three of the front row seats had 'Reserved' signs on them—booked for teachers and parents. Nathan, Junie, and Sachin took their seats in the fifth row—they also booked one seat for Aida—and settled down to enjoy themselves. After all, Bollywood Night only came once a year, and it's not always one gets to enjoy being in a place where the audience was as brightly dressed as the performers. Soon, the entire hall was filled. They nudged each other when two attractive and sharply dressed people—a man and a woman—entered the hall and sat in the front row, just beside the principal. They had no doubt these were the Korean talent scouts; nobody could look so good and dress so well in designer clothes, unless they worked in the K-Pop industry. Junie whispered knowingly, 'They are wearing Versace!' Her eye for fashion had become more sophisticated after spending more time with Aida.

The orchestra played the opening piece—the theme song of the show, 'Jai Ho!' When the curtains opened, the audience clapped enthusiastically. Ms Rosela, who was the emcee for the event, walked to the centre of the stage and announced, 'Good evening, ladies and gentlemen! Allow me to welcome you to Noble Hall's Bollywood Night! The school celebrates diversity by featuring a different culture every year and this year, the student body has chosen to celebrate Bollywood. However, we are opening the show with a contemporary Italian operatic song, "Nella Fantasia". After all we are all about culture and diversity! Ladies and gentlemen, please welcome Aida Anargul to the stage!'

Aida opened the show with 'Nella Fantasia'. Most of the students had never heard the song before and although a few giggled at the back because of the unfamiliar Italian lyrics, Aida's light clear voice carried the deeply moving song to its conclusion. Both Nathan and Junie were in tears and Sachin pretended there was dust in his eyes. When it was over, everyone clapped politely but Nathan, Junie, and Sachin, jumped to their feet, cheered and clapped enthusiastically. They were even more surprised when Aida sang another song—Bruno Mars' monster hit, 'Just the way you are'. The beautiful love song won over the entire audience, who gave her a standing ovation.

Maiandra took the stage after Aida, and gave a beautiful rendition of P. Ramlee's song, 'Getaran Jiwa'. Her rich strong voice was controlled and emotive, creating an audio landscape with resonating lows and soaring high notes, and the three friends were surprised when they found themselves shedding a few tears. This was followed by a Hindi song, 'O Sajana'. It was such an old song, no one had ever heard it before. Maiandra had learnt the song from her grandmother, who had come from India to Malaysia as a young bride. The beautiful song moved everyone to tears; but they were tears of happiness. 'O Sajana' was a song full of the joy and hope of spring. Maiandra received a standing ovation as well, she had legions of followers among the students.

Aida joined them after her performance and sat down to enjoy the rest of the show—one dazzling spectacle, followed another until they reached the finale. The four friends had to grudgingly admit that the Jin Jeanies rendition of A.R. Rahman's catchy and uplifting song, 'Jai Ho!', was the show stopper. The song had taken the world by storm and now, it swept all of them along. The three girls were dressed in brightly-coloured, richly-embroidered, and sequinned lehengas: Zara in peacock blue, Minji in emerald green, and Maiandra in vermillion red. Identical embroidery patterns on the lehenga, and a fitted black choli, pulled the look together. Zara's mother had bought the outfits at a shop in Brickfields which specialized in Indian costumes.

All three were superb dancers. Zara and Minji had fairly good vocals, but Maiandra stole the scene with her soaring, powerful voice. Their performance was supposed to be the finale, and the three girls went backstage, after bowing and blowing kisses to the audience. But the audience asked repeatedly for an encore. Finally, twelve girls emerged onstage, all wearing bejewelled black choli but paired with a pair of black salwar. A black dupatta was wrapped around their head and the ends of the long scarf used to cover their faces.

Junie whispered, 'I think it's the entire cheerleading team!'

Nathan said, 'Cool! They look like bandits!'

The audience gasped and then cheered wildly. The twelve girls with their faces covered, gave another rendition of 'Jai Ho!' and the whole school stood up and cheered, and sang along with them. The air was electrifying.

When the show was over at around seven in the evening, Aida stood up and said she had to return to the lab because she had forgotten something. Junie offered to accompany her, but Aida replied, 'It's okay, Junie. It's just a notebook I need to pick up. I'll meet you later at the car park.'

Junie agreed readily. She felt uncomfortable in her elaborate salwar kameez and wanted to change into her jeans and cotton blouse as soon as possible.

Aida did not go to the lab, instead she rushed to the secluded pond at the back of the science lab. She reached the bridge near the pond and paused. Suddenly three masked figures in black costumes, emerged from the shadows. Aida gasped, they were dressed like the performers at the 'Jai Ho!' encore, but these girls wore *kitsune*—fox demon—masks. The stark white masks had pointy ears with two almond shaped openings for the eyes—outlined in gold and scarlet, which swept upwards towards the ears—with a small triangular nose painted in red at the bottom. The mask left the lower part of the face exposed lower part of the face exposed. Tiny, beautifully drawn scarlet and gold spider lilies decorated the left side of the mask. Despite their beauty, the masks made the figures look even more sinister. Aida called out, 'Hello! Are you from the show?' She felt silly and apprehensive at the same time.

One of them walked towards her and slapped her hard on the face.

Aida gasped more in shock than in pain, 'Why are you hitting me?' She tried to pull off the mask of her attacker, but the second girl came and slapped her on her other cheek. This time, Aida managed to shove her away but the third one kicked her in the knee. Aida cried out in pain again. But her survival instinct kicked in—she had to defend herself. So she forced herself to ignore the pain and kicked her nearest assailant back. The girl cried out in pain and fell on the ground. The voice sounded familiar but none of them spoke. She knew this was to prevent her from identifying them, but she had a hunch about who they were. Three tall, athletic, and slender girls with incredible muscle tone . . .

Then two of them grabbed her by the arms and dragged her to the pond. Aida tried to snatch their mask and kicked out wildly. She screamed in fear, 'Let me go! Help me! Help me!'

They threw her into the pond. She fell into the muddy water with a splash. Her head sank under the water. Fortunately, the pond was shallow, and she managed push her head out of the water, coughing and spluttering. She pulled herself up by grabbing at the lotus roots and leaves. She tried to trudge out of the pond, but the ground underneath was too soft. Aida screamed again as loudly as she could, 'Help me! Please help me!' She was a singer and she screamed louder than she had ever before. The three girls stood around the pond, slightly shocked by their own actions.

Alex, who was alone in one of the science laboratories heard her and rushed out of the lab. He saw the three masked figures standing by the pond; they started running when they saw him. Alex heard the scream again and realized someone was struggling in the pond. He sprinted towards the pond and saw Aida struggling inside. He tried to pull her out of the pond by extending a stick he had found on the ground. He yelled, 'Aida! Calm down! Don't struggle and try to grab this stick.'

When he realized that it was futile, Alex took out his handphone and called Junie, she was the only one in the class who bothered to talk to him. Junie bolted out of the toilet and called Nathan on her handphone as she rushed towards the pond. When she reached the pond, she still had her costume in a plastic shopping bag. Junie yelled, 'Aida, grab this!' And she threw one end of her shawl to her. Aida managed to grab it. Then Junie and Alex slowly pulled her out of the pond. When she was near enough, they grabbed her hands and pulled her on to the bank. By then Nathan and Sachin had arrived to help them. They took the soaked and muddy girl to the school clinic.

On the way there, Alex told them, 'There were three girls in black costumes and wearing masks, standing around the pond!'

Nathan, Junie, and Sachin were stunned. Nathan said, 'You mean they were doing nothing to help her?'

Alex replied, 'They ran away when I came . . .'

The students who were still lingering in the corridors outside were stunned into shocked silence when they saw Aida being led to the Nurse's office. Then all of the students started sending out SMS to their friends. Fortunately, the nurse was still at the clinic and helped Aida to clean up thoroughly and change into her regular clothes. She also removed some of the leeches and bugs that had stuck themselves to her, cleaned the cuts and scratches she had sustained with antiseptic wash, and used antibiotic cream and band aids for the larger cuts. The nurse also called her parents, and it turned out that her driver had been waiting for her in the car park for over an hour. Once Aida spoke to her parents and they were sure that she was all right, the driver was instructed to take her to their regular hospital where her parents were going to meet her.

When she was ready to leave, Junie asked her, 'Aida, what happened?'

Aida burst into tears, she had been in survival mode until now and had been reining in her emotions. But now she could no longer hold back her tears and her body shook with the intensity of her emotions. Nathan, Junie, Sachin, and Alex watched helplessly as she wept.

When she could finally speak, she gasped out, 'They attacked me! Their faces were covered but I know it's them. They tried to kill me!'

Junie felt sick to her stomach. She knew who Aida were referring to. But weren't they supposed to be friends or at least frenemies? She couldn't believe they would go so far. She couldn't help asking, 'Are you sure, Aida? That it was the Jin Jeanies?' She didn't want to mention names in case anyone else was listening in.

Aida replied, her voice shaking, 'Yes! They wore the same costumes as the "Jai Ho!" dancers, but they had *kitsune* masks . . . and they never spoke. But I know it's them.' Then she started crying again, she was shaking in anger and shock, and she realized that she was in pain as well.

Alex suddenly asked, 'Why did you go to the pond by yourself?' They were all surprised to hear him speak. Alex spent more time with computers and in the lab than he did with other students. But by rescuing Aida, he had become one of them now.

Aida hesitated and then said, 'Someone said he had an important message for me.'

Junie asked quickly, 'Who sent you the message, Aida?'

'I'm . . . not sure now . . . he said he knew something about a cat—'

Before she could complete the sentence, her driver had shown up at the door. Aida said, 'I have to go now.'

The driver helped her up and led her to the car. Nathan, Junie, Sachin, and Alex followed her out of the building to the shaded outdoor walkway, leading to the car park. They stood in the walkway, in a tight knit group and watched as the car drove away.

Then they looked at one another. Nathan said, 'I think she's hiding something . . . she didn't want to tell us who the guy was.'

Junie replied sombrely, 'I know. And I can guess who she went out to meet . . . or thought she was going to meet.'

'Who are you talking about?' asked Nathan.

'It's Jin,' she said in a choked voice.

'Jin set her up? That swine!' burst out Sachin.

'I thought Jin had been grounded,' replied Alex. The news of one of the Popular Posse being grounded had been the hottest news and had made its way through the school.

Nathan agreed with him, 'I didn't see him in the hall. I mean, why ask someone to meet you, when you can't actually meet them?'

'So it can't be Jin?' Sachin asked.

Junie nodded, 'Besides, he likes her too much. I mean, it was kind of obvious at the *Kaidankai* gathering. My brother is a big show-off but he's not a bully . . . well not the type who sets people up to be bashed.'

'So you think it's someone pretending to be Jin,' said Nathan.

'Yes, but how did they trick Aida to go out and meet them by the pond? I mean she's quite smart and not the type to be easily fooled by a fake note,' said Junie.

'Someone could have sent her an SMS,' said Sachin.

He realized it was improbable, even before Junie said, 'How would somcone clone his number? Besides, I don't think Aida has his phone number. He never gives it out to anyone, except his swim teammates and the Jeanies.'

Sachin suddenly had a flash of insight, 'Facebook!' he said. 'They used Facebook to lead her into a trap.'

Junie and Nathan looked at him, blankly. 'How?' asked Nathan.

Sachin replied, his voice raised slightly in excitement, 'This is cool! It could be someone pretending to be Jin!'

Realizing that he was going off track, he explained, 'What I mean is you can create a false identity, and no one would guess, unless they decide to investigate that is.'

Alex objected, 'But wouldn't Jin find out if someone was pretending to be him? I mean, you have to have some friends in common.'

Sachin looked slightly disappointed when he realized that Alex was right. But he persisted, 'We don't actually know that Jin has a Facebook account. I mean, the person could just send friend requests to everyone while pretending to be him!'

Nathan turned to Junie but she guessed what he was going to say, 'Yes, I know Nathan. I have to find out if Jin has a Facebook account.'

At that moment, there was a honk from Nathan's mother. She was picking up Nathan, Sachin, and Junie. Alex's mother was also waiting for him. They waved goodbye to him and yelled, 'See you on Monday, Alex!' said Nathan.

'Yo, Alex! Don't study too hard, you hear?' Sachin yelled for good measure.

10

Cats Galore

The next morning, Junie called Aida on her handphone and found out that she was in hospital. She had not informed Jin about what had happened to Aida at the school after the Bollywood Night concert.

When she walked into the kitchen, she was surprised to find that Jin had actually prepared breakfast—mugs of warm Milo, with toast and soft-boiled eggs. She sipped the Milo and thought it was delicious—he had added more Milo than their mother would normally have. Then she cracked two eggs into a bowl and was slightly dismayed to find out that the yolks of the eggs were runny. She sighed, added salt and pepper and dipped her toast in the mixture.

Jin commented, 'I thought you like soft-boiled eggs?'

Junie replied, 'Soft-boiled eggs are supposed to have semi-solid yolks and slightly runny whites. Poached eggs a.k.a. Onsen eggs have runny yolks and solid whites.'

'Oh, says who, a.k.a. Ms Know-it-All?' Jin snapped at her.

'Says Gordon Ramsay, and that's Chef Ramsay to you!' Junie said.

'Oh, the chef with a four-letter word coming out of his mouth with every sentence! I personally think Anthony Bourdain is a better cook, I mean who actually needs to learn how to boil eggs?' Jin said with a sniff.

Junie was about to snap back but changed her mind. She was actually secretly impressed that Jin had heard of Anthony Bourdain. He was slowly turning into a nerd without even realizing it. Instead, she said, 'The Milo is great though! You added extra Milo and hot fresh milk, I can tell.'

Jin was silent so she asked him casually, 'All of us got into Facebook—it's a social media platform—last week and I've already got about two hundred friends! Erm . . . have you heard of it?'

'I know what Facebook is and I had an account a few months ago. But it's not exactly happening—Facebook is for people with no life,' Jin said, slightly dismissively.

'You mean you haven't added anyone lately?' Junie asked innocently.

'Why? You expect me to add you and all your nerdy friends?' He asked. 'I'm busy with homework and swimming practice,' he added.

'But Facebook is different now, I mean people are really into it. Even Hafiz and Minji have FB accounts!' Junie pressed on.

Junie mentioning that Hafiz and Minji being on Facebook actually made Jin sit up and look at his sister. Finally, he admitted, 'Actually, I sort of forgot my FB password for some time now. I guess I have to create a new account and add them again.'

Junie nodded. This was what she wanted to know. She knew that Jin hardly had any time to himself nowadays. Outside of school and swim practice, he spent most of his time with their mother and was only allowed to watch TV an hour per day. She even went through his homework with him almost every night and he had to accompany her on errands and help out in the house as well.

She mentioned casually, 'There is an unspoken competition among all the Form Five and From Six students, to see who can amass the most number of friends and Aida seems to be winning so far.'

Before Jin could reply, he heard his mother yell, 'Jin! Are you ready? It's time to go for your swimming practice!'

Jin got up and picked up his bag. As he walked out of the dining room, Junie called out, 'And oh, a group of girls pushed Aida into the pond last night!'

Jin spun around, 'What? Is she okay? Why would anyone do that?' He sounded genuinely shocked.

'Some girls bullied her. She's in hospital for observation. Nathan and I are going to visit her today,' Junie replied. Jin looked like he wanted to ask her more questions, but his mother had already started the car engine.

Jin got into the car and they drove off. He mentioned to his mother, 'One of the students from school is in the hospital now. Is it okay if I drop in to visit her after practice?'

His mother said reluctantly, 'Okay, I'll drop you off at the hospital after practice. You can take a taxi back home but make sure you come straight home, okay?'

Jin was surprised that his mother had actually agreed to let him be on his own on a Saturday. He found himself talking a lot more to his mother on their trips to the club as well as on grocery shopping trips, which she used to do with Junie. And he was even more surprised that he had stopped resenting her so much for grounding him.

When she was alone, Junie texted Nathan.

It's not Jin. He's clueless & he even forgot his FB password.

Nathan texted back.

That's no surprise. Someone could have taken over his FB account and sent messages to Aida.

Junie

> Looks like it. Can you pick me up, to visit
> Aida in the hospital?

Nathan

> Sure. My mother will be driving us.

Within the hour, Nathan had arrived with his mother to pick Junie up. Junie got into the car and Nathan's mother drove them to the hospital. She had bought a bouquet of flowers and, on Junie's advice, a box of salted caramel cupcakes for Aida.

When they entered the room, Aida was propped up on the pillow, reading a book. She looked much better than she did the night before. She cheered up when she saw Nathan and Junie. 'Good morning, Auntie! Hi guys! I'm so happy to see you!'

According to Aida, she was just in hospital for observation in case she accidentally swallowed some of the pond water and also because of the bruises and small cuts and scratches on her hands, arms and legs, which might get infected. She had been given an anti-tetanus shot and was being treated with anti-biotics at the moment to ward off potential infections. Once she had completed the anti-biotics, she might have to take additional medications in case of parasites.

Nathan's mother asked casually, 'Did you recognize the students who pushed you into the pond?'

'No, Auntie. They were all in costumes with their faces covered with *kitsune*, I mean fox masks,' she replied in a subdued voice, her eyes lowered. She looked crestfallen, as if she blamed herself for her misfortune.

'I see. I understand that you are still in shock. Maybe you'll be able to remember in a few days' time,' she replied.

Aida said sadly, 'Guys, I might have to leave Noble Hall. My parents think it's not safe for me to continue in the school any more.'

Nathan and Junie looked shocked. Junie said, 'Aida, you can't leave! Not after we've become such good friends!'

Nathan added, 'You shouldn't be the one to leave! It's those mean girls who bullied you who should leave the school!'

Nathan's mother said, 'Wait, you mean the ones who pushed you into the pond were girls?'

Aida nodded but remained silent. Nathan's mother continued, 'Even if you don't have proof, you should tell us what you know, Aida.'

Nathan burst out, 'We're pretty sure it's the Jeanies who did this, Mum!'

'Who are the Jeanies?' asked his mother.

Junie was about to say something but Aida stopped her, 'No! We don't know who they really are because I never saw their faces and . . . and . . . I don't want to ruin anyone's life when I'm not sure about this!' Aida insisted.

'You shouldn't try to protect them . . .' said Junie, but her voice trailed off and she looked troubled.

Nathan and Junie felt depressed in the car as Nathan's mother drove them home. They spent the rest of the day completing their homework and the project report about the mummified bird.

* * *

That same morning, Minji and Maiandra were at the school gym practising. They had special permission to use the gym for themselves that morning. They, together with Zara, usually spent their weekend's mornings at the Rhythmic Gymnastics Club at Holiday Villa, where they trained under Coach Ean. It was well known that Coach Ean also trained national rhythmic gymnasts, and it was Minji's dream to make it into that elite team. The two of them executed a series of impressive synchronized rotations on one toe while twirling their ribbon and ended with a leap and mid-air twist before landing neatly on their feet.

Perspiring and with hearts racing from the exertion, they decided to take a break.

Minji walked to her backpack, picked up her towel and wiped her face before quaffing half the content of her bottle; it was an isotonic drink. She took in a deep breath before remarking, 'That was amazing, wasn't it? Where's Zara? She was supposed to be here at 9 a.m., and it's already 10 o'clock! I thought we agreed to practice some RG before the rest of the team arrive for the cheerleading practice at eleven.'

Maiandra put her water bottle down and said, dismissively, 'I heard that she has gone into hiding! She is so unreliable! Backbone like a jellyfish! We should never have agreed to help her with her plan to get even with that girl from Kazakhstan.'

'Well, I understand Zara's motivation. Jin has been a part of our group since the beginning and is a friend to all of us. We all agreed that we wouldn't try to make any moves on him. I felt upset too. Aida is an interloper,' remarked Minji resentfully.

'I was never into Jin, well not in the way Zara and Aida seem to be. I just wanted to be . . . popular. But her being chosen to open the show, without even auditioning and only weekly practice was a bit much. We have to compete and work like mad but everything is so easy for her! It's bloody unfair!' Maiandra spoke with resentment.

'Even though she's only in Form Five, all the teachers are bending over backwards for her! I can't believe one of the annoying know-it-all kids got the better of us!' Minji added vengefully.

'I bet she was only interested in performing when she found out that K-pop talent scouts were attending,' Maiandra said bitterly. 'I've been working my whole life for this moment, and I'll really have a fit if it turns out that she got picked by the talent scouts. And there better not be any rumours about this because these people are super picky about their girl groups—'

She stopped herself from completing the sentence when Zara walked into the gym. 'I'm sorry to be so late, Minji, I wasn't feeling well this morning,' Zara said.

'Don't worry about it, Zara. Maiandra and I have finished practicing for rhythmic gymnastics. We are just going to complete the choreography for the year end sports carnival, when the rest of the cheer team arrive,' replied Minji coldly.

They were silent for a couple of minutes as Zara changed into her cheerleading outfit. Maiandra said casually, 'So, how is our dear friend from Kazakhstan faring?'

Zara said with a catch in her voice, 'I'm really worried, guys! Junie said that she is in hospital!'

'She's in the hospital just for being dunked in the lotus pond? Isn't she a total drama queen! I would have thought a good wash and shampoo and some meds would have been enough!' Minji said in a dismissive voice.

'Guys, it was really bad! She's actually traumatized! What if she had been stuck in the pond? She could have died!' Zara said, sounding genuinely worried.

Both girls walked towards Zara and stood in front of her. Minji with her hands on her hips, Maiandra with her arms crossed.

'Hello! Stop freaking out on us! We would have pulled her out, if that Alex hadn't come running there like some kind of hero! We just wanted to teach her a lesson, not kill her!' Maiandra protested.

'And don't forget this whole thing was your idea; you catfished her! You sent her the message to trick her into coming to the pond,' Minji said, sounding quietly menacing, her eyes narrowed.

'Yes, I know, I know it's my fault! But I never intended for it to go so far!' Zara said, her voice rising in anxiety.

'Well, what did you expect will happen? That we'll give her a couple of slaps then shake hands and say that we love and respect each other?' Maiandra said sarcastically.

'Well, make sure you don't tell anyone about us just because you're feeling guilty all of a sudden. We're about to graduate this year and I can't have this hanging over my head in the future. Everyone whines about Alex's Singapore tiger mother and forgets about my Malayan tiger mother,' Minji added, sounding bitter.

Zara faced them defiantly, took in a deep breath and said, 'Guys, I'm not telling anyone about the two of you, not even to my mother. You have my word.'

At that moment, someone knocked on the door. Maiandra called out, sharply, 'Who is it?'

'It's me, Hafiz. I'm coming in,' and he entered the gym. Hafiz looked worried, he was not his usual confident, laid-back self. He stared at them and noticed their tense body language, although they tried to smile and act nonchalant.

'Guys, have you heard? A group of girls beat Aida up and pushed her into the lotus pond . . . and rumour has it that they were part of the 'Jai Ho!' dancers at the Bollywood concert!'

The three girls tensed up even more. Zara cast her eyes down and Maiandra clenched her fists.

Minji said finally, 'You can't really think it was us, Hafiz!'

Hafiz said, 'I don't know what to think. But the other girls in the group said the three of you were missing for almost an hour after the concert.'

They were silent, and Minji lowered her eyes. Hafiz continued, 'How could you? It's three against one and that's not sportsmanlike!'

Minji rushed towards him, took his hand in hers and said, 'Please, Hafiz, can we talk about this later?'

Hafiz squeezed her hand but then let it go. He said, 'No! I really don't want to know, I can't know. I'm the Captain of the rugby team and I'm applying for a scholarship. I can't be involved in what looks like bullying. I'm really sorry, Minji, but it's best that we . . . we break up the Popular Posse and not see each other again!'

He left the room, leaving Minji looking devastated. Maiandra ran to her and put her arms around her to comfort her. She said, 'We can face this together, we don't need Hafiz and the rugby boys!'

They heard footsteps coming down the corridor and fell silent. The door opened and the cheerful faces of the other nine members of the team appeared. They called out, 'We're here! We cheer to chase our blues away!'

'We cheer to pledge our allegiance as one!' yelled Minji, Maiandra, and Zara. They rushed towards each other and did a group hug. And the group magic was so potent, they truly forgot their anxiety, resentment and guilt and felt only the warmth camaraderie.

That evening, Sachin decided to stop at McDonald's for his favourite snack—Spicy Chicken McDeluxe. It was uniquely spicy and uniquely Malaysian. Both Nathan and Junie had disavowed fast-food, but Sachin occasionally had a craving for it. He had to eat alone at those times, although he avoided eating beef. Anyway, he had an idea. He texted Alex before placing his order and paying for his food. Then he sat in a secluded corner, took out his laptop and surfed the Internet while munching on his food. Alex joined him after about fifteen minutes; he had a tray with a burger, fries, and large glass of coke. Sachin said, 'Glad you could make it.'

Alex said, 'My mother will kill me if she finds out that I sneaked out. Anyway, show me what you got.'

Sachin showed him the IP address he had written down, from the picture of the dead cat which had been sent to Nathan days ago. They both sat to work, trying to trace its origin, while consuming large amounts of coke and fries. It was time consuming and there were thousands of leads to track down, furthermore they weren't quite sure what they were doing. They exchanged ideas while working.

Finally, after about an hour, Alex said, 'The IP address seems to be located in Kota Kemuning. I think the computer it came from is in a shop.'

Sachin said excitedly, 'It's a pet shop! With a name like Cats Galore, it must be a pet shop!'

'Well, that makes sense, although I can't imagine why they would send a picture of a dead cat to Nathan,' Alex added.

Sachin suddenly had an idea. He took out the piece of paper he had written down the numbers Nathan's mother had given him and showed it to Alex. He said, 'I can't figure out these numbers, but do you think this is an IP address as well?'

Alex looked at the numbers closely, 'I don't think so. Where did you get this?'

Sachin said, 'It's from Nathan's dad. Apparently, it's supposed to help us locate Souchong.'

Alex sat up and said excitedly, 'You know what? I think these are actually GPS coordinates! Nathan's dad is cool! He even gave his cat a GPS tracker. Let me try to locate him . . .'

Sachin waited with bated breath while Alex did a search with his computer. After several minutes, Alex exclaimed, 'This is weird! According to the GPS, Nathan's cat is next door to the IP address of the person who sent the cat picture!'

'Are you sure?' Sachin asked again. He could hardly believe it—the fact that the GPS pointed to the same place as the IP address.

'Quite sure. Check this out,' Alex said and turned his laptop to show Sachin his discovery.

'You're right. That place must be a cat napping outfit. We'll have to let Nathan and Junie know soon, but not tonight. Knowing Nathan, he might try to go on his own,' said Sachin.

They both felt elated at having solved something difficult and which might even lead to something which might help a friend. 'Wow! I'm hungry after all that work! How about some chips and apple pie? The apple pies here are the best—crispy shell and chock full of apples,' Sachin said.

Alex hesitated, 'I'm quite late already. My mother might notice I'm not in my room, not even in the house, and throw a fit.'

'Well, if she hasn't noticed you were not in your room, earlier, she's not going to notice it now,' and he walked over to the counter to place his order and paid for them. He noticed that there were fewer people around—it was almost 10 p.m. He walked back a few minutes later, with the potato chips and two apple pies and sat down. They munched on the chips first, 'These are good, crispy on the outside and soft on the inside,' Sachin remarked.

Alex nodded in agreement, 'I've never eaten potato chips so late at night. It feels different—sort of fun.'

'How's it going with you? I mean your studies?' Sachin asked.

'Well, that's all I do—study. I'm kind of tired,' he replied, darkly.

Sachin nodded. 'It's not easy trying to please parents. My father wanted me to be a cricket player but luckily, we moved to Malaysia and I found out—much to my relief—that no one plays cricket in this country,' he said with a grin.

'Well, you're lucky. My mother's from Singapore, where people are super *kiasu*, so there's nowhere for me to run,' Alex said.

'What's *kiasu*?' asked Sachin.

'It means, "afraid to lose" but what it actually means is staying ahead at all costs. There are probably a lot of mothers out there who are like my mother,' he added sombrely.

They were silent for a while and focused on eating up all the chips. By now the apple pies had cooled down and they started eating them.

Alex said unexpectedly, 'My mother wants me to do well enough to study medicine in Oxford or Cambridge. In fact, we visit those places on school holidays every year—if I actually get accepted to either University, I'll be able to find my way around, no problem. That's all I've been preparing for since I was young.'

Sachin nodded. He had seen Alex's mother when she was angry, and it hadn't been pleasant. He said, 'It must feel like a huge weight around your neck, you know just like in that book we read, in Ms Jones' class—the man had to walk around with a giant bird around his neck.'

Alex said, 'Yeah, *The Ancient Mariner*,' and fell into a brooding silence.

'My father wants me to go to MIT. I mean, I would love to go to MIT, but I feel it's out of my league. I would be happy to go to Caltech, actually.'

Surprisingly, Alex nodded. 'I'd prefer to do something in IT too. It's a new field.' He looked at his watch and said, 'It's past 10 o'clock! I need to go home.'

'Maybe you should just take a break and just chill? I have the latest Assassin's Creed at home. Want to have a game?' Sachin asked.

Alex looked stunned. The idea of playing a game late at night, without his mother's permission seemed inconceivable to him. If she found out, she would go berserk. But at the same time, he felt tempted. Hanging out with Sachin, Junie, and Nathan was the most fun he had had in a long time. He just said, 'You actually have Assassins' Creed: Brotherhood? I didn't even know it's already available in Malaysia!'

Sachin said, 'Yup, and it's original too. It's quite late for you to cycle back and my place is just five minutes away. You can cycle back tomorrow morning. Anyway, what's the worst thing your mother could do to you? Lock you up in a dungeon?'

Alex was silent. But he came to a decision. Perhaps it was because of the chips and apple pie, but he made up his mind to have as much fun as he could. He didn't get many invitations to play PC games, in fact he didn't get any invitations at all. He needed to have friends, desperately. He didn't feel that he had a life and he wondered what it was to spend time with real people instead of a computer. They cycled to Sachin's place which was in a condominium just across the road from McDonalds. Sachin and Alex stayed up until 2 a.m. in the morning, playing Assassin's Creed: Brotherhood, before falling asleep on the sofa.

Early the next morning, which was a Sunday, Nathan was awakened by a loud ping on his phone. It was a text message from Sachin. He sat upright when he read:

I've had some news about Souchong from my network. Meet me at the 100 Yen Shop at around 10 am. If you can't make it, let me know

Nathan texted back that both he and Junie would be there.

He called Junie and showed her the text message when she arrived at his place and she perked up as well.

After breakfast, they cycled to the 100 Yen Shop. Sachin and Alex were already there, enjoying a large bowl of melon-flavoured shaved ice. Nathan and Junie were surprised to see Alex. Sachin waved at them and said, 'Here! Come and join us!'

Both Nathan and Junie ordered strawberry-flavoured shaved ice. They sat down at the same table as Sachin and Alex and looked at them expectantly. Sachin said, 'Alex figured out the numbers were GPS coordinates! I mean the numbers in your father's message. I feel like kicking myself for not figuring that out earlier!'

Junie looked stunned but Nathan looked blank. 'What's GPS?' he asked.

'Global Positioning System. Technically, you can locate any object on Earth through GPS coordinates via satellites. In this case the coordinates point to this.' Sachin had brought his laptop with him and showed them a message from one of his 'network'. It was a picture of a pet shop.

Nathan grabbed the laptop and said, 'Let me take a look at this!' Junie peered over his shoulder, with her eyes wide open. It was not just a pet shop, it was one specializing in cats— Cats Galore.

'Where was this picture taken?' asked Nathan with bated breath.

'It's supposed to be right here in Kota Kemuning, according to the coordinates,' replied Alex.

Junie said, 'Here? Are you sure? How can we be sure Souchong will be in this pet shop?'

Nathan insisted, 'I know that Souchong is here! I saw him at the window, during the *Kaidankai*. Somehow, he must have been attracted by all the candles and the cat stories. The *Kaidankai* is supposed to open a window into the spirit world and cats are supposed to be able to see spirits . . .'

Alex, who was busy eating his ice cream, looked up. 'You all had a *Kaidankai*? I've read about it, but I never thought anyone would have the guts to reenact the ritual here.'

Junie tried to explain, 'We were not intending to open a window into the spirit world, but to find closure—'

But Nathan cut her off, 'I think we should focus on finding this pet shop and rescuing Souchong, like now!'

Junie gave in, 'I guess there's no harm in checking the shop out. We might get lucky.'

'I'm looking up the address now,' Sachin added, taking the laptop from Nathan.

'There can't be that many pet shops here!' Nathan protested.

'There are four actually and this could be one of the more secretive ones,' replied Sachin.

His phone pinged and he quickly read his text. He jumped up, 'I have it!' and showed them the text. It was an address in a remote part of the huge housing estate. They dashed out of the shop and got on their bikes. All four of them pedalled furiously in the direction of the pet shop. It took them over half an hour to reach a row of shop houses, and they were drenched in sweat from the exertion. The shop house was shuttered but they had no trouble locating it from the stench of cats. They parked their bikes and Nathan, Junie, and Sachin entered the shop as calmly as they could. Alex decided to wait outside in case the owner got suspicious with so many people entering his shop. Nathan was now experiencing the beginning of an anxiety attack. He remembered what his mother had said about consciously calming down by controlling and slowing down his breathing.

They were stunned by the number of cats in the shop. There were large cages filled with the most extraordinary looking cats they had ever seen. Nathan and Junie stood and gaped, while Sachin stood by the door, pretending not to know them. Junie ran down the cages, admiring the cats, followed by Nathan a short distance away from her. They were larger than domestic cats and most of them had the strange part-leopard part-python like markings of wild cats. The owner—an affable, good-looking, and young man—came towards her, 'Are you looking for a cat? We specialize in Bengals.'

Junie said brightly, 'These cats are so exotic and gorgeous! But what are Bengals?'

The man laughed and said, 'According to one story, these cats are natives of Bengal in India. They were specially bred by royalty who loved cats and wanted to create a unique breed. We import the best Bengals from reputable breeders in India into the country. Of course, the Bengal is the favourite among cat fanciers here.'

Junie nodded and said, 'But do you have other cats, besides Bengals? I mean the more ordinary ones, like Persians or Siamese?'

The man looked bemused. Then he replied, 'We don't have any Persians, but we do have a Siamese and even a Burmese. The Siamese is the old-fashioned apple-headed variety, and quite rare now.'

Junie smiled and said sweetly, 'Can we look at this Siamese cat, please? We're really interested in old fashioned Siamese cats.'

The man took them to the back of the shop, Junie walking by his side while Nathan walked behind them, and showed them a sleeping cat in a cage. Nathan's heart gave a leap of hope, he was sure this was Souchong, even though he had grown thinner,and his collar was missing. The cat sensed their presence and lifted up his head. He rose and took a step towards them. Nathan held his breath—the crystal clear blue eyes set in the diamond shaped mask was unmistakable. Being a cat, Souchong did not show any emotions. He simply sat down and gazed at him calmly with his blue eyes. Nathan's heart was pounding, what was he going to do? Nathan clenched his fist; he felt like yelling, 'What have you done to my cat?!'

Junie grabbed Nathan's arm to calm him down and interjected brightly, 'He's just what we were looking for! How much would it cost to buy a cat like this?'

The man said, 'I'm sorry, but he's not for sale. In his own way, this cat is quite special. The man who brought him in gave instructions to look after him very carefully. We intend to breed our own line of Siamese cats.'

'Doesn't he have a collar?' asked Nathan. Junie gave him a warning look and the man looked surprised.

'Well, no. Only dogs have collars, you know,' the man replied, patronizingly.

Junie suddenly exclaimed, 'Since this cat is not for sale can you show me the Burmese cat with blue eyes, like the one over there?' and she ran towards the far corner of the shop. Nathan was about to protest when he realized that this was a ruse.

When they were out of sight, Nathan found that his hands were shaking. He forced himself to calm down and unbolted the cage stealthily with faintly trembling hands. He held his breath and gently lifted Souchong out of the cage. He covered the cat with his shirt and walked swiftly towards the door. Sachin was standing beside the door, and he pressed the pad to open it for him, after that he pretended to be part of a family who were browsing for a fancy cat. Nathan rushed out with Souchong hidden under his shirt. Alex was waiting outside. He pointed at Junie's bike because she had a small carrier in front and Nathan placed Souchong inside. Alex waved as Nathan peddled furiously away, passing rows of houses, which he hardly noticed. A small car passed him, Nathan was so nervous, he almost missed a turn but managed to find his way home.

When he reached his house, he rushed Souchong into his room, turned on the air conditioner and closed the door. He ran downstairs into the kitchen to get a can of cat food, and the cat carrier, now laying in a corner. Nathan rushed upstairs, put the carrier down, opened the can and placed it on the floor, next to the cat. He watched the cat eating his food carefully—he had always been a neat eater—while texting Junie, Sachin, and Alex to come to his place.

Sometime later, Junie came up to his room, her face shiny with perspiration. She sat on his bed and exclaimed, 'Wow, I've never cycled so hard in my life! We had to rush out before he realized that the cat was missing!' After she had calmed down a little, she inspected the cat and said, 'So, it's really Souchong!'

Sachin came into the room, five minutes after Junie. He gave both Nathan and Junie a high-five. Nathan noticed that Alex was not there. 'Gosh, I hope Alex got out of the shop in time as well. Where is he, anyway?'

'His mother called him to come home. Apparently, he has to do revisions,' said Junie.

Sachin shook his head, 'Poor Alex! He has the ultimate Tiger Mother . . .'

Junie added, 'I sometimes feel sorry for him. His mother shouted at him in front of everyone last year, on Prize Giving Day, just because he wasn't the top student that year!'

Nathan nodded, 'You were the top student last year, Junie! I guess it can make you feel guilty if your winning causes someone else's misery.' He stopped short because Junie looked upset.

'We must always do the best we can, even if someone else needs to win more than us. That is the nature of sportsmanship!' Junie asserted, even though she sounded slightly defensive.

'At least, this win shouldn't cause anyone any misery,' said Sachin.

'I wouldn't count on it. The owner of Cats Galore is going to be furious when he finds his cat missing,' she mused.

'Hello! This is my cat! I'm pretty sure this is Souchong! And you can't steal what is yours to begin with!' Nathan protested. He picked up Souchong and placed him on his lap, protectively. Souchong butted him gently and curled up on his lap to take a nap. Nathan murmured, 'I'm never going to lose you again!'

Sachin said with a sigh, 'It was incredibly lucky for us that Alex figured out what the numbers meant.'

'But why would Uncle KC leave such an obscure clue? We wouldn't have found Souchong if not for Alex!' said Junie.

Nathan said thoughtfully, 'It may not have been "obscure" for Dad. Sometimes he just assumes we know what he knows.'

Junie nodded in agreement, 'He is like that.'

Nathan sighed, 'But you know what? We've got Souchong back and I'm happy. It's okay that Dad is in Kazakhstan, as long as I know that he is happy with his job and that he is safe there.'

Sachin said, 'After what we went through, we can't afford to lose Souchong—I think I almost got a heart attack waiting for Junie and Alex to come out of the shop.'

He paused and added, 'Nathan, you need to turn him into an indoor cat and only take him out on a leash.'

Junie said, 'But cats don't have leashes . . . oh wait . . . there are dogs which are as small as cats and they have leashes for them!'

Nathan nodded, 'We need to get a leash for a small dog, as well as a collar, or maybe a body harness will be better.'

'We can go later this afternoon, but I'm famished now. Let's have some lunch first!' said Junie. Nathan carefully placed a sleeping Souchong in his carrier cage. He stroked his head and murmured, 'We'll be back soon.' When they left the room, Nathan was the last one and he was extra mindful to close the door behind him.

They dashed down the stairs and discovered that Kak Yam had made spicy sardine sandwiches for the boys and some egg sandwiches for Junie. All three were famished. They gobbled up the sandwiches and all of them had a glass of cold juice. After the meal, Nathan felt unexpectedly tired. He said, 'I'm so full, I don't think I can cycle to the pet shop right away.'

Sachin said, 'Yeah, I'm pretty exhausted from all the cycling and it looks like a late afternoon thunderstorm is approaching, from that distant rumbling noise.'

Junie had to agree, she was exhausted too. She decided to take a nap in the guestroom, and quickly fell into a deep sleep while the storm raged outside. Nathan and Sachin sat in his room, where Sachin told him about the latest game of Assassins Creed. Then they both dozed off without intending to.

Nathan dreamt that Souchong was outside the house, he was running again. He climbed over walls, through overgrown gardens, among the rows of empty houses on the outskirts of Kota Kemuning . . . it looked so familiar, where had he seen this place before? Before he could figure it out, a loud thunderclap made them all jump awake in fright. Sachin quickly looked at his phone, it was almost 5 p.m.!

Junie suddenly knocked on the door and announced, 'Guys, wake up! It's almost five! Time to go to the pet store!'

After making sure Souchong was all right, Nathan, Junie, and Sachin dashed out of the house and cycled to Nathan's regular pet shop, Patsy Pets. The owner, Patsy, recognized Nathan and Junie, and greeted them. Nathan introduced her to Sachin.

Sachin promptly asked her, 'Hi Patsy! We are looking for a body harness for a Chihuahua!'

Junie gave him an annoyed look, 'Chihuahua? Really? Those are the size of rats.'

Nathan quickly corrected him, 'Do you have a body harness for a small Shi Tzu? And those long extendable leashes?'

Patsy looked surprised, 'Oh, you have a dog now!' She added quickly, 'So sorry to hear that you lost your Siamese cat.'

Nathan looked slightly taken aback, 'How did you know?'

Patsy said, 'We all heard about it; it was in the community news.'

Nathan replied, 'Erm . . . yes, we have a Shi Tzu now.'

Patsy nodded, and while searching for a suitable body harness and leash, remarked, 'Dogs are easier to handle. They can't climb fences and trees to run away and fall sick less often, if you take care of their diet.'

'You're right about dogs being easier to control,' said Sachin.

'I've heard that there are a number of new pet shops opening up around here,' Junie butted in.

'Yeah, *lah*! They are sprouting up like mushrooms. I'm supposed to get the exclusive right to sell Science Diet but now all the other shops are also selling them!' Patsy sounded disgruntled.

'We even saw one selling fancy cats! I mean the cats were really different, their markings were almost . . . like a python's,' added Junie.

'We heard about this shop but we don't know much about them or even where it's located. Some say, maybe they are even bringing in wild cats,' replied Patsy.

Junie said, 'These are Bengals, imported from specialized breeders in India.'

Patsy gave her an appraising look, 'That's just the cover story. My vet friends say that Bengals are actually cross breeds of wild cats with certain domestic cats.'

Junie gasped, 'Wild cats are endangered and it's against the law to capture or sell these cats!' She was outraged and her hands were clenched into fists.

'I hate people!' muttered Nathan.

Patsy sighed and said, 'Some people don't really care about animals, only how much money they can make. But we all got to eat—although some people want to eat abalone and wagyu beef all the time.' She walked down the aisle and finally found a small enough body harness and took it with her to the cash register. Nathan took the body harness from her, checked it, and decided that it was small enough for Souchong and paid for it.

After leaving the pet store, Sachin decided to cycle straight home while Nathan and Junie cycled to his house again. They ran to his room to try the harness on Souchong. It fitted perfectly.

Feeling pleased with his new purchase, Nathan decided to train Souchong to walk with the harness on. The poor cat looked confused and annoyed initially but soon realized it was another game and walked around the room with him—especially when he held out small pieces of cat treats in front of him to spur him on.

Junie who had been keeping quiet all along suddenly burst out, 'We can't let them get away with it! We just can't!'

Nathan stopped what he was doing and turned around to face her. He said, 'Who? Get away with what?'

'Cat smuggling and wildlife trafficking! I'm talking about Cats Galore! We have to stop them!' she raged.

'It's true they kidnapped—er or is it catnapped?—Souchong but we kind of stole him back and we don't have proof any more,' said Nathan.

'Besides, they are mainly selling Bengals. Who knows? Maybe they did import them from India,' he added.

Junie insisted, 'We have to investigate them! We can't just pretend that nothing happened just because we got Souchong back! If you won't do it, I will! By myself!'

Nathan was alarmed. He said, 'Okay, we all agree to go back there and investigate Cats Galore, but not today or even tomorrow. I mean they might get suspicious to see us again so soon. We also have to ask Sachin first. I mean, we might need his help again.'

Junie impulsively hugged him and said, 'I know. I'm kind of tired too, so I'm going home. Can you ask Sachin about this while I do some research on the Bengal?'

Nathan nodded. He ran his fingers through his hair and said, 'Don't worry, Sachin won't let us down. I'll look up the Bengal myself as well. There's clearly some kind of wild cat in its genetic make-up, I've never ever seen domestic cats which look like that.'

He walked with his cousin downstairs and accompanied her to her house. Nathan spent some time at Junie's place before walking back home.

His mother was already home when he returned. She was seated at the dining room table which had already been laid out. She said to him, 'You might as well have your dinner now and wash up later. Kak Yam said that you've found Souchong . . . anyway, she's already fed him. Nathan, I'm really happy you got Souchong back, but how did you find him?'

Nathan decided to tell her the truth about Cats Galore. His mother sighed, 'You know you're not supposed to do something like that. Even if we can prove that it's Souchong, it's still not right to sneak him out like that. Anyway, we can't file a complaint against the shop because we've broken the law ourselves.'

'I know what I did was wrong, Mom . . . well, technically wrong. But if we had waited, they might have sold Souchong or taken him elsewhere, or worse,' he replied.

After dinner, he went up to his room and sat on his bed, holding Souchong on his lap. He didn't feel like taking a bath, in fact, he didn't feel like doing anything. He stared at the wall blankly but his mind was made up. Junie was right, they had to stop these people.

11

The Hour Between the Cat and the Tiger

The next day, Sachin's mother drove Sachin and Alex to school. Sachin met up with Nathan and Junie. They discovered that most of the students were agog with excitement as rumours of what had happened to Aida had spread throughout the school. Aida was still in hospital and during break, many of the students were openly staring at Nathan, Junie, and Sachin. Some even came up to them to ask how Aida was and if 'the authorities' had found out who the bullies were. It was a strange and uncomfortable sensation for them to be at the centre of attention.

Junie commented, 'Ever since we came to Noble Hall, I've wanted to be popular, you know, the "It" girl but now I can't imagine why anyone would ever want to be popular.'

Sachin said, 'It's not so bad when I'm with the rugby team, cause Hafiz deals with it, but this is downright uncomfortable. I kept on checking to see if there was something in my hair or my shirt was out. The last time everyone stared at me, a bird had pooped on me or maybe it was that time when I wore socks which did not match . . .'

Nathan agreed, 'It's creepy. I can hardly wait to go back to being nerdy nobodies.'

'But it's actually not us they are interested in, it's Aida,' Sachin pointed out.

'Yes, I get that, and maybe that's a good thing,' said Junie.

The three friends realized that Zara, Minji, and Maiandra were avoiding them. Zara seemed tense and preoccupied, while Minji and Maiandra were colder than their usual selves. Junie was glad because she was conflicted about how she felt about Zara now. Surprisingly, Jin joined them for lunch, although he looked more subdued than his usual self. Junie and Sachin were feeling a little glum as well. They didn't know what to talk about with Jin. Nathan on the other hand had perked up considerably after securing Souchong during the weekend. He had slept well for the first time in weeks and the dark rings around his eyes had started to disappear.

They were relieved when the bell rang and they could return to class. Sachin remarked, 'Saved by the bell!'

Nathan said, 'Thank goodness for classmates who still continue to ignore us.'

Junie remarked, 'I thought Alex was going to join us for lunch today. Since he helped us to find Souchong, he is our new best friend!'

Sachin said, 'I heard he had been summoned to the principal's office.'

'But why? He is the most lawful student we know. Alex is not a rebel or a rule breaker,' said Nathan.

Sachin had not told them that Alex had actually spent the night at his place. Alex's mother had called the school in hysterics when she discovered that he had been missing the whole of Sunday until Monday morning. She was about to make a police report when the principal told her that he was in school. She spoke to Alex briefly on the phone and had sounded as if she was crying. He was shocked, his mother had never cried or shown any weakness to him before. He didn't even think that she cared about him, only about his grades. His mother drove to school to pick him up, but they both had to see the school's student counsellor.

While walking back to their classroom, Nathan, Junie, and Sachin saw Alex walking with his mother to their car. Sachin called out, 'You okay, Alex?'

Alex nodded and waved back at him. This in itself was unusual. They were even more surprised when he replied, 'I'm fine! We're going to have lunch at a restaurant! And maybe watch a movie later!'

Sachin whistled. 'Alex's mom is actually allowing him to skip school and taking him out for lunch at a restaurant and even perhaps catching a movie later.'

'I wonder what happened to him?' Nathan wondered out loud.

He said, 'Well, I'm going to let the cat out of the bag now.'

'What do you mean?' said Junie suspiciously.

'Alex and I spent the entire weekend playing video games, that is apart from trawling the world wide web looking for Souchong and helping you guys rescue him from Cats Galore.'

'What! Why didn't you tell us earlier?' Nathan said.

'You mean, he never went home?' asked Junie, who was quite shocked.

'I didn't want to implicate you two, in case his mother actually called the police. She thought he could have met with an accident or even been kidnapped,' Sachin replied.

'That was kind of cruel, I mean to his mother. But I'm glad that it worked out in the end. I'm not sure you should have done that,' Junie said, sounding conflicted.

'I was worried he was going to have a breakdown . . . I mean it's not normal to cry just because your classmate scored three points more than you. Besides, he kind of reminded me of myself before I made friends with you two!' Sachin said.

'Are you kidding me? You're the most confident person in our group!' said Junie.

'That's because you two are way bigger nerds than I am,' said Sachin in a deadpan voice.

'What!!!' Both Nathan and Junie gave him a friendly punch, bursting into laughter after that.

'By the way, don't forget you promised to help me investigate Cats Galore this week. Remember, you promised!' Junie reminded them.

'Umm . . . I can only do that this coming Saturday. I have to do my homework and a ton of assignments to complete, not to mention rugby practice. You can't spend an entire weekend chasing cats and playing video games without paying a price for it. Besides, Mom said I have to do better this term. Remember, I have a mother too,' replied Sachin.

Junie was forced to concede, 'That's a good idea. That will give us time to complete our homework and assignments as well.' She paused and added, 'We have to be careful because the owner of the shop has seen us . . . well, he has seen Nathan and me.'

Nathan said, 'I think we could disguise ourselves, dress differently and change our hairstyles. I mean, try to look older maybe.'

'Considering, we were only there yesterday, that's not going to be easy,' said Sachin.

Nathan waited impatiently for the weekend to arrive. On Friday evening, he looked himself in the mirror after dinner. He took out a box of hair dye he had asked Junie to buy during the week. It was meant to turn even the darkest hair to platinum blonde. He was fed up with being overlooked and inconspicuous. Despite the uncomfortable feeling of being at the centre of attention recently, it was a refreshing change to be less ordinary. He debated on whether to create a blonde streak in the centre parting of his hair or to turn the two sides, blonde. He decided on the later, the blonde streak at the centre reminded him of a skunk, which he didn't mind, but he didn't want to hear skunk jokes for the last few weeks of school.

He read the instruction on the label and carried it out carefully. It took him almost an hour, but he was satisfied with the result—the lower half of his hair was pale platinum blonde on both sides and the blonde band extended to the back of his head. However, his bathroom was a mess, and he had to spend another half an hour cleaning this up and rinsing the towel out.

On Saturday afternoon, Junie walked to Nathan's house after completing the last of her homework. She gasped, 'Your hair! You've dyed it! You look so different!'

'That was the intention and also because I was fed up with being ordinary!' Nathan replied with a grin. He also wore a fitted black long sleeved T-shirt with white lightning bolts and daggers circling the round neck, and a pair of khaki pants. The effect was to make him look surprisingly edgy.

After a quick lunch, they put on their dark glasses and cycled to the 100 Yen shop, where Sachin was waiting for them. He was wearing dark glasses as well. Nathan was even more pleased with his hair when Sachin couldn't recognize him, that is not until he saw Junie. He punched Nathan on the shoulder and said, 'This is rad, Nate! When you mentioned disguise, I didn't think you would go so far!'

'I dyed my hair to evade recognition,' Nathan replied.

'Well, if your aim is to look inconspicuous, you failed miserably cause half the room is looking at you!' Junie pointed out with a suppressed smile. Nathan realized she was right; all the girls in the room were staring at him. He quickly turned towards the counter and ordered shaved ice for the three of them.

The first fifteen minutes were devoted to eating their favourite shaved ice cream. Junie carefully scooped up a spoon of red shaved ice smothered in luscious strawberry sauce and remarked, 'I don't know how they do this. The shaved ice is so smooth and soft, it's like snow and the flavour of the sauce is like distilled strawberry. Yum!'

Nathan nodded. 'It's not as creamy as ice cream but the intense flavour makes up for it.'

Sachin nodded. 'So, what's the plan? We hide our bikes and spy on them from behind some bushes?'

Nathan said, 'The problem is the area is quite open, you know they cut down all the trees when building houses.'

'We just need to find a place where we can spy on the shop, without being seen,' said Sachin.

When they had finished their shaved ice, they cycled to the street near the pet shop and hid their bicycle behind the few trees left standing. They scanned the shop nervously, expecting a bunch of hoodlums or shifty mad scientists to emerge from within, but nothing unusual happened. There were a few cars parked outside the shop. Occasionally, a car drove up, but the people looked perfectly mundane. They walked into the shop, then walked out after about half an hour, carrying bags of cat food, got into their car and drove off. After more than thirty minutes of waiting and watching, they wondered if they were wasting their time. It was getting uncomfortably warm too.

Nathan was so bored he decided to pay more attention to the surrounding houses—neat, identical double-storey terrace houses. He realized that a few were occupied from the curtains at the windows and the neater yards. The majority were probably empty though. However, in the late afternoon, cars started to enter the yard of the occupied houses and parked inside. They had returned home from lunch.

Finally, Junie said, 'I'm sorry but I think this is a waste of time. We need to go nearer and take a look, maybe even from the inside.'

Nathan objected, 'But the owner has seen us and probably realized that one of us abducted the cat!'

Sachin volunteered, 'Well, I don't think they will remember me since I pretended not to know you guys, so I could walk inside and take a look, and maybe distract them.'

Junie said, 'Notice that Cats Galore is the only shop which is open. But I think all the shop lots in this row belong to them. There might be something going on there.'

After a brief discussion, it was agreed that Sachin would have to enter the shop to look around. Nathan and Junie would scout around, outside. They put on their dark glasses and cycled to the shop. Sachin parked his bike outside the front door and went inside to 'browse some cats', while Nathan and Junie cycled to the back of the shophouse. They parked their bikes and peered through the louvered windows.

One room was an office, with a desk and two chairs. There was a man in the office, occupied with a computer on the desk. There were also files of paper stacked on the desk. The second room looked like a pet clinic of some sort, with a few cages with large cats, who were even more exotic and fabulous than the exotic cats in the store. Junie held her breath and clenched her teeth, she recognized the strange markings on the coats of these cats. A woman dressed in a lab coat and overalls, obviously a vet, was tending to them. Another man, who seemed to be a worker, was cleaning the cages.

Junie took out her camera and started taking some photographs. Somehow, even the almost imperceptible noise made by the camera caught the attention of the cats. They looked at Junie and the worker noticed their reaction and turned around as well. Nathan and Junie ducked to avoid being seen. They bent down, and stood absolutely still for about a minute, which seemed to stretch on forever. Then they looked at each other and quietly walked back to their bikes, still bent down. They grabbed their bikes and cycled to the front of the shop.

They only waited a about a minute when Sachin dashed out. He said, 'Let's get out of here! I don't want to attract more attention. The guy isn't too friendly.'

The three of them cycled away from the shop, as quietly and quickly as possible. When they were at a safe distance, they stopped to rest at a coffee shop and ordered iced lemon tea.

Sachin picked up his story from where he left off, 'Like I said, the dude in charge clearly suspects something, and kept following me all over the place. I guess after the "Souchong snatch" they are not going to trust any young people in the shop, but I did get about ten minutes to myself. There were dozens of Bengals but I honestly didn't see any actual wild cats, and oh—'

Nathan cut in, 'We found the wild cats. They were in cages in the rooms at the back!'

Junie who had been keeping quiet all this while and looked preoccupied, burst out furiously, 'Guys! Those cats are not just wild cats; those people are keeping Asian leopard cats! These cats are critically endangered, and a protected species under not just Malaysian but also under international law!'

Sachin said, 'What? Leopard cats! Those scumbags!'

Junie said, 'They could be F1 Hybrid Bengals or first generation Bengals.'

Nathan replied, 'You need a wild Asian leopard cat to get a F1 Hybrid. And F1 Hybrid Bengals are worth over $10,000 in the wildlife trafficking black market.'

Sachin whistled. He said out loud, 'Wow! 10K for a cat! Who knew you can make big money from breeding cats! Anyway, what is an F1 Hybrid?'

'I see you haven't been paying attention in Bio class. Filial 1 Hybrid, it means the cat is 50 per cent Asian leopard cat and 50 per cent domestic cat. But only the females are that valuable, because the males tend to be sterile. But many don't know that and end up being cheated. It takes four generations of breeding Bengals with domestic cats to produce a true Bengal cat,' Junie explained, sounding irate.

Sachin whistled. 'That's a ton of money sitting around in that shop! There are around thirty Bengals there—guys they are worth 300K!'

She glared at Sachin, 'You shouldn't think about animals in terms of money! One should always put the welfare of the animal first!'

It was Sachin's turn to be annoyed. 'Excuse me, I never said I was about to embark on a mass cat breeding project! Anyway, who helped you locate Souchong? And would you even have located this place without my help? Not to mention helping both of you, with your IT assignments for the entire term?'

Junie snapped, 'You forgot to mention, Alex! He figured out the GPS!'

Sachin scowled. Nathan decided he had to diffuse the tension, 'Hey, chill you guys! You're attracting too much attention!'

When they were both silent, Nathan added, 'You know it's true, Junie! Sachin did give help us to find Souchong and locate Cats Galore. Alex wouldn't have done it without him. And he did give us a helping hand to catch up with their IT class assignments, which let us do other stuff.'

Noticing that she was looking annoyed, Nathan said, 'And it's great that you did all that research on Bengals, Junie! And figuring out that the cats were F1 Hybrids. But there's nothing we can do about this, ourselves. If the cats are really worth that much, these guys might be dangerous—they are not going to give up those cats without a fight! It's better to alert the Wildlife Protection Department. Let's go home.'

Junie calmed down a bit. She realized that she was actually angry with the people at Cats Galore who were willing to cage those wonderful animals for profit. She said, 'You're right, Nathan. And I'm sorry for losing my cool, Sachin. But I feel we need to do something for the poor cats ourselves!'

Sachin who was relieved that Junie had actually apologized to him, said, 'You were triggered by the amazing cats, Junie. I sort of expected it to be Nathan . . . but yeah, it's not just Cats Galore, the people who are willing to pay exorbitant sums for these exotic cats are also to blame. They created the demand for the cats.'

Nathan replied, 'But will the Wildlife Protection Department do something for the cats? I mean, they might not take us seriously. Do we have any proof?'

Junie said, 'You mean PERHILITIN? They sometimes take forever to take any action. I took some photos but I need to download them into my computer to check.'

Sachin said, 'You have photos? That's fantastic! All we have to do is to send it to them, with the address of Cats Galore attached!'

Junie cheered up when both Nathan and Sachin seemed onboard about the need for them to do something to save the cats. Junie said, 'Maybe I'll send the photos to Mr Yeoh and see what he says first. He did mention that he sometimes follows the PERHILITIN people on raids.'

Nathan nodded, 'That's a good plan. Mr Yeoh will know what to do. Um . . . I think we should go home now. I need to take Souchong out for his walk soon.'

When they were about to leave, Sachin suddenly said, 'By the way, how exactly do we get a Bengal? I know they are leopard cats crossed with normal cats, but what type of cats? Tabby cats?'

'No, not Tabby cats! From what I read Bengals have Egyptian Mau or Abyssinian parents,' Nathan said.

'And where exactly are these people going to get Egyptian Mau or Abyssinian cats in this country? I kind of forgot to mention this, but there was another non-Bengal cat inside the shop and I'm sure it's a Siamese!'

Junie said, 'You mean the Burmese? I saw that cat before.'

'There was one which had blue eyes like Souchong, but with white socks, I guess that's the Burmese. But this other one looks exactly like Souchong, right down to the dark socks and mask!' Sachin insisted.

Nathan was stunned. 'Why didn't you mention this before?'

Sachin looked sheepish, 'Um, because we were obsessing over the F1 Bengals? Sorry, everything else flew out of my mind. Besides you've already rescued Souchong!'

Nathan sighed but the dream he had about Souchong came back to his mind. The three of them cycled to their respective homes in silence; it was late afternoon. Nathan took a quick bath and helped himself to food; he wasn't going to wait for his mother. He waited for Junie to send him a message.

As he waited, something his father had said suddenly sprang to his mind, 'The old saying that, "It never rains, but it pours" is completely unscientific but perfectly true. For example, no matter how well I try to plan and schedule everything, I will end up with all my customers and suppliers wanting to meet me on the same day at the same time. At other times, there will be nothing going on for days.'

Nathan thought about what his father had said and replied, 'Mum said something similar, that things always come in threes, but people always say that when something disastrous happens, like a car crash or a plane crash.'

His father had replied, 'Actually that's not true. It isn't always about bad things; good things can come in threes too.'

* * *

When Junie reached her home, she raced into her room and locked the door. She took out her handphone and camera. She uploaded the pictures she had taken with her camera onto her laptop as quickly as she could. Then she examined the pictures carefully. She had managed to capture seven images; three were good and showed the cats in detail. Her heart pounding, she dialled a number on her handphone.

A voice answered at the end of the line. 'Hello! Yeoh here.'

'Mr Yeoh! It's Junie! There is something I have to tell you. A group of people are rearing Bengals in the neighbourhood, F1 Bengals! I'm sure these are critically endangered species!'

'Calm down, Junie. How sure are you that these cats are F1 Bengals? Did you actually manage to identify them? People are allowed to rear F4 Bengals, it's legal.' Mr Yeoh replied in a measured voice.

'Mr Yeoh, these cats are much bigger than domestic cats, and have markings like leopards and some even like err . . . pythons. I'm sure a few are leopard cats and the rest are F1 Bengals. I've already emailed you a few pictures I took.'

'Okay, hold on. I'll check my computer now,' Mr Yeoh replied.

Junie waited impatiently for him to resume the conversation. She heard her mother calling her to come down for dinner and replied, 'I'll come down for dinner a bit later, Ma! I'm not feeling so well now and need to take a rest.'

Her mother replied, 'Okay, we will set aside some food for you, but don't take too long, and remember to clear up after you finish eating!'

It was five minutes before she heard Mr Yeoh's voice on the phone, 'You could be right, these could be F1 hybrid Bengals; first generation designer cats with wild blood.'

Junie suppressed her feelings of excitement. She tried to speak calmly. 'Mr Yeoh, the kittens could be hybrids but I'm sure at least two of the grown cats are leopard cats, *Prionailurus bengalensis*. I've seen pictures in magazines and wildlife documentaries.'

'Hmm . . . all right. From your description, they could be leopard cats. It's actually listed in IUCN's red list as of least concern but it is still endangered and worth investigating. There is a lot of trafficking in rare and endangered wildlife species these days. Junie, where is this pet shop located?' Mr Yeoh asked.

'It's called Cats Galore. They specialize in fancy cats. It's located in Jalan Mokara in Kota Kemuning. I'll send you the address now,' Junie replied.

'The name sounds familiar. Okay, I'll go and check it out. I'm calling Karen and a few friends at the Wildlife Protection Department, as well,' Mr Yeoh replied. 'Thanks for the tip, Junie!'

Junie was puzzled about who Karen was until she realized that he was referring to Miss Jones. 'Mr Yeoh, I want to be there as well! I know where the shop is!' Junie pleaded, disappointed that he did not want to take her along.

'It's too risky, Junie. If they really are trafficking in leopard cats, it's a criminal offence and they might get violent,' Mr Yeoh replied. 'I can't take a student with me on such a risky venture. But, don't worry. We'll make sure the cats are rescued and released into the wild.'

'Mr Yeoh, are you actually going there tonight?' Junie asked.

He added, 'Yes, we need to check this as soon as possible. I'll call you later to let you know if we manage to rescue the cats.'

'Thanks, Mr Yeoh. Can you also let me know if they agree to do the raid?' Junie asked. Mr Yeoh did not reply. Junie sighed and switched off her phone, feeling slightly crestfallen but relieved that she had done something about the cats. Junie decided to spend several more minutes researching Bengal cats now that she was sure that Cats Galore was actually breeding them.

Junie was stunned by what she found and sent a series of texts to Nathan.

Junie

Found out more about the Bengals; hidden info. A rare type - Bengal Snow/Bengal Silver—Bengal Snow/Bengal Silver from F2 female Bengal crossed with male Siamese

Nathan

What? Those scumbags! They wanted Souchong for breeding!!!

Junie

leopard cats are classified in the IUCN Red List as Least Concern

Nathan

What is IUCN? What is Least Concern?

Junie

International Union for the Conservation of
Nature. Least Concern means not critically
endangered i.e. found everywhere in
the region

Nathan

Never seen one in the wild before

Junie

Me neither. Maybe they are not as
common as IUCN thinks . . .

Nathan

We have to rescue those cats!

She walked out of her room, down the stairs and into the
kitchen to have her dinner. Her mother had placed a large plate
of pasta, with a side dish of roasted peppers and mushrooms on
the side. She sighed placed her phone on the table and sat down
to eat her dinner.

When she had finished her meal, she picked up her phone and
checked impatiently to see if Mr Yeoh had sent her a message.
He hadn't. But she realized that hardly half an hour had passed
and he was probably on his way there. Just as she was putting her
phone down, it pinged. It was Mr Yeoh.

Mr Yeoh

> We are rescuing the cats today.

Junie's heart soared. She thanked him via an SMS and sent another SMS to Nathan.

In his room, Nathan heard his phone ping. He picked it up and read the message from Junie.

Junie

> Called Mr Yeoh about the pet shop. They are raiding the place, tonight. Do you want to go?

Nathan replied.

Nathan

> Yes! See you in 15 mins

Junie's message was the impetus for Nathan to act. He thought, *Things happen in threes.*

Nathan sneaked out of the house quietly, making sure no one heard him. He had brought Souchong with him in his backpack, with his harness and leash on for added security. He cycled along the deserted street and stopped in front of Junie's place. She was already waiting for him. They cycled away silently, along the familiar streets of his neighbourhood. As they approached the park, Souchong lifted his head and gave a low meow. Nathan and Junie were surprised to see a group of cats, seated in a row on the low steps leading up to the park. The five jet black cats looked like they were related; the largest appeared to be the mother with four of her off-springs—kittens of varying ages and sizes. Nathan worried that they might make a dash across the road, which would force him to turn back. He wished he wasn't so superstitious. But they looked calm and composed, even when the headlight from their cycles caught their eyes, which glowed eerily in the dark. He breathed a sigh of relief as they passed them.

But the minute they passed the cats, Nathan and Junie saw a lane ahead of them . . . it was Chempaka Lane! They couldn't find it during the day, but they could see the tree lined lane quite clearly now. Both of them stopped and looked at each other hesitantly. The black cats they had passed earlier followed from behind towards the lane and stood in a row along its side, almost as if asking them to follow that path. They suddenly yowled in unison and Souchong followed suit. On an impulse, Junie nodded to Nathan and said aloud, 'Nothing ventured, nothing gained!'

Nathan said, 'Chempaka Lane, here we come!'

And they turned into the lane, their headlights lighting up the path ahead.

The neighbourhood they thought they knew so well looked completely unfamiliar in the dark. They cycled stoically, the long row of trees looked menacing, the night was dark, and they were grateful for the full moon which shone through the gaps in the canopy and lighted the narrow lane for them. Even then the long shadows were unnerving. A mysterious wisp of mist suddenly emerged from among the distant trees, spread throughout the grove, slowly encroached into the lane. Nathan wondered if they had made a mistake and said out loud, 'Maybe we should turn back . . .'

Junie was about to answer when she suddenly froze and gasped. She had come to a standstill. Nathan stopped, looked in the direction she was staring at and froze in fear as well. His heart was in his throat, and he could barely breathe. A dark shadow was emerging from the mists, slowly materializing. It seemed to be a tall female figure, dressed in what looked like ancient hunting garb. What was even more terrifying was that she seemed to have a cat's head with pointed ears. An animal, walking beside her, emerged from the mist as well. It looked like an enormous cat.

Nathan thought, *Bastet*, and he went cold with fear. Even though he found the ancient Egyptian goddess fascinating, he really did not want to meet her in real life. But Junie whispered in a hushed voice, 'Cat Sith!'

Nathan calmed down slightly. She was only a witch, not a real-life goddess. He could deal with a witch.

The figure in the mist seemed to gesture to them, pointing at the path ahead. They suddenly unfroze and were about to turn around and peddle away when they heard a loud humming sound. Both Nathan and Junie jumped with fright, and Nathan suddenly realized that it was coming from his backpack! It was Souchong! He was purring like a little engine. Junie burst out laughing, but quickly stopped herself—it was taboo to laugh in the wild. Nathan felt his anxiety lift when he realized that Souchong must feel secure to purr so loudly!

The mysterious figure touched the side of her head with two fingers of her right hand and then stretched out her arm in the air, it was a salute. Then she slowly vanished into the mist, accompanied by her giant cat. Soon the mist dissipated, and the clear light of the moon shone through the trees again.

Nathan and Junie gave a sigh of relief and decided to continue with the journey. Nathan finally found his voice and whispered, 'Do you think it was really Cat Sith?'

'I thought it was her at first, but maybe she's human? I think she was wearing a mask,' she whispered.

'But no one we know has a cat that size, and what about the weird mist?' he whispered. He didn't want to mention that he had thought of Bastet.

They came to the end of Chempaka Lane quite unexpectedly and were surprised to find themselves in a familiar part of the neighbourhood. The road in between the rows of terrace houses was well lighted and they could see the main road a short distance ahead. They cycled out of the neighbourhood and into the main road which led them directly to Cats Galore. Nathan and Junie realized that Chempaka Lane seemed to be a short cut to Cats Galore.

Out of breath, they paused to stare at the shop. They saw a familiar car and a large van with the Wildlife Department crest on it, draw up outside the shop and realized that the place was being raided. A man and a woman got out of the car, while five men got out of the van and headed towards the back of the building. They were carrying torches.

Nathan and Junie got off their bikes and hid them behind a tree. Then Nathan took Souchong out of the backpack and gently put him on the ground. He placed the harness on the cat to make sure that Souchong did not run away again. At the same time, the harness had an extendable leash, so the cat could move freely. The cat paused for a few seconds as if trying to regain its bearing. A gust of wind blew, and the cat raised its head and sniffed the air. Nathan was reminded of the time when Souchong was still a kitten and he had taken him out for the first time. The cat had been startled when a gust of wind had ruffled its fur, looking around for whatever could have touched him without being seen. But now he seemed to be enjoying the breeze.

Junie said, 'We can't go near the shop now, we don't want to be seen by them.'

'They are going to the shop lots at the back; that's where all leopard cats and F1 are. They won't see us if we enter through the front door,' Nathan replied.

Junie nodded, 'Let's go! Souchong, lead the way!'

A few moments later Souchong ran down the street and headed unerringly towards Cats Galore, followed closely by Nathan and Junie.

At the same time, a massive SUV, a Toyota Alphard, suddenly appeared out of nowhere and drove away from the parking lot of the shop. The SUV raced away at breakneck speed and came whizzing past them, almost brushing against them. The SUV stopped briefly, the front window wound down, and a man shouted, 'Damn you, kids! Trouble makers! I'll get you one of these days!' and sped off before they could say anything.

Junie said, 'I recognize the shop owner, and there was a woman sitting beside him.'

Nathan said, 'It was the vet.'

Souchong was startled and bolted towards the shop, straining on his leash. Nathan and Junie ran after him. He dared not call out to the cat and his heart pounded from fear and exertion. The cat reached the front door and Nathan wondered what to do next. Junie pushed it and was surprised when it opened. The owner had forgotten to lock it in the mad rush to leave the place before they were caught. Souchong dashed inside, but Nathan managed to grab him on time.

They passed rows of cages, almost all of them were empty. Clearly, the owners had managed to take the valuable Bengals with them in carriers—probably at the back of the Alphard. Souchong seemed to know exactly where he was going and led straight to the last cage in the row.

'Look, there's a cat in that cage! And it's not a Bengal!' Junie called out.

Nathan felt a huge sense of relief when he saw the cream-coloured Siamese in the cage. He had been afraid they might have taken it away as well. When Nathan drew closer, he realized that Sachin was right, this cat had an uncanny resemblance to Souchong. By now, Junie had already opened the cage and was carefully taking the cat out in her hands. He was surprised to see that her hands were shaking. Junie had trained herself to be calm, she said a scientist who had no control over their emotions and their hands, was pointless. Junie must be really nervous, he thought. Souchong stood up on his hind leg and was leaning against Junie, he looked up at the cat, meowing softly. Nathan took down his backpack and opened it. Junie placed the cat inside carefully and Nathan secured the backpack. He lifted the backpack onto his back, while Junie took Souchong's leash from him. Then Junie picked Souchong up and they ran towards the door as quickly as they could. Junie looked out to make sure the coast was clear before opening the door and dashing out, followed by Nathan.

They raced all the way to their bikes. A man came out from the door of the shop lot further down and saw the two of them dashing away. He flashed his torch light at them and called out to them to stop, '*Berhenti dulu! Apa awak dua buat di sini?*'

Nathan and Junie were horrified, what if they got arrested? What if they took Souchong away?

The guy asked, 'Where do you think you're taking the cat? All the cats in this place must be surrendered to PERHILITAN.'

Nathan replied defiantly, 'This is my cat! They stole the cat from me!'

At that moment, they heard a familiar voice, 'Nathan and Junie are my students. Their cat got kidnapped and they came to rescue them, in fact, they were the ones who told me about this place.'

Nathan and Junie felt a huge sense of relief when they realized that it was Mr Yeoh.

The man appeared hesitant, then he shone the torch at Souchong and realized that he was not a Bengal. He said, 'Oh, *kuching biasa saja! Tak apalah, Encik* Yeoh, normal cat only,' and he gestured to them to leave.

Mr Yeoh told them, 'Please return home as quickly as possible and do not come back to this shop again!'

Junie replied, 'Yes, Mr Yeoh . . . and we're sorry for not listening to you.'

The two of them left the scene as quickly as they could. When they reached their bikes, Junie placed Souchong in the carrier in front, secured the leash to the handle before cycling away. Nathan had no trouble getting on his bike with the cat in the backpack, but he waited for Junie to leave before cycling away behind her. He felt his spirit soar as they raced towards home.

He said, 'That was a close call! We could have been detained!'

'I know! Thank goodness for Mr Yeoh! Luckily he recognized us and came to our rescue!' she replied.

'I wouldn't have given the cats away, even if we were caught. After all, they have no jurisdiction over Siamese cats!' Nathan said with a laugh.

'Yeah, a Siamese is not going to be able to survive in the same space with Bengals,' Junie said.

The ride home was relaxing and oddly exhilarating, with a cool wind blowing into their faces. They had the road to themselves, and Nathan felt surprised that the same road which had looked so sinister before, on their way to Cats Galore, now looked quite calm and peaceful. In fact, under the moonlight and the bright streetlights, he thought everything looked so beautiful.

When they reached Junie's home, she handed Souchong to Nathan, and quietly walked inside with her bike and parked it beside the front door. She entered through the front door using a spare key. Nathan got off his bike and walked all the way home, holding on to Souchong and the bike, while carrying the rescue cat in his backpack.

When he reached home, the porchlight was on and he was shocked to see his father waiting for him, just outside the front door. Nathan unlatched the gate and entered the compound. His father was home; it was almost too good to be true. 'Dad, you're back!'

His father walked towards him and hugged him, before latching the gate behind him.

'Nathan, what are you doing wandering around alone in the middle of the night? It's almost midnight!' Souchong ran to him, rubbing himself against his legs. If Nathan had any doubts about the identity of his cat, this proved to him beyond a doubt that this was Souchong. His father picked the cat up and added, 'Let's go inside and we can both have a hot drink.'

Nathan left his bike under the porch, and they went into the dimly lit house. The two of them walked straight to the kitchen. His father turned on the lights while Nathan put his backpack with the sleeping cat in it on the floor and sat on one of the four stools arranged around the island. His father noticed his hair for the first time and remarked, 'Wait, what happened to your hair? Never mind, there are worse things . . .'

'I dyed it myself,' Nathan said, feeling a little self-conscious.

'Oh, actually it looks quite erm . . . edgy! Let me boil the water to make some coffee.'

'Dad, I don't drink coffee!' Nathan said.

'Oh, sorry, I forgot. But you seem more grown up now, even though I've only been gone a few erm . . . months.' He got up and started opening and closing the doors of the overhead cabinets where Kak Yam stored the jars of coffee and Milo. 'Ah yes, found the coffee and the Milo.'

Nathan was so pleased about seeing his father that he had forgotten about the cat in his backpack. Souchong sniffed and pawed at it until the backpack overturned, when the cat tried to get out. Nathan bent down to unbuckl the strap, letting the cat out. The two cats pawed and sniffed each other curiously. Nathan stroked the new cat before taking his seat again; his father had already made him a large mug of Milo and a smaller mug of instant coffee for himself. He was slightly stunned to see two cats in the kitchen, but he calmly placed the drinks on the island.

'Where did the second cat come from? He looks like Souchong's doppelganger!' he remarked as he took a seat opposite Nathan.

'Dad! It's really bad luck to meet your doppelganger! Besides, they are not identical! Souchong's mask is diamond shape, while the new cat has a clover-leaf shaped mask—actually a four-leaf clover which brings good luck!' Nathan pointed.

'Okay, it's a handsome cat and I'm not going to even ask if you grabbed it from somewhere! But what were you doing out so late?' his father asked him again.

'We went to a place called Cats Galore, where they were breeding Bengals—these are domestic cats crossed with Asian leopard cats! These people are wildlife traffickers! Anyway, we found out people from PERHILITIN were there to raid the place tonight to rescue the wild cats and we decided to rescue this cat, in case it gets abandoned and starves in the cage,' Nathan explained.

'Oh, okay. As long as it is a rescue and not, ahem, a theft! But you need to find if the cat has an owner first. And your mother may not agree to having two cats in the house, anyway, don't ever do this again!' his father said firmly.

'Dad these people are ruthless! When Souchong went missing, they sent me a picture of a dead Siamese cat to tell me not to look for Souchong any more! In fact, they were the ones keeping him in a cage!' Nathan protested.

His father seemed genuinely shocked by this piece of information. He said, 'What? That's terrible. I wonder why anyone would do something like that? I guess it's possible that they wanted to keep Souchong for themselves. He has a fantastic pedigree of the old type Siamese.'

His father fell silent for a while to mull over what Nathan had just told him. He sipped his coffee slowly—without sugar but with a bit of fresh milk. Nathan drank his Milo; he was surprised to find that he was quite hungry and actually needed the beverage, he also felt like eating some food. He went to the fridge and took out two potato buns and brought it to the island. His father took one while Nathan ate the other—he dipped the bun into the Milo before eating the Milo infused bun. He thought that was the best bun he had ever tasted.

His father remarked, 'Quite a delicious bun, must ask your mother to buy more tomorrow.'

His father continued, 'I came back from Astana because your mother said you were really stressed out about losing Souchong. Anyway, I'm glad you found him. By the way, who located him via the GPS? Your mother said that no one could figure it out. I was out in the field for a while and I didn't check my emails.'

'Oh, it was Sachin and Alex. You've never met Alex before but he's another student from my class,' Nathan replied.

His father nodded, 'Smart boys, it's good that you're making more friends.'

Nathan suddenly asked him, 'Dad, did you complete your job there? Was it a big project?'

His father perked up when Nathan asked these questions, 'No, and yes. My work has just started, in fact we are going to build a factory in Astana—a high tech microchip making facility. It's going to be big! I came back home to see how you and your mother were, and to sort out my business over here. I will be spending most of my time over there now.'

'I guess this is what you always wanted, Dad. But why can't you continue working here? I want us to be together,' Nathan said. He felt conflicted; he was proud and happy his father was involved in a big project, but felt sad that he would not be seeing him so often.

His father looked down at his feet. He cleared his throat and said, 'I wish I didn't have to spend so much time away, but I guess you never get to have everything you want in life—those who do, usually cheat! But the truth is, I haven't been doing well in Malaysia . . . in fact I owe people money . . . a lot of money.' He paused and sighed. 'The reason I didn't want to contact you and your mother was because I didn't want my calls to be traced.'

Nathan turned pale. 'Dad, are you in danger?'

'I'm okay now. I hate not being here for you but you seem more than capable of taking care of yourself now. But please don't ever go out by yourself at night again. Even though this is a quiet place, we don't know what is out there.'

Nathan nodded his head. They finished their drinks, washed up and went to bed. Nathan carried the cats with him to his room. He put the new cat in Souchong's carrier and allowed Souchong to sleep at the foot of his bed, as he usually did.

12

Confessions of a Popular Girl

On Sunday, Junie decided to visit Aida in the hospital again. Aida was supposed to be discharged that evening, but she had told Junie that she would not be going to school for the rest of the week because she still could not face school after what had happened. Junie decided to have a chat with Aida before she returned home. Mrs Kwan dropped her off at the hospital entrance, after dropping Jin off at a café to 'bond' with his friends. Their mother had decided not to ground him any more. Junie walked in and got on the lift to Aida's ward. When she stepped out of the lift, Zara was walking down the corridor towards the lift. Junie felt the now familiar awkwardness and conflicted emotions whenever she came across Zara. But Zara looked like she had been crying and Junie remembered that they used to be friends. Junie took a deep breath and said as cheerfully as she could, 'Hi, Zara!'

Zara gave her a wan smile, 'Hi, Junie, take care!' and entered the lift. The lift door closed behind Junie, but she was relieved that Zara was all right, in spite of everything that happened.

Aida looked up and smiled when Junie walked in, 'Junie! I'm so happy to see you!'

Junie pulled up a chair and sat down by the bed, 'You look so much better since last week! And I brought you a book to read too. It's actually by a Malaysian writer called Tash Aw. The title is pretty cool too—*The Harmony Silk Factory*!'

'Wow, thanks! I haven't read this book before, but I love the cover,' replied Aida.

'It's actually for adults, and a bit complicated. But Nathan and I have decided to graduate to reading books for adults and we're starting with the well-known Malaysian writers, not just Tash Aw but older writers such as Lloyd Fernando, and probably a few Singaporean writers as well,' added Junie.

Aida nodded, she turned away, looking slightly preoccupied. There was a moment of awkward silence before Junie said, 'I just saw Zara walking down the corridor and she looked like she was crying.'

Aida turned to look at Junie and nodded. 'Zara admitted that she was one of the bullies and she said she was really sorry for what she did. She said she didn't know they were going to go so far. She thought they were only going to scare me.'

'Did she confirm that the other two were Minji and Maiandra?' Junie asked.

'No. She said it was not up to her to tell people who the other two were. They have to do that themselves, besides, she thinks the entire rhythmic gymnastics team will get really angry with her if she gives them away. I think she's right in a way,' Aida said.

'No,' said Junie. 'I don't think it's right to protect people like that, people shouldn't be allowed to get away with bullying!'

'It's complicated, Junie. Because my parents are friends with Minji's parents. They don't want to involve the authorities or anything like that, because they don't want Minji's future to be affected,' Aida said with a sigh.

Junie nodded, but she felt conflicted again. She felt awful that Minji and Maiandra would get away with their vicious behaviour but realized that Aida was right, it was complicated.

'Anyway, Zara wanted to tell the school Principal about what she did, and she thinks she's going to be suspended for the whole term but I told her not to do it. I didn't want her to be punished for what the other two did.'

At that moment, Junie felt real admiration for Aida. She didn't think she would be that forgiving. Before she could say anything, Aida continued, 'She also confessed that she was the one who sent me the Facebook message. When she went to your place for the *Kaidankai*, she saw the laptop and realized that Jin had not logged out of his Facebook account so she just changed the password and took over his account. I feel so stupid for falling for that kind of thing.'

'Don't be sorry and you're not stupid at all. Lots of girls do silly stuff when they're around Jin,' replied Junie, with a grin. 'It's like they see Jin and their IQ drops by about fifty points. One girl I knew sprayed so much Marc Jacob's "Lola" on herself that she fainted and her mother had to take her to the doctor!'

Aida burst out laughing. 'Boys are just as bad. According to Nathan, they spray Axe on themselves, in the Boys locker room and expect girls to throw themselves at them, just like in the TV advertisements.'

'You could lose your head over the Axe Effect!' exclaimed Junie and they both burst out laughing.

Junie and Aida did not notice Jin outside the door. He was holding a bouquet of flowers in his hand. Jin quickly hid himself behind the wall when he heard his name being mentioned.

When Junie and Aida managed to compose themselves, Aida said, 'So how is Jin doing? Is he okay, after being grounded for so long?'

'Oh, Jin is okay. Actually, he's doing better than okay. His swim time has improved, his grades have improved and he's getting along with Mum really well. And, he even learnt to do grocery shopping and make soft boiled eggs properly,' said Junie.

Aida laughed and said, 'That's so amazing!'

'Actually, there's something I need to share with you about how Jin got grounded,' and Junie told her about the shisha/ *beedi* incident.

Aida listened to Junie's account with rapt attention. Her expression alternated between amusement and alarm, and she burst out laughing at the end. She suddenly realized something, 'You mean, Jin hasn't found out how you set him up till now?' asked Aida.

'Nope. And I don't intend to tell him either. Well, maybe not until I graduate from school,' said Junie.

Aida said, 'It's so much fun, listening to all your stories. I'm really glad we became friends.'

'But you're not going to leave Noble Hall?' Junie asked.

'No. I persuaded my Mum and Dad, that I'm going to be okay at Noble Hall. I mean I have friends there—like you, Nathan, Sachin, and Alex . I showed them all the Facebook posts I received from students in the school, and they all pledged to protect me (and other bullied students) and not allow this to happen again. I think, they sort of realize that bullying can happen in any school and one has to deal with it. Besides, Minji and Maiandra are leaving at the end of the school year, in a few weeks' time.'

Junie hugged her.

Jin took a deep breath and walked away. He tossed the flowers into a bin located on the corridor on the way to the elevator. At that moment, Nathan and Sachin walked out of another elevator, behind a few doctors and nurses. Jin was too preoccupied to notice them, but Nathan and Sachin noticed him and exchanged glances. Jin got into the elevator and the door closed.

They passed the wastepaper basket on the way to Aida's room and Sachin picked up the flowers Jin had tossed. 'No point wasting some perfectly good flowers, especially since we forgot to buy some . . . and we can't afford flowers, anyway.'

Nathan commented, 'Jin must have bought them for Aida. I wonder why he threw them away?'

Sachin shrugged, 'Who knows? But as they say, "don't look a gift horse in the mouth".'

Aida and Junie greeted the two boys cheerfully when they entered the room. Aida was delighted with the flowers, 'Thanks! They're beautiful!'

'Guess who we just saw, going into the elevator?' asked Nathan.

'Zara?' said Junie.

'No. It was Jin,' replied Nathan.

'Was Zara here?' asked Sachin. Aida nodded at him, but she decided not to say anything.

Junie looked puzzled, 'You mean you saw Jin in the hospital?'

Nathan said, 'Yup! But we don't think he saw us. We hid behind some doctors and nurses.' Junie looked slightly alarmed when she heard this.

'But he never even said "hello" to me,' said Aida, sounding slightly hurt.

Junie's phone pinged and she took it out of her pocket to check it. She said, 'It's urm . . . an old friend. He's in the hospital café and he wants me to join him there.'

She got up and said, 'I have to go now, Aida! Get well soon!' And she gave Aida a hug and rushed out of the room.

Sachin remarked, 'What was that all about? It's not like Junie to ditch us like that.'

Nathan and Sachin pulled up two chairs and sat down. Without Junie around, they felt slightly awkward. Sachin said, 'You look amazing . . . I mean for someone who's just recovering from trauma.'

'The doctors said I'm all right physically and I'm going to be discharged tonight. I just feel sad and angry . . . and scared. I keep on seeing them in my mind. I wish they would just go away . . .'

Aida face contracted and looked like she was about to cry. The boys were relieved when she pulled herself together and continued, 'Junie said that you've found Souchong? That's one of the best news I've heard so far!'

'Yup! And we helped to shut down a wildcat trafficking network as well. Alex and Sachin are getting quite good at cyber detective work,' said Nathan.

'It was a team effort, really. But yeah, the breakthrough came when we realized Souchong could be tracked by GPS,' Sachin replied.

Nathan noticed a book lying on the bed and picked it up. 'Oh, *The Harmony Silk Factory*. I'm reading this as well, and another book called *Scorpion Orchid*, by Lloyd Fernando.'

Aida said, 'Junie gave it to me. She said it won the Whitbread Prize and it's quite famous. I've only just started reading it.'

Nathan nodded, 'It's quite a complicated read, set in Ipoh, during World War II. There's another book which is getting a lot of reviews—*The Gift of Rain*. I think it's also set in Malaysia during the Japanese occupation as well.'

'I wonder why so many books are set during the Japanese occupation? It's not like they were such great times either. I've read most people were starving . . . or dying,' Sachin said.

'No idea. I've wondered about that as well. Maybe it allows writers to write more interesting antagonists instead of the usual gangsters and corrupt politicians,' replied Nathan. 'Anyway, Junie and I have decided to challenge ourselves to read all the famous Malaysian books published after September 1963—the year Malaysia actually came into being.'

Aida looked up, 'Junie mentioned the challenge as well but I was under the impression that Malaysia gained independence from the British in 1957.'

Nathan replied, 'That is correct, but that was just Malaya, or what we call "Peninsular Malaysia" now. Sabah and Sarawak became part of the country in 1963.'

'Actually, Malaysia as we know it came into being in 1965, because Singapore left the Federation in that year. But you can ignore that part because I was just being confusing,' added Sachin with a grin.

Aida looked confused but she knew Sachin well enough by now not to be annoyed. She replied brightly, 'Well, I think I get the gist of things now and I've decided to take up the challenge as well. I want to know more about this country.'

An attendant walked in pushing a trolley with Aida's lunch on it. Nathan and Sachin suddenly felt hungry and realized that it was lunch time. Nathan's phone pinged at the same time. It was a text message from Junie. They excused themselves and walked to the elevator.

* * *

Jin took the elevator down, fuming with rage. He wanted to go somewhere where he could sort out his conflicted thoughts and feelings. He thought about taking a taxi to a cineplex nearby but changed his mind when he saw the hospital café. The delicious smell of food wafted from the kitchen. He sat down and ordered the set lunch. Then he had an idea and sent an SMS to Junie.

When Junie walked into the café, Jin was eating a large plate of chicken chop with potato chips and coleslaw. She ordered a cup of tea and sat down opposite him. She said, trying to sound as casual as possible, 'So why did you want to meet me?'

Jin came straight to the point, 'It was you who set me up! I heard what you said to Aida!'

'So you admit to eavesdropping?' said Junie.

'Pot calling the kettle black much?' retorted Jin.

Junie flushed. She hated that expression. 'I never actually told Mom anything. She found out for herself,' Junie said defensively.

'You made sure she found out! You really think you're so clever, you and your smart-ass friends. What made you think you had the right to do that to me?' Jin almost yelled at her. The people at the restaurant looked up at them.

Junie glared at him. She didn't get angry often but Jin was rubbing salt into her wound. She said in a low furious voice, 'I did it to get even with you. It's not enough that half the school wants to be your friend, you have to steal the few people who actually want to be my friend. First it was Zara, and then it was Aida.'

'What are you talking about? You have Nathan and Sachin to be your friends . . .' he was genuinely confused.

'You really don't get it, do you? I may want to have more friends. I like stuff like clothes and shoes, and want to have friends who can talk about these things. But I always end up being left behind as your plain and boring sister.' She was still glaring at him.

Jin snapped back, 'So what do you expect me to do? Pretend I don't like them?'

'Yes, that's exactly what I expect you to do! It's not enough that you're the favourite at home, and the most popular boy in school . . . no, that's still not enough for you! You have to make my life miserable as well!' Junie had turned white with fury.

Jin sighed in exasperation. 'No, Junie. You don't get it. I'm not the favourite at home, not always. Mom and Dad already decided to send you overseas for Uni.'

For once, Junie was speechless. She had always believed that Jin would be the chosen one. They only had enough money to send one child abroad for studies and Jin was the eldest and Mom's favourite.

Jin continued, 'Mom told me while she was driving me around. She said, I have to win a scholarship to study abroad.'

Junie was still speechless. She thought to herself, *It can't be true . . . I don't believe you . . .'*

Jin continued, 'Anyway, your trap actually helped me. Thanks to Mom chasing me to swim faster and study harder, my swim time has improved and even my grades are better. A corporate sponsor may even offer me a scholarship to study in the US . . .'

By now, Junie had decided to stay mum. She knew to keep her peace when she was ahead. She gave a sigh of relief when she saw Nathan and Sachin and waved to them to join her at the table. They pulled the chairs and sat down awkwardly with Junie and Jin. There was a long pause where Nathan and Sachin gave Junie quizzical looks, and Jin took the opportunity to finish his meal. Nathan and Sachin took advantage of the lull in the conversation to order their meal. Taking a cue from Jin, they both decided to order chicken chop as well.

Finally, Jin got up, 'I'm really glad you found your cat, Nathan. I've grown to like that dark mask of his and those cool blue eyes!'

Nathan and Sachin stared at Jin in surprise. He had never shown this side of him before and Nathan wasn't sure what to say. He was almost relieved when Jin added with a trace of sarcasm in his voice, 'And pay for the lunch since I paid for the flowers . . . my allowance was cut, thanks to Junie.' And he walked off.

'Are you okay? What was that about?' Nathan asked in a stunned voice.

'Jin found out I was the one who set him up. He heard me while I was talking to Aida,' Junie said.

'Phew! Imagine Jin eavesdropping! Hope he didn't give you a hard time,' said Sachin.

'Actually, it kind of backfired on me . . . or maybe it didn't. Thanks to Mom's constant breathing down his neck, he might get a scholarship to the US, to train for the Olympics well more likely the Commonwealth Games.'

'Gah! That's not good news! He'll be even more swollen headed than ever,' said Nathan.

'Actually, it is. It means, I get to study abroad for my medical degree . . . erm . . . according to Jin, they were going to send me overseas, anyway, not him,' said Junie hesitantly. She added ruefully, 'All this time I was the chosen one and I was resenting my brother for nothing . . '

'Wow! Good for you, Junie! Your parents are true progressives! They have more sense than I ever gave them credit for,' said Sachin.

Nathan and Junie burst out laughing. Then Junie said, in a slightly contrite voice, 'I kind of feel bad about setting him up like that. Somehow, Mom not punishing me actually makes me feel bad.'

Nathan replied, 'You really did not "set him up"! Jin was smoking shisha, I mean *beedi* and the evidence was genuine. You only placed them where Auntie would find them!'

Junie felt better. She said, 'That's true. Jin was the one who said it was shisha, and made Mom even more confused! They smelt of cloves, so I think they were just *beedi* with a dash of spice.'

Sachin added with a grin, 'You can trust Jin to get things mixed-up, although to be honest, all of us were taken in for a while . . .'

Then he decided to change the subject, 'So Junie, you'll be applying to Oxford or Cambridge, then? Apparently, Alex's mother had practically told him that he would be disowned if he didn't get into one of them, although she has probably—hopefully—changed her mind now.'

'Not really. I'm probably going to apply to both Imperial College and University College in London. They're known for their science courses and also for being pro-women. Anyway, it's in two years time, so I still have time to decide. What about you, two?' Junie asked.

'I'm thinking of SOAS—the exotic School of Oriental and African Studies, probably to do history or something equally pointless. My mother thinks I should try law, though. What about you, Sachin?' said Nathan.

'I might end up in the same place as Jin—California. Gah! Can you imagine that?' He made a face.

He was about to continue, but the young wait staff had arrived with their food—two plates of perfectly done chicken chop covered in black pepper sauce, accompanied by potato chips, and coleslaw. The aroma was irresistible, except to Junie, who rolled her eyes. So Sachin changed the subject, 'Hey, let's eat! It's been so tense, I even forgot I'm starving!'

They were silent until they had finished their lunch. Then Junie remembered something, 'Hey, how is the new Prince of Siam? I didn't get a good look but he must be stunning!'

Nathan nodded enthusiastically, 'He's doing great. I fed him this morning, but I'm keeping him in a cage for the moment.'

He paused and added more quietly, 'Dad came home, last night.'

Sachin burst out, 'What?!! He's back and you never told us?'

Junie hissed 'Shush!' and placed her index finger on her lip as a sign to keep his voice low, because people had turned to look at them.

'Is he okay?' Junie asked in a low voice.

'Actually, he's really busy but seems to be doing great! Apparently, he's going to set up a high-tech facility at Astana to make microchips. He's got partners and funding and everything.' Nathan told them briefly what had happened during his late-night talk with his father.

Junie asked, 'Does anyone else know about this?'

Nathan replied, 'Only Ma, and now the two of you. I'm sure Dad would have called Uncle KB and Auntie Fei by now. It's weird but that party at Aida's place turned out to be really useful for Dad.'

Junie and Sachin nodded thoughtfully. Sachin remarked, 'So what your Dad said is true, about the value of networking.'

Junie remembered about what Aida had said about her parents being friends with Minji's parents.

* * *

A few weeks later, a package arrived for Nathan in the post. It was from Amazon. He and his mother sometimes ordered things from Amazon, but he didn't remember ordering anything recently. When he opened it, he found a book, entitled *The Great Silk Road* inside. But there was another smaller packet with the book. He was puzzled because he had definitely not ordered this book, maybe his mother had bought it for him. It was in hard cover and lavishly illustrated. He turned his attention to the other packet, which had another layer of wrapping on it. When he opened the package with the help of a letter opener, he was surprised to find a packet a tea with the words 'Lapsang Souchong' on it.

Nathan was about to call his mother but decided to investigate the packet himself. He carefully opened the packet and was disappointed to find that it was filled with dried tea leaves—rich fragrant lapsang souchong tea, scented with pine smoke—but still boring tea leaves. He thought for a minute and then decided to go to the kitchen. He found the jar where Kak Yam kept the tea leaves and poured out the contents into the jar. However, among the tea leaves was a card. He picked it up carefully from among the loose tea leaves and placed it in his pocket. Then he closed the tea jar and replaced it in the cupboard.

When he was alone in his room again, he studied the card carefully. It was the usual product information about the special method to make lapsang souchong tea, and what made it so enticing. However, there appeared to be a number at the bottom, which appeared slightly different from the print on the card. It said 93. Nathan pondered over it for a while. Then on a whim he reached out for the book about the Silk Road and opened it at page 93. It was a map of Astana, the bright new capital of Kazakhstan.

The End

Acknowledgements

I would like to thank Nora Nazerene Abu Bakar, Publisher at Penguin Random House SEA, for accepting the manuscript entitled *Lapsang Souchong* and allowing it to see the light of day in the form of a book.

Also, many thanks to Thatchaayanie Renganathan, the structural editor whose insights and suggestions (and sometimes insistence) helped to take the story further than I thought possible. The final result is a more rounded, cohesive and, I hope, funnier book.

My thanks also to Swadha Singh, the copy editor, whose painstaking work is much appreciated.

And a huge thank you to Divya Gaur, who is part of the Penguin Design Team and who created the brilliant cover for the book.

I owe a debt of gratitude to Tuen Mong, former banker and avid reader, who first told me the real life story of the cat and the hummingbird, and the cat parent's desperate attempt to preserve the bird, when we were living in Havana, Cuba in 2010.

Beta readers played an important role in shaping this book, so my gratitude to the following: Don Bosco, Children's Book author and entrepreneur; Kok SenWei, Psychiatrist and visual storyteller, and Sharon Bakar, Editor, Publisher and cat parent.

And I owe a debt to Teoh Choon Ean, Children's book author, and former teacher and National Gymnastics coach, who helped me gain an insight into the hothouse world of Rhythmic Gymnastics.

As it takes a village to produce a book, I am lucky to have the support of two book groups: The Classic Challengers, headed by the indefatigable, Naz Ghazali; and The Paper Back Book Club, headed by Swagatha Roy.

Finally, I would like to thank my readers, who have always been so generous with their time, interest, and support.